NO BACKING DOWN

BECCA SEYMOUR

—— RAINBOW TREE PUBLISHING ——

NO BACKING DOWN

ZONE DEFENSE
BOOK 4

BECCA SEYMOUR

RAINBOW TREE PUBLISHING

ALSO BY BECCA SEYMOUR

Cover Design: BookSmith Design

Editors: Hot Tree™ Editing

E-book ISBN: 978-1-922679-72-7

Paperback ISBN: 978-1-922679-73-4

Alternate Paperback ISBN: 978-1-922679-77-2

No Backing Down is set in Minnesota and uses both fictional and real locations and references. The basketball league in both the Zone Defense and Fast Break world is called the League, not the NBA. While I loosely followed the NBA structure, I created my own league and team names, my own competition names, and took liberties to make my fun, low-angst world work.

THEN....

CHAPTER 1
DYLAN

AGED 15

Sitting on the muddy bank with my feet in the water, I grinned over at Cassius. He stood, holding his rod, gently reeling in his catch. A wide smile stretched across his lips as he gazed at the moving line.

"Looks like a big one," I said with a chuckle, focusing on the splashes.

"That's what he said." His response was quick, just like it usually was, the amusement there but disappearing a second later as I jolted in surprise at his words, head turning quickly toward him.

He. He said *he.*

Wide-eyed, Cassius stared at me, color in his cheeks and a look in his eyes I'd only seen once before. Fear. That time was when he'd stolen a bottle of vodka from his folks' liquor cabinet, only to realize a little too late that there was no chance his parents would believe a raccoon got into the house and knocked the bottle over, hence the reason the bottle was empty and in the garbage.

No, sir. Not in our bellies.

"The line."

My words snapped him out of the silent stare off, but it was too late for his catch. The line went slack, the fish having wriggled off, making its escape.

Continuing to stare out at the water, my pulse loud in my ears, I held my breath. Aware of every movement my best friend made, I waited. Waited for him to make a joke. Waited for him to address the giant mammoth between us.

Was it a slip? Was it a jesting?

And still I waited.

At the clearing of his throat, I finally sucked in air, the action loud and shuddery.

"So yeah…." Sitting beside me, our shoulders brushing like they always tended to do when we were together, Cassius trailed off.

Discomfort rolled off him. I felt it in the tension of his arm against mine. Realized it in the shuffling of his ass as he went to put some distance between us.

Reacting on instinct, I clamped down on his forearm and finally angled to glance his way.

His deep brown eyes were wide, the strange fear in them easy for me to read. Because of course it was. But I didn't like that particular emotion one bit.

Cassius and I spent almost every waking moment together. We had for years.

We knew almost—*almost*—everything about each other.

He. He said *he*.

Punching out "Holy shit," I held him tighter. I couldn't let go. Couldn't organize my words fast enough.

The terror I saw staring back at me every time I looked at myself in the mirror splintered. Cracked wide open. It usually sat heavily on my chest. A dense boulder that threatened to catch my breath and make it disappear for good.

How could it not?

My parents—

Fuck, I couldn't even think about them without breaking out into a sweat of self-hatred and loathing.

But this was Cassius.

My Cass.

He was the brother I never had. My best friend always.

The one person who I knew I could finally share my truth with.

"Dylan."

The worry in his tone snapped me out of my spiral. Though it did nothing to calm my pulse or my fast breaths as they sawed out of me.

"I'm gay."

The wind caught my words, so quiet, almost whispered, but so loud in the couple of inches between us.

A moment of stillness. Of absolute quiet. Even the flowing water of the Zumbro River didn't truly register.

The flare of understanding in his eyes had me catching my breath.

Fuck. What if I was wrong? What if it *was* a joke?

I swallowed hard, reminding myself this was Cassius. Even if he wasn't… even if he had been joking around, he wouldn't push me away, right? Wouldn't share my secret in our small-ass town.

The barest of movements had me bracing.

I landed on my back, a heavy grunt shooting from my mouth at Cass's weight.

A whoosh of breath later, relief, pure and oh so joyous, raced through me.

Cass hugged me hard. With his face buried in my neck and the gentle brush of his breath against my skin, I felt him grin. Right before I heard his words. "I'm so fucking proud of you."

Tears burned my eyes as I wrapped my arms around him, right here on the muddy bank of the river, in our favorite fishing spot. Unable to speak, I hugged him hard, hugged him so tightly that he started to chuckle.

"Can't. Breathe."

"Shit." My arms slackened, and I reluctantly let him go.

As he pulled away, I kept my gaze on him, needing to see his face. Needing to see the truth of his reaction for myself.

A tender smile and warm eyes. Just seeing them loosened my muscles even more.

"I'm pretty sure I'm bi."

My eyebrows shot up at his words. They damn well nearly touched my hairline at the deep pink flooding his brown cheeks. Embarrassment and Cassius in the same sentence didn't compute.

My best friend could be a cocky, self-assured asshole.

Truth was, he put on that mask every single day when we were around others.

He was Cass, the basketball captain. Cass, the guy who was already being watched closely by colleges, despite that, when going back to school after the summer break, we'd just be sophomores.

He was also Cass, the handsome guy who always had girls trailing after him and all the guys wanting to be his friend.

Because along with all that, he was good and kind.

But he was also Cass, one of ten Black kids in our school. He was also Cass, who dealt with ignorance every day. That shit exhausted him and pissed him off more than he let on. Well, to anyone other than me.

"Pretty sure?" I asked, my brain coming online.

"Yeah." He shrugged. "I know there's a shitload of queer labels, and bi seems to fit."

A huff of a laugh escaped me, the exchange surreal.

"And you're gay?"

Heat burned my cheeks as I nodded. "Yeah."

He studied me, gaze roaming my face, a concentration in his gaze that threatened to make me squirm. "So when you kissed Zoe last year?"

Embarrassed, I rubbed a hand over my face. "Gross and awkward."

At his gentle chuckle, I glanced at him.

"I bet. Did you already know by then?"

I swallowed hard, my heart flipping around a

little, still not believing the secret that had held me terrified and frozen for so long was finally out there. I felt light, like I'd been filled with helium and could float away at any second.

"Sort of suspected over the last couple of years. I suppose I wanted to be sure."

With his brow drawn low, Cass looked perplexed. Once again, he studied me. "I'm sorry you didn't feel able to tell me till now."

Emotion clawed at my throat. "You're a fucking asshole."

"What?" A burst of confused, incredulous laughter joined his question. "Why?"

"You." I laughed, the sound watery, my vision blurry. I shook my head, not hiding my reaction from him. When we made eye contact, he smiled softly and reached out and squeezed my arm.

My eyes almost closed at his reassuring touch. I'd been so terrified I'd lose him, that this one simple gesture would be my undoing as a fresh wave of relief trapped in my throat.

"You," I started again, but it was no good; I had to clear my throat. "Thank you for being an asshole."

His lips twitched. "A bi asshole." He bounced his eyebrows. "This revelation puts a whole new meaning to assholes."

I shoved at him, laughing loudly. His ridiculousness wiped away my threatening tears.

As we stared at each other, each grinning, nothing but relief and contentment between us, I tilted my head, sobering a little. At the change in my expression, Cass's amusement faded, though a small smile remained on his lips.

"I'm not ready to tell anyone yet."

Understanding filled his gaze, and he bobbed his head. "Your folks are going to lose their shit."

An understatement if ever there was one.

Lose their shit? More like get me locked away and their church group gathered around me to call forth the devil from my soul or some bullshit.

"You come out when you're ready. You know I've always got your back. Friends forever, right?" He held out his hand, and I just knew he was going to do the tricky handshake we'd invented when we were eight—a series of taps, fist bumps, and ending in a shoulder check. One we created in solidarity after a particularly nasty confrontation with Christopher Fuckface on the playground, whose whole family were racist fucks.

The day they'd left town and moved to Florida had been one we'd celebrated.

We did our epic handshake. "Friends forever." I grinned and hugged him tightly before we picked up our rods and tried to catch some trout for dinner.

CHAPTER 2
CASSIUS

AGED 16

Holy shit. I burst out laughing and peered over at Dylan. "This was in the bag of DVDs that your folks got?"

Poor Dylan didn't seem like he could land on one particular reaction. It hovered between mildly horrified and morbidly fascinated. Then his lips twitched, and he snorted out a loud laugh at the ridiculously hilarious movie playing.

"Fresh from the garage sale." Still chuckling, he shook his head and picked up the DVD case.

"We should absolutely get them to watch it." The desire to shove it in their DVD player and watch his asshole parents' reaction itched at me. I would have loved to see their faces. Dylan's pearl-clutching mom would have curled over in horror. Probably smashed the TV from throwing the controller at it.

His dad, that weak fucker, would have broken into a bullshit lecture, spouting off scripture about sin and sex before marriage, I suspected. The asshole would probably then go on to pretend to throw the DVD away, only to jack off to it later.

I didn't trust the fucker one bit.

I'd seen the way he'd eyed Josie Marion's mom's tits in her low-cut top.

Dylan held up the DVD, the image of the group of teenagers looking fairly low-key and not giving hints to the hilarious nastiness of the movie. "Maybe they thought the movie was legit wholesome, all-American goodness."

A teasing twitch of his lips followed, just as we both snapped our gazes to the fucking epic development of Jim's dad catching him with his pants down as he fucked an apple pie.

"Jesus." I shook my head, my cheeks hurting from laughing so much.

"Looks like a waste of perfectly good pie to me." Dylan arched a brow and peered at me.

I snorted beside him, sitting up on my bed. "I don't know. Third base is pretty fucking hot. Worth wasting a pie to get that feeling."

"Even when it's Tanya trying to suck your brains out?"

I held back my smirk that Dylan managed to only scrunch his nose a little at the mention of Tanya. He'd never been a fan of Tanya Carol's. Sure, she was a loudmouth, a cheerleader, and hella popular at parties. She always offered a good time. Especially as she legit didn't want a boyfriend and chased fun and easy like most of the guys I knew.

"I think the fingers in the pie are more about the feel of pussy. A pie can't exactly suck you off."

This time, Dylan's face scrunched so damn fast and tight, I couldn't help but laugh.

"And Jim fucking the pie is what it's like to fuck a girl?" Looking genuinely horrified, Dylan shook his head and hit Pause on the remote. "And that, right the fuck there, is why asses are so much better than vaginas. Who wants lumpy and squishy? Like…." An over-the-top shudder followed, and fuck if I didn't laugh harder.

"You're such a doofus. Pounding any orifice sounds like dick heaven." I still hadn't gotten that far yet. Not for lack of trying. I'd gotten to third base with Tanya. Dylan was right about that. There hadn't been a chance with a guy yet.

I was the only out person at school. While Dylan was gay, he remained firmly in the closet. And I suspected there'd be other guys at school in the same position. What that meant was I hadn't had any chance to experiment.

I couldn't wait to leave for college to take full advantage of all the dick and pussy on offer. I suspected Dylan couldn't either, though his plans of being a cop pointed in a whole different direction to my League plans.

"Hmm." Dylan stretched out his legs, crossing his ankles. "I'll take your word for it."

"You know, I expect slipping into a guy is more like sticking your dick into chocolate."

Dylan spluttered out a cough, his chest wheezing. "The fuck," he managed with a choke.

Realizing he'd choked on his own spit, I leaned over, laughing almost uncontrollably while smacking him on the back.

"Jesus." He edged away from me, clutching his throat. "Warn a guy." Bright red, he coughed some more. Shaking his head, he stared at me with watery eyes. "Chocolate? The fuck, Cass?"

"What?" With my mouth stretched wide and laughter in my gut, it was hard to pull off an innocent look, let alone voice. "What's wrong with chocolate?"

"Nothing's wrong with chocolate, but how the hell is fucking a guy like fucking chocolate? Like a chocolate cake or a pudding?"

A pudding had merit but wasn't what I was thinking. Not that I'd given any thought to fucking food before this moment.

"Not sure that would be tight enough." I bounced my eyebrows up and down, and still red-faced, Dylan huffed out a strangled laugh. "And rather than the tightness, I was thinking more about how fucking delicious and tasty chocolate is. And the velvety smooth sort you can get... yeah, it would be like fucking the good stuff."

"Jesus H. Christ. I best not leave you alone in the company of baked goods or anything if this is going to be a new fetish of yours."

Shooting him the bird, I chuckled. "Fuck off." Even as the words spilled out of me, a ludicrous fucking thought trickled into my brain.

Mom had been baking for her book club. She'd said there'd be extra. Hell, the house smelled divine —it always did when she baked.

"Oh hell. What's that look in your eyes?" Looking resigned and only slightly worried, Dylan shifted forward from where he'd been leaning against my headboard. He collapsed back on my bed and covered his face with his arm. "Just don't tell me. I don't want to know."

I jumped up, settling on my knees beside him,

and bounced the mattress for good measure. "Fuck that, you know I have the best ideas."

"No." He removed his arm so I could see his face. Wide-eyed, he stared up at me. "No, you seriously have the worst ideas."

"I so do not."

In response, his eyebrows jerked high. "Really? Take a moment and think about that."

I tutted and pounced on him, lying fully on top of him, feet to head.

Since this position we found ourselves in was all too common, he didn't even bat an eyelash. With my elbows settled on the bed, wedged under his armpits, I clasped my hands and settled my chin on top of them as I peered down at him.

"Don't look at me like that."

That resigned voice was back, this time paired with a "fucking hell, what's he going to do this time" look on his face. Because Dylan wasn't wrong. I could grudgingly admit to myself—and sometimes him in the past—that I'd done some stupid-ass shit over the years.

Consequences were always a tomorrow's Cassius's problem.

"You don't want to know what it feels like to fuck food?"

And there it was. One of my not-so-awesome

ideas. Yet I still happily shared said crazy ideas out loud to my best friend. But if I couldn't say them to him, who could I say them to? Obviously the answer was nobody. Maybe the answer should have also been "don't share your fucked-up, or weird, or dangerous, or ridiculous ideas with anyone. Ever."

But screw that.

Life was for living. Being young was for fucking up and having a good time.

Once I joined the League, I'd be under scrutiny. It meant now was the time to stir things up and do spontaneous shit that usually got me into trouble.

Realizing Dylan remained silent, I frowned. "What? You don't want to fuck food with me?" I stuck out my bottom lip, earning me an eye roll. "Come on. Let's call it experimenting."

His scrunched nose was back. "Me doing any sort of masturbating with you in the room does not get me going. I love you, man, but it doesn't mean I want to get my dick out in front of you."

My grin was quick and wide. "I love you, too, and fuck if you not getting a stiffy because of how fucking sexy and awesome I am doesn't make me happy, because uhm, awkward much, but this will be funny."

"Funny? Really?" He wasn't buying it.

It was time for a different approach. I jumped off

him and headed for the door. "Wait here," I hollered as I hauled ass toward the kitchen.

Somewhere deep in the crevices of my brain, I wondered why the hell I was so determined to do this. Not once, not ever, had I jacked off with or in front of Dylan. As my best friend, he was firmly in that zone of "do not go there," and it worked.

But I was also a dog with a goddamn bone. Once I had an idea in my head, letting the thing go was almost impossible. I had few qualms over making a dick of myself at the best of times. In front of Dylan? None whatsoever.

I peered around the kitchen door and grinned when I saw it was empty.

The fresh scent of cooked pastry greeted me, and my stomach rumbled. Fucking and eating baked goods. Score.

Mom always made extra, especially when Dylan was around. And since he stayed here more often than not, and the two of us had hollow legs according to Dad, I had no issues with grabbing the first two pans my hands came in contact with.

I shoved them on a tray, the foil still a little warm to comfortably carry. As I stepped past the cutlery drawer, I stopped and tugged out two forks. I considered getting the cream out of the fridge but thought better of it.

Hightailing it to my room, I smirked when I realized one of the pies was actually a chocolate pie. *Heck yes.* Mom's chocolate pie was the best. It was also huge, like four inches of thick, gooey-when-warm deliciousness.

I all but slammed my bedroom door closed behind me. Dylan startled, shooting up in bed. When his gaze landed on the food in my hand, he closed his eyes and collapsed back onto the mattress.

"Fuck no. Just give me a fork and I'll eat the damn thing. No way am I putting my dick anywhere near it."

Holding the tray, I stepped forward, ignoring Dylan's hesitation. Not that I'd force him to do anything. I wasn't that much of an asshole. Not that I couldn't be, but I never was to him. I placed the tray on the bed and eyed the contents.

"You're not seriously going to do it, right?"

I shrugged, eyeing the pies. Curiosity was a hell of a thing. Yes, I knew it killed a cat or something, but with nothing but two delicious pies to be worried about, I figured I'd be safe.

I flicked my gaze at Dylan, who was staring at me warily, his gaze traveling between me and the tray. "But they're here now."

"God, give me strength." He shook his head at me. "Just because they are doesn't mean you have to follow through. Just eat the damn thing and let's watch more sketchy DVDs my folks thought were wholesome and savory."

"Yeah, but…." I so wanted to do this.

"Fucking hell, Cass. Fine." He sighed in defeat. "Just not in front of me."

I grinned, swiped up the chocolate pie, and headed toward my small en suite my folks had fitted for me last year, 'cause apparently, they couldn't cope with my teenage grossness. No idea what they were talking about.

I dropped the pie quickly on the closed laundry basket. The foil was a little hot, but that made sense. Heat always stuck to metal stuff, right? Lingered a little.

It meant the pie would be deliciously warm.

Fucking perfect.

I tugged out my cock, already half hard. It didn't take much for my sixteen-year-old horniness to kick up a gear. Any thought of fucking usually did the trick.

Figuring I needed to go in at some sort of angle to get the full experience, I bent my knees and held the end of the foil with my fingertips. I gripped my cock and scooted forward. With my dick eager and throbbing, I grinned.

Fucking showtime.

I slid in, and delicious heat surrounded me as the smooth chocolate molded around the first few inches of my dick… and fuck.

Fuck.

"Fuck!" A strangled scream escaped me. I jerked away, my dick hurting like it had been scorched. I dropped the pie, eyes wide in horror as I looked down. Chocolate covered me, looking so much like shit, I gagged. But holy fuck, the pain.

"Fuck. Dylan. Fuck!"

I grabbed a towel, trying to wipe the chocolate off. Stinging agony made me go cross-eyed, and I whimpered. Or hell, I could have wailed.

The bathroom door flew open. Dylan's pale skin turned ashen, his lips parting as his gaze dropped to my chocolate-covered dick.

"It fucking burns. I've burned my fucking dick." A sob caught in my throat.

Then Dylan was moving, and thank Christ he was, since my feet were frozen as tears spilled down my cheeks.

He tugged open the shower door, turned the cold faucet on, and shoved me into the small cubicle. Right beside me all the way, he dropped to his knees, an action I would have given him shit for any other time. He tugged down my loose sweats before lifting his hand.

"Pass me the showerhead."

I ignored the tremble in his voice, just relieved he was doing something, anything that would stop the burn and prevent my dick from falling off.

I groped for the head, passing it to him with shaky hands.

I didn't know whether my tears had stopped, the shower water having soaked me. But with the cool water on my dick, I exhaled. The sound was gasping and a little desperate.

When he tentatively held my dick, all I could think was I hoped it didn't come off in his hand.

He gently washed away the chocolate. I winced the whole time, my lip trembling while I tried like hell to keep it together.

"Jesus, Cass."

"Fuck." I sniffed. "Is it bad?"

I didn't want to look. Fear holding me captive, I stared instead at Dylan's worried expression.

When he darted a glance my way, he tried to school his reaction, but it was too late.

"I think we need to go to the hospital."

I blanched, the blood draining from my face. "No fucking way."

Emotion shifted in his eyes, a resolved look that I knew all too well. Sure, I could be a fuckhead and a loudmouth, but Dylan could be a bossy shit. I shuddered at the thought of shit, the chocolate on my dick having looked far too much like it for me to ever be the same again.

I swallowed, trying to cling back to my thoughts.

Dylan. Bossy. At times stubborn.

And Dylan who was soaking wet, my dick in his hand and genuine worry in his eyes.

"You've scalded yourself. There's a few blisters here already."

"Fuck." The word punched out of me. "I can't go to the fucking ER." I shook my head. "Can't we just get some cream or lotion or something?"

I could see he wanted to argue, even as he glanced once more at my sore cock, his gaze roaming it clinically.

"Please, Dyl."

Maybe it was the clear desperation in my voice or just plain old sympathy, but he nodded, passing me the showerhead.

"Okay. Just keep the water cool and flowing gently. I'll head to the pharmacy."

I nodded solemnly, knowing he'd have to drive all the way to Rochester, as they were the closest town with a late-night pharmacy. Our small town of three thousand didn't have much open after 5:00 p.m.

"You know where my keys are."

He stood and nodded. My folks had put him on my car's insurance—something they'd done without even asking when they'd bought me the car. Dylan was absolutely a part of our family, and I didn't think it would have been possible to appreciate that any more than in this moment.

"You're going to be okay."

I latched on to his quiet certainty and accepted his hug gratefully.

When he stepped back, his lips twitched. "Don't let your dick freeze off."

And hell if I didn't appreciate him even more for being a funny asshole.

CHAPTER 3

DYLAN

AGED 17

WHITE-HOT ANGER BURNED MY VEINS. I SHOULD HAVE known they'd have done something like this.

I was a fool to think them discovering I was gay would have been any different. Fuck, I was an idiot.

Ensuring the wooden wedge was firmly under the door so they couldn't get into my room, I tugged out my flip phone with trembling hands.

My heart stuttered hearing Paula's loud crying. My kid sister was just fourteen, and I hated that she'd be stuck here. But I couldn't stay.

She was tougher than me. And I'd do everything in my power to make sure she was okay.

Fleeing was my only option.

I just hoped she could forgive me.

Not having the patience to work through the digits needed to send a text message with my ancient phone, I keyed in Cassius's cell number, hoping I had enough credit for the call to connect and for me to ask for help.

"Yo," he said on answer. "I was just about—"

Hearing his voice, I heaved out a sob, cutting him off.

"What's wrong?" A steel I rarely heard from Cass hardened his words.

"Pastor Neil's here. They've packed my bag. Said they're sending me away."

The beat of silence lasted not even a second before Cass erupted. His expletives filled the line. "The fuck they are. Fucking assholes. They'll have to get through me. Pack your shit or leave it all. I'll be there in five minutes."

A shuddering breath tore out of me, turning into a sob. Relief mingled with my tears. "Thanks, Cass," I managed, not questioning anything.

"You never need to thank me," he said, voice soft, the sound of the outside traveling down the line, letting me know he was on the move. "Just stay safe. I've gotta go so I can call Mom."

"Okay."

The call cut off, and I placed the phone in my pocket.

I couldn't think, couldn't work out what to do, where to start.

All I knew with a certainty that helped me keep breathing was that Cass was coming for me.

A pounding of feet up the steps had me holding my breath. A jiggle of my handle followed.

"Dylan. It's me."

Paula.

I rushed to unwedge the door and let my sister in.

Red-faced and teary-eyed, my sister stared at me, bottom lip trembling.

"Hey." I reached out and tugged her into my arms, fixing the wedge immediately after. "It'll be okay."

Clinging on to me, Paula nodded against my chest, her tears soaking my tee that I hadn't changed out of since coming home from basketball practice. Being accosted by my parents and their pastor made showering low priority.

"It's all my fault."

I shushed her, holding my sister even tighter. "It isn't. You couldn't have known. It would have come out eventually."

My gut clenched at her blaming herself. Two nights ago, I had been discussing *all* the hot merits of Jenson Ackles, which Paula had scrunched her nose at. We hadn't realized Mom had overheard until it had been too late, resulting in my folks discovering I was gay.

I should have known their two days of ignoring me was the calm before the storm.

But fucking conversion therapy?

Had I thought they'd accept me? It was an easy no.

But the crushing disappointment, the burn of betrayal tore through me with the speed of wildfire.

I guessed, deep down, some small part of me had held out hope that they would surprise me. Grab on to those values they always spouted. That they would wrap me up in their arms and tell me they loved me no matter what.

I was a fool to even dream it.

Instead, rather than ignoring my existence for a few more months until I graduated, they had to *change* me. *Fix* me. Save my fucking soul.

It wasn't like they truly gave a shit about me or Paula for anything other than how we impacted their image.

I pressed a kiss to Paula's head, needing the connection to center me. The same white-hot anger was too close to the surface, and I needed to get out of here intact. The last thing I wanted was to make life any more difficult for Paula.

"Are you leaving?" she whispered.

I heard her fear loud and clear and hated it. "I'm sorry. I can't—"

"It's okay." The speed of her words cut me off. "You need to leave, and I'll be fine. I promise." She angled back, her swollen eyes breaking my heart. It was her tentative, brave smile that had my tears spilling, though. "I'll be fine," she repeated, a sternness in her voice that pulled a shaky laugh from me.

"I know you will."

"Promise to see me at school."

"I promise."

A small, watery smile appeared, and she bobbed her head. "Okay. What's the plan?"

"Cassius."

She rolled her eyes. "Of course." She reached behind her, tugging out trash bags from her back pocket. "Let's get everything together."

This kid sister of mine was the best. She was also too damn smart for her own good, and hell if I didn't adore her.

We made quick work of emptying my drawers, shoving the contents into bags. Paula threw them out my bedroom window, a grin on her face.

"Fuck our parents," she all but hollered with each bag thrown.

Despite my world imploding, I laughed, so grateful for her. As I crammed my belongings into the black garbage bags, I made a silent promise to myself that when I finally became a cop, I'd do everything in my power to make sure kids like me and Paula were protected.

I was grabbing my schoolbooks when the squeal of tires drew my attention to the window.

Mom, Dad, and Pastor Neil had yet to appear outside, despite the raining trash bags of clothes, but the squealing tires and Cass charging across our lawn finally got their attention. I peered out, seeing the front door open.

Fuck. I needed to move.

My parents had never been fans of Cassius's. They'd never given him a chance, not seeing beyond his dark skin or how his parents attended a more liberal church.

But Cass being here now, my best friend in shining armor who I knew wouldn't hold back his opinion of my parents, could end up in disaster. And likely with him arrested, because of course my parents were assholes and would have no hesitation in calling the cops.

Grabbing my heavy schoolbag, I darted for my bedroom door. Shifting the wedge, I yanked the door open, hightailing it out of there, Paula on my heels with a couple more bags.

By the time I hit the hallway, raised voices filtered past my dad blocking the doorway.

Not hesitating, I pushed past my dad, shifting out of his reach when he made to grab me.

I didn't look back. Didn't respond to his yell of my name. My eyes were all for Cass as he stood, arms folded, in front of the garbage bags on the ground.

"Seriously, you hate your son so much you don't want him to have his clothes?" The bite to Cass's voice was colder, sharper than I'd ever heard before. "You're a goddamn hypocrite."

"Don't you talk to me like that. It's all your fault, taking my son away, turning him to sin."

I welcomed the rage building in my veins at hearing Mom's vileness. It was better than the hollow pit trying to form in my chest. Better than tears trying to spill, knowing this was it. Likely the last time I'd speak to my parents again.

Cass's eyes snapped to mine, his gaze softening as he checked over me, wanting to know if I was okay. My smile was tight, as was my nod.

Less than a handful of steps later, I was beside Cass and before my mom, the pastor by her side. Paula had managed to bypass Dad and was ignoring us all, dragging two bags to Cass's car.

"Dylan, I forbid you to leave. You need help. Let

Pastor Neil help you. All you need is clarity and to let the good Lord show you the way. You're better than this."

At her side, Pastor Neil solemnly bobbed his head. His sharp features seemed more prominent, sinister in the fading light. "Let God save your soul from eternal damnation. We've saved others. Led them to the path of salvation."

Cass's scoff was more of a sneer. "You're sick in the head, all of you. There's fuck all wrong with Dylan. He's fucking perfect, despite being brought up by you sick fucks."

"I will not be spoken—"

"What the fuck ever. Come on, Dyl. Let's go home." He reached for me, squeezing my cold, clammy hand.

"I knew it. He's corrupted you." Mom pitched her voice high. "If you leave this house now, you will never be allowed back. You'll be—"

The sound of an engine cut her off and tugged all our attention away.

My heart stumbled in my chest.

Mama T was here, Cass's mom.

Fresh tears sprang to my eyes.

Mama T was the mom I'd always wished for. She was kind and strong and so loud. She also showered me with affection, something I lapped up and which Cassius had always done too. The two of them were the biggest cuddlers with the kindest souls.

It made their protective streak so much more of a surprise when it came with such fierceness.

"You're in so much shit now." Cass's words were quiet, his amusement clear.

But I couldn't smile. Couldn't really feel relief. Not now when everything was changing and my parents were disowning me.

Out the corner of my eye, I saw Mom tense.

While I got a sliver of satisfaction at that—she'd always been intimidated by Mama T—it wasn't enough to soften the blow or the hurt.

Mama T took in the scene as she stepped closer. She took in the bags at my feet, my sister hovering by the open door of Cass's car, my quiet dad in the doorway not seeming to give a shit about anything. When her gaze met mine, nothing but love and care shined back at me, and when she snapped her attention to Mom and Pastor Neil, a flinty hardness shot their way.

"Cassius," she started, "get all of Dylan's things and put them in your car."

Wordlessly—something of a rarity for Cass—he did as his mom said, leaving me standing in front of the woman who'd birthed me. I stared down at my training shoes, focusing on the scuffs, wondering how I'd ever be able to replace them.

I could leave school. Get a job. When I'd earned enough, I could get a small rental, look at moving Paula in with me. The quicker I could get her out of here, the better.

Mama T's "Dylan, honey" dragged my attention up and to her.

Her words were warm, her dark skin blemish free, making her smile seem brighter. Kind eyes peered over at me.

"Yes, Mama T?"

"Don't you go calling *that* woman—"

"Dylan." Mama T cut through Mom's tirade, her voice still gentle. "Do you know where your birth certificate is, honey?"

I nodded.

"Excellent. Why don't you just go on inside and grab it. It's something you're going to need."

I shot a wary glance at Mom, then Dad still in the doorway.

"It'll be fine, honey. These people aren't going to create any more of a scene unless they want even more curtains twitching and folks in this town knowing exactly how they treat their flesh and blood. You know, Major Trenton is hosting the first LGBTQ rally next June. His brother, Marcus, is coming out especially. You know Marcus, don't you, Rita? He's dating Lionel, Cassius's godfather. It'll be so great for our small town, showing the city folk just what it means to be a supportive, inclusive community."

It was impossible to look away from Mom's bright red face or ignore her hesitancy. Mom liked to think she was an important figure in the community, but that was so far from the truth it was laughable.

"Dylan, honey, go on and get that paperwork."

I nodded a little numbly, sidestepping Mom. When I edged closer to the doorway, Dad met my gaze for a brief moment. Sad eyes peered back at me, but a hollowness lurked so close to the surface that he'd never say anything. Never defend me or stop what Mom was doing.

Swallowing when he stepped out of the way, I refused to feel sorry for him. Refused to feel anything for him. He chose Mom every damn time. Hid behind his "devotion" or some shit.

He was a coward and didn't deserve a single ounce of emotion from me.

Picking up speed, I headed straight for the small office where my folks kept the important documents. It didn't take long to find my birth certificate. While I was there, I snagged my checking account details and hesitated at a framed photograph on the sideboard.

It was of me and Paula, taken a few years back when we were at a church fundraiser. For once, we'd had a great time, having had our faces painted and been allowed to eat so much candy that my tummy had hurt. But it hadn't dimmed my smile as I wrapped my arm around my kid sister for the photo.

I snagged the pic, concealing it beneath my paper-work. With long strides and a confidence I didn't feel, I walked away, leaving my house that I suspected I'd never return to again.

Cass waited by his car, eyes immediately on me. My skin tingled, needing one of his hugs. Not once had I ever complained about how much of a snuggle monster he was. Sure, I'd laughed and teased him about it, but I loved every second of warm comfort I got from him.

I always had and always would.

But not now. Not until we'd left this place.

I darted a look at my sister. Tears trickled down her cheeks, but her smile, fuck… her smile was wide and proud. I shot her a wink, the movement releasing a fresh tear. I left it. The tear was for her, not them. She deserved to know how much I loved her.

But I'd see her on Monday and every single school day. I'd seek her out and make sure of it.

Mama T stood vigil as I got into Cass's car, arms

folded, gaze on me, a gentle smile on her painted lips.

I didn't spare a glance at my parents. I couldn't.

"Let's go home."

I nodded at Cass's words and closed my eyes when he squeezed my leg.

I'd be okay. I always would be with Cass by my side.

CHAPTER 4
CASSIUS

AGED 18

"You're going to need it."

I folded my arms, refusing to take the ball. "Nope. Nuh-uh. Not happening. Keep it here."

Dylan huffed out an annoyed sigh when I shook my head.

Since we'd been battling over our joint lucky basketball, he'd been getting more frustrated. Did I love getting a rise out of my best friend? Hell yes. It was fun. Especially as he was the epitome of cool. Not to be confused with closed off.

He was too loving and giving for that.

Case in point: he wanted me to take our lucky basketball away with me to Michigan U. No way was that happening.

It didn't matter that I was going to play B-ball on a full-ride scholarship, and I absolutely would go pro to play for the League. He needed our ball here.

Was I being ridiculous? Quite possibly. But it was bad enough that I was leaving while he was staying home to go to the local community college in Minneapolis. The thought of leaving him without our lucky ball was a step too far.

"Fine," he relented. "But take my jersey."

I grinned, snagging his high school team jersey from his bed. As far as I was concerned, his jersey, number twelve, was just as lucky as the ball. While I was the one chasing my pro basketball dream, he'd been the one supporting me all the way.

Hell, my best friend was at my side every game, making sure I got the cream of the play while watching my back the whole time.

That he didn't really like playing wasn't lost on me. It didn't mean he hadn't been great at it. What it meant, his commitment, was that he was the best fucking friend ever. He'd played for me. To be *my* support.

Fuck, I wondered if there was anything else of his I could steal to take with me. How the hell was I going to cope with not seeing him every single day?

I swallowed hard as I watched Dylan busy

himself with my iPod. He was putting together a new playlist for my twelve-hour drive to school.

"Can I have your pillow?"

Dylan snapped his attention to me, his brows shooting high before they settled into a semblance of understanding.

I was a needy asshole at the best of times. These past two weeks in the buildup to me leaving tomorrow at dawn, I was practically certifiable.

"My favorite pillow?" he clarified.

I shamelessly bobbed my head.

The look he sent my way indicated he understood. How could he not?

We'd been two peas in a pod since the day we met. But that was nothing compared to the past eighteen months since he'd moved in. While Dylan had technically taken over one of the spare bedrooms, it was nothing more than a glorified closet.

Every single night, we shared a bed. I gravitated toward his warmth, hung on to his calm and his sweetness. Not once had it ever been weird or awkward. How could it when it was simply us?

"That's fine, but only if you leave me yours."

Grinning immediately, I launched at him, arm wrapping around his chest. All six foot three of me landed on top of Dylan, tearing a grunt from him. "You promise to call or text every day?"

"As if you'd let me get away with not doing that." He clung to me, his grip strong and familiar. While Dylan didn't have my height, his shoulders were wider than mine. They helped him give the best snuggles.

"Knock, knock." Since Dylan's door was already angled open, Mom eased on in. Her smile settled on us immediately. "You need a Dylan-sized body pillow."

I lifted my head off Dylan's chest and grinned at Mom. "You have the best ideas. You think we can have one made, one that's just as squishy as Dyl?"

"Dude." Dylan jabbed my side, his fingertips digging in. "I am not squishy."

"Not an insult, just fact."

While I expected the shove, I still landed to the side of him with an "*Oomph.*"

"Only firm, bulging muscles could manage flipping your bulky ass."

I reached over and flicked Dylan's ear. "I think you meant perfect ass."

Dylan's snort matched Mom's.

"Hey, no agreeing with Dylan. It'll only go to his big head."

All my pouting did was earn me an eye roll from Mom and a pillow smacked in my face.

"Come on. Guests are due to arrive any minute. I

need your help downstairs." Mom smiled softly. The moment I saw her get teary-eyed, I was up.

"Don't get sad, Mom. I'm leaving my better half right here with you. It'll be like I'm not gone at all." I embraced her, dotting a kiss on top of her head.

"True, I suppose." Mom chuckled and angled to peer up at me. "Better looking too."

As I scoffed, Dylan stepped up, engulfing us both in a hug. "Thanks, Mama T. Always knew you'd see the truth of it."

Rather than calling them out, I settled into the love.

I was going to miss them both so much. And Dad.

"Right. You two need to let me go and get your butts ready." Mom wriggled free, but I didn't miss her affectionate smile. I was so grateful Dylan would still be here, keeping my folks wrapped up in love. If I couldn't be here, he would be equally the best thing.

Left alone, I stared at Dylan. "Wish we didn't have this farewell thing."

"I know. But it makes Mama T happy."

It did. I knew that. My folks had invited some of our close family. Paula was coming, too, having made up some bullshit to her parents to let her break free from the confines of her house.

"You think we can escape to the river after?"

The river was our spot. Our quiet place away from home and school and the pressures of the game. It was tucked away around one of the larger curves, and over the years, we'd been lucky enough to never have anyone discover us while we were there.

It was the place where we came out to each other.

Hell, we even stored an old cooler under a bush, complete with beers and snacks.

"You think that's wise? You need to be on the road by six." While concern filled his tone, he didn't conceal the want in his eyes. He wanted the escape with me too. The last night I was still technically living at home. With him.

The last night before—if I had my chance—my world would burst wide open with possibility in the pursuit of my League dream.

"I'll be fine. Just an hour," I promised, inwardly smiling at his protective streak.

He was going to make such a good cop.

"Then yeah. Of course. Whatever you want."

Dinner was fun and loud. We didn't break free until just after ten, but my tiredness would be worth it.

The gibbous moon sat high in the cloudless night sky. Plenty of light spilled to the dry ground, making visible the uncharted path we followed by rote.

Before long, we reached our spot and sat on the

grassy bank. Side by side, we pressed against each other, the position familiar and comforting.

"You know you're going to be amazing, right?"

Dylan's deep voice cut through the high-pitched whines of the cicadas, but it didn't pull my attention away from the moonlight spilling onto the slow-moving river.

Looking at Dylan right now was impossible.

With a fear I never prepared for, an anxiety I never expected sparking in my gut, there was no way he wouldn't spot it.

When I remained quiet, though, it was just as bad. It was as big a tell as me simply laying bare my soul for Dylan to see.

His strong arm looped across my shoulders. A tight squeeze of my arm followed, enough for me to exhale and lean my head against his shoulder.

We sat in silence, my gaze on the moon's silvery reflection as I took comfort in Dylan's embrace and the sound of his steady breathing.

"What if I fuck it all up?" I ignored the uncertainty in my tone, the quiet catch.

"What if you don't?"

I huffed out a breath, a small smile pulling at my lips.

"*You* are an incredible player. You're the best guy I know, and I'm not blowing smoke up your ass." He punctuated his words with a tender kiss against my head.

Another twitch of my lips and a little tension loosened in my chest at the familiar gesture.

"And we'll be okay, right?" The question wasn't one I'd ever asked before, despite it plaguing my mind.

"Are you serious?" He rocked me a little, amusement lighting his tone when he said, "As if we'll never not be okay. You're my best friend and always will be."

"Yeah, I know." I rolled my eyes at myself, more than aware that I sounded like a prepubescent teen, but Dylan meant everything to me. I loved him as much as I loved my folks but differently. I couldn't even compare it to being like the love of a brother as I didn't know what that was, but it seemed more significant than that.

My thoughts were jumbled as I tried to figure out how I'd cope away from him, from home and my folks. The words "Do you believe in soul mates?" spilled out of me.

When Dylan's breath froze, I stilled, wondering what the fuck I'd just asked.

It wasn't like I was in love with the guy. It wasn't like that. Hell, we'd never even kissed. Not that he wasn't a good-looking dude, because he was all levels of sexy. I objectively knew that.

But fuck if I knew what I was thinking or feeling.

This was my last night. My emotions were doing a number on me. Making me spin out. Making me—

"Yeah, I do."

My shoulders jerked when he spoke despite his words being whisper soft, and fuck if my pulse didn't pick up and dart through my veins at the speed of light.

Shit, I needed to look at him, see his face, read his expression. Not that I thought he was fucking with me—that tended to be my role in our relationship.

Moving my head from his shoulder, I shrugged off my awkwardness. This was Dylan. I told him practically everything. Even stuff he didn't really want to know.

Hell, just a couple of years ago, he'd saved my dick from third-degree burns and hadn't told a soul. He'd even checked my sore dick during the healing process when I struggled to see through the mirror at the underside of my soft cock.

Now, that right there was a friendship like no other.

The memory, and the gazillion others, bolstered my confidence. "Me too. I think you're mine."

Dylan's eyes widened a fraction before they

settled, a gentle smile softening his features. "You do, huh?"

I narrowed my gaze at him and snapped out my hand to dig my fingers into his side. The asshole laughed as he caught my hand before I could tickle him.

With a wide smile, he clasped our palms together and lightly squeezed. "I think you're my soul mate too."

"You do?"

"I do. It's why I know you're going to achieve everything you ever dreamed of. It's how I know we'll always be best friends. Next year, in ten years, and fifty years from now."

His words were cheesy as fuck—the whole exchange was—but I held on tightly to them. Snatched them from the gentle breeze and tucked them deep inside me.

"You ever need me and I'm there for you, okay?"

I searched his gaze and nodded. "Same goes for you. And I swear to god, when you've finished your associate's degree and become a cop, you keep yourself safe and don't make me come and force you into early retirement or some shit. Because I totally will."

An amused snort fell from Dylan's curved lips.

"That right? The hell would I do in early retirement?"

I shrugged. "What's the equivalent of a house husband for a best friend?" I ignored his raised eyebrows and carried on. "Well, that. You'll be that. I'll be pro before you know it, kicking ass on the court, rolling in endorsements, which means I will absolutely make it happen."

"Uh-huh. And you think I'll just roll with it?"

I tutted and shoved at him. "As my soul mate, you'll do so willingly, knowing it'll make me happy, as all I want to do is keep you safe."

Pursing his lips, Dylan was clearly holding back a laugh. "How about I just stay safe so we don't need to worry about me being a kept man, 'cause if you think I'll ever do your laundry, we need to reassess this whole soul-mate deal."

"Keeping you safe would be the ideal solution." I was nothing if not magnanimous. I'd be sure to remind him of it at some point.

"In that case, we have a deal. Stay safe and have each other's backs."

Sighing happily, I wrapped my arm around him and settled my head once again on his shoulder. "Deal."

CHAPTER 5

DYLAN

AGED 19

I FELT GUILTY BLOWING SOME OF MY SAVINGS ON AN airplane ticket, but Cassius needed me. The ninety-minute flight was a heck of a lot faster than a twelve-hour drive. And while I didn't get a bargain, it would be worth it—I'd just have to pick up some extra work shifts.

Thankfully, I was ahead in school and on top of my assignments for my associate's degree in law enforcement and criminal justice. It meant the early weekend I was taking shouldn't be a problem.

Not only that, but since Paula moved in with me and Cass's folks a couple months back, life was a lot less stressful.

What I hadn't done was tell Cass I was actually coming.

Last night he'd been freaked out, had some sort of meltdown or existential crisis or something, and since then, his phone had been off.

But he needed me. Sure, he hadn't asked, but this was my best friend we were talking about. Every word he didn't say, I heard.

Basketball season was over, which was something. It meant I didn't have to worry about him being in another state at a game. Plus, I'd visited his campus three times before over the past couple of years, so I knew my way around a little.

I also knew his schedule, because of course I did.

I had a copy printed off and stuck to my bedroom wall.

A quick look at my watch told me I had ten minutes to get to his current class that he'd soon be leaving. He only had one more class later this afternoon, giving me enough time to figure out what exactly had happened last night.

After his last class of the day, we'd then kick back and catch up with some much-needed soul-mate bonding.

As dippy as it sounded, I truly believed we were the other half of each other's souls. Not that I'd ever say that to another single human beyond him.

A glance at the building name told me I'd reached the right place. I just needed to figure out the right exit. With classes still in session, I dipped inside the building, trying to look for room numbers.

It didn't take long to find the right one. Since it was closer to the south-side exit, I ambled over, stepping back out into the late-spring air. Spotting a wall a few feet away, I headed over, perching on the brick, gaze not wavering from the exit.

A short while after, the doors opened and students spilled out. Conversation filtered around the campus, the sound loud and interrupting the small gathering of birds darting around one of the nearby picnic tables.

I stood, not wanting to miss him, ready to call out and run if he passed by without seeing me.

I'd never been happier that Cassius had grown another three inches since leaving home. At six-six, he towered over most of the students.

Wearing a Minnesota Eagles jersey, our home team, he was straight-faced, looking like he was only paying half attention to whatever the blonde at his side was saying. She was animated, laughing, reaching out and touching his arm a couple of times.

I held back my sigh. I was used to the attention Cass got. Not only was he hot, but being such a fun guy pulled people into his orbit without fail.

And all that was okay. Even the girl flirting with him.

What made my stomach swirl and my heart pang was the despondency on his face.

I moved through the crowd side-on to my best friend. Pitching my voice loud enough to be heard over the conversation and laughter of the flood of students, I called, "Cass."

More than a few heads snapped in my direction, but the only one I cared about was Cass's. He stopped walking, and his head turned with a speed that I was sure caused whiplash.

And then he was moving, pushing through the throng, and grabbing me in a hug.

"You're here." The words whispered against my neck tugged at my heart.

What the hell had happened yesterday?

"Of course I am. You needed me." I held him close, ignoring the curious glances and some slack-jawed looks.

This right here, affection, PDA and all, was me and Cass. It always had been.

Fuck anybody who felt the need to do a double take or had an opinion.

I felt his reluctance as he pulled away, but his smile was real when I finally glimpsed his face. "Let's go to mine."

"Don't you have another class?"

He shook his head. "It's been canceled."

I nodded, happy to get more time with him. "Lead the way."

With his arm around my shoulders, he did just that, ignoring everyone around him, not sparing a passing glance to the few who called his name.

During the whole walk, tension pumped through me. Coming here had been the right thing to do, especially given his reaction. The unknown filled me with dread, though.

Cass didn't lose his cool. Ever.

Sure, we'd laughed and cried together over the years, but whatever happened yesterday was different.

Twenty minutes later, we were in his house just off campus. It was a place he shared with four of his teammates. The house was untidy but not dirty. I was relieved when Cass led the way straight to his room, though.

When we were in his space, I relaxed immediately. It wasn't home, but his room smelled of him. His Axe body spray mixed with all things Cassius. Sure, his old pair of running shoes needed throwing out, but still, this was very much a space I felt comfortable in.

"I can't believe you're here." He stood with his back to the door, eyes wide as he shook his head.

"How could you think for a second that I wouldn't be after our conversation yesterday?" I said softly.

His flaming-red cheeks surprised me. His wince worried me.

"Get your ass over here and tell me what's going on."

For the first time in the history of ever, Cass hesitated. The action pulled at my gut.

No fucking chance.

"Cass," I said sternly, preparing to whip out the big guns. "Ass on the bed, give me a cuddle, and talk to your soul mate, yeah?"

The words out of my mouth deserved to be mocked. Any other time, we would have done exactly that. But in this moment, I meant them. Needed him to believe them and follow through.

I kicked off my Chucks and made myself comfortable, relieved he had a full-size, not only because of his height but because we'd be sharing this weekend.

With my back to the headboard, I opened my arm and arched my eyebrow in silent order.

When I received a lip twitch, my pulse evened out a little. When he toed off his Nikes and clambered onto the bed, I exhaled in relief. And when he finally planted his head on my chest and snuggled into me, for the first time in three months since I'd last seen him, I felt like I could breathe again.

We lay in silence, the soft rasps of our breathing the only sounds. It took but a few moments for the speed to match, our inhales and exhales syncing, and my worried heart calmed.

"So I hooked up with a guy last night," he started, taking me by surprise. A flurry of questions sparked in my brain, but I clamped my mouth shut, having no idea where he was going with this.

"It was great. Hot, you know?"

I trailed my fingers through his short hair, my blunt fingernails scratching lightly over his scalp in the way he found comforting.

"And it was all fine, and you know it's not the first time I've hooked up with a guy."

I did know that. While we didn't exactly kiss and tell and share details of our conquests, we knew enough about what was going on in each other's lives.

There'd only been a couple of guys Cass had hooked up with—until last night, apparently. And nothing beyond mutual hand jobs. His experience with girls was vastly different. Not that he fucked around majorly. He was too terrified of knocking a girl up to take full advantage of what I knew was easy pickings.

"Okay," I prodded when he remained quiet. "Did something happen? Something not okay?" My hand froze as dread curled in my gut. Fuck, what if he'd been hurt? Just because he was a big guy didn't mean he was invincible. What if—

"Whatever you're thinking, you need to stop." He wriggled his head, his not-so-subtle way of letting me know he wanted me to carry on petting him. I did so with a shaky breath, relief escaping in the heavy whoosh of air.

"So what happened?" I asked quietly.

"I freaked the fuck out, that's what happened."

I jerked my head back in shock, trying to angle to see his expression. At my movement, he shifted his face from its position on my chest, and his gaze met mine. "Freaked out?"

"Fucking humiliated myself."

"What, like you shot your load too soon or something?" Confusion rang loud and clear in my voice.

Cass scoffed. "I fucking wish."

The expression on his face hurt my heart. He looked honest-to-god mortified. "You can tell me anything, remember. No judgment."

His gaze searched mine before he bobbed his head and resettled his cheek on my chest, cutting off our eye contact.

"It was great, until he asked me to prep him. When it was clear I was unsure, he went about it himself, and I freaked."

I didn't understand and was so confused by this whole conversation. Grasping for the right thing to say, I settled on "Well, sex doesn't have to mean penetration. If it's not for you, then that's o—"

"But that's the thing," he said, cutting me off and lifting from my chest to look me in the eyes. "I want to fuck so bad. Hell, just the thought of sinking into a tight ass makes me want to jizz my pants."

I couldn't hold back my lip twitch, reassured by Cass's familiar bluntness.

"All I could think about was my dick covered in skin-destroying chocolate that looked like lumpy fucking shit and the memory of the pain…." Wide-eyed, he shook his head. "I fucking heaved. *Heaved.* In front of this cute guy who wanted my cock, and I heaved, freaked out, threw him a half-assed apology, and raced on out of there like my ass was on fire. The fuck is wrong with me?"

Speechless, I parted my lips before slamming my mouth shut.

The last thing I wanted to do was remember that night when I legit thought Cass's cock was going to drop off. Just the thought of his pained scream and desperate sob was enough to make me wince. But it was the chocolate covering his dick that had hardened to a lumpy goo that wasn't the best visual in the world.

There was no denying it looked like shit. So that, with the pain, not only in the moment with the heat but those sore, wince-inducing welts on his dick after…. Hell, there was a lot of trauma there to unpack.

And something he'd never shared with me before.

"All I could think about when I was so close to his ass was my cock covered in chocolate shit and being in agony. Who the fuck thinks that? It's screwed up, right?"

The fuck was I supposed to say? The last thing I wanted was to say the wrong thing, but this conversation, what he shared, had thrown me for a loop.

Once he'd fully healed a few years back, we'd never discussed it again. Not once.

That clearly the event had such a lasting effect worried me, especially as he associated it with anal sex. If I dug deep, I supposed I could understand why he made the association. Anal sex could be messy, and accidents could happen.

And it was something I'd discovered in my fairly limited experience since being in college that any unpleasant messiness wasn't talked about. It was one of those undiscussed rules that I assumed queer guys knew and followed.

You prepped. You cleansed. But literally, sometimes shit happened.

You'd quietly deal with any messiness and pretend everything was peachy.

Was it nice? Not exactly. But sex—good, amazing sex—was so worth it.

I grasped hold of my thoughts, settling on "It's not fucked-up. Considering what happened to you, I get why you'd link the two."

"Even though it's irrational?"

His despondent tone made me so sad that I hauled him into another hug, then petted his hair. "Trauma has its own set of rules," I said gently, grateful for the psych class I'd studied last semester. "That it's made you wary of anything ass related isn't so much of a surprise, especially when it's to do with your dick. Rational or not. Have you felt this way for a while?"

He shrugged. "Maybe. I don't know. It's not like I have issues crapping or anything. I have no drama watching porn and seeing guys get off. Yesterday was just the first time I got close. I think my reaction took me by surprise so much, I panicked even harder. Talk about being fucking humiliated."

"Hey, you've nothing to feel humiliated by or ashamed of. You couldn't have known." I cleared my throat, thinking about the guy he'd been with yesterday. "What did you say to the guy?"

"Apologized and said I was feeling unwell. Said I thought I had food poisoning."

"That'll be all the sketchy shrimp you ate, huh?"

When he chuckled, I dotted a kiss on his head, thoroughly pleased with myself.

His laughter died off, and he glanced up at me. "What if I can't get up close and personal with a guy's ass?" Wide-eyed horror filled his gaze. I would have laughed at this whole conversation if he wasn't being absolutely genuine with his fear.

"How do you feel about a guy getting close to *your* ass?" I hated the heat touching my cheeks as I asked the question. Sure, we were close, but this level of detail was way out of the norm. But he needed this openness. Needed me to be frank.

"I'm not sure. Never considered bottoming, really."

I quirked my eyebrow at him, calling bullshit. Surely every queer guy had thought about it at length. Whether they decided if it was for them or not meant they'd had to have put thought into it, right?

"Fine." He rolled his eyes at me, some of his stress seeming to melt away. "I've put plenty of thought into it. I'm not sure if I ever want to." It was Cass's turn for his cheeks to flush. "Maybe for the right guy I would. But after yesterday and the more I think about it, I think I'll be so fucking terrified of my reaction, I'm not sure I could go through with it."

My heart ached at his truth while being so proud of him for sharing this with me.

"Maybe put yesterday behind you, and eventually you'll just get there." My words felt lame and not at all helpful. I tried again, thinking about some of the things I'd learned from one of my psych classes. "You need to be able to talk out your worries with whoever you're with." I winced, even though I was sure my advice was solid. "Which I know isn't exactly great for a one-night stand or a casual hookup."

Cass stared at me in silence, his expression letting me know he was thinking hard. "That makes sense." When he nodded, I gave myself a metaphorical pat on the back. "So I need to trust the person."

"Yeah. Enough that you can be honest with them about douching and your worries."

Once again, he nodded. I grinned, on a roll with

this advice-giving shit. Hell, maybe I should skip out on the police academy and be a sex therapist or something instead.

Humming in response, Cass pressed back against me, returning to his snuggle position. "Thanks, Dyl."

With a happy exhale and a soft kiss to his head, I held him tighter. "Any time, Cass. You know that."

CHAPTER 6

CASSIUS

AGED 20

EVERYTHING WAS CHANGING.

Excitement sparked to life in my gut whenever I thought about what lay ahead. That didn't stop the slither of unease. Whatever happened in the next hour with the draft pick, it was likely I'd be thousands of miles away from all that was familiar.

Sure, I entered the draft early, much to Mom and Pop's frustration, but this was what I always wanted. Had spent years dreaming about. My degree credits would keep. Maybe in a few years I could finish my degree, once life had settled and I was a shoo-in for the starting five.

If I ended up on the West Coast, those changes I

was both nervous and eager for would take some getting used to.

"You okay?"

Dylan's soft question was for my ears only. Not that anyone else would be able to hear, considering the volume in the arena.

"Yeah." A shaky breath huffed out of me. The buzz zipping around was like nothing I'd ever experienced before. And I suspected I never would again.

This was it. The League draft.

Looking past the tables complete with other players and their family and friends, I wiped my sweaty palm on my thigh, hoping I didn't stain the fabric.

"Not long before they start."

My gaze connected with Dylan's when he spoke. His eyes were wide. There was little doubt in my mind that he felt almost as nervous as I did. We'd already discussed the possibility of me moving away and what that would look like.

Hell, the very thought of not being able to see him regularly was difficult to imagine. More than that, discomfort, heavy and unfamiliar, sat on my chest, constricting my lungs. We may have lived apart for almost three years, but that hadn't stopped me being needy to spend time with my best friend.

I didn't expect anyone would ever understand the

pull Dylan had over me. In fact, I didn't even know how to explain it or attempt to put it into words.

For the first time, I was hyperaware of my inability to reach out to hold his hand. It fucking sucked. He was my best friend. Hell, if my best friend was a girl, I was sure I'd be able to cling on to her hand, seeking the support I desperately wanted.

And while I usually fought against even the tiniest hint of prejudice, with so many cameras around, and soon to be millions of Americans watching the draft from their screens, I reluctantly knew now wasn't the time.

What I would do was hug the shit out of him, though, as soon as my name was called.

Grateful, I smiled at Dylan, relieved he was here. For sure, my folks being here meant everything, right alongside my friend Colton, who I'd met last summer at Montview Academy. We'd become good friends, despite us being on different trajectories after his injury.

But it was Dylan who helped keep me grounded. Helped to keep my breathing steady.

Paula, dressed in a lit suit and kickers that I knew had rainbow laces in them, leaned over the table to get my attention.

I angled forward, taking in the mischievous glint in her eyes. At almost eighteen, she absolutely knew who she was. Back then, I thought I did, but compared to Paula, who'd come out as lesbian last year, told her parents to fuck off, then moved in with Mom and Pop, I swore she was more clued up than I ever was.

"You think anyone would notice if I slipped out before they start and smuggled in some pizza?" She bobbed her eyebrows for good measure, and I grinned, appreciating her cutting through the tension.

"Unless you're prepared for it to get squashed by hiding the tray under your jacket, it's likely you'll get tackled."

"Ooh… there was a cute security guard near the door. Maybe I should make sure I walk past her, wait till I get her attention."

"What, with your alluring cheesy stench? Sounds delightful."

Paula flipped her brother off, only to hide her hand quickly at a raised brow from Mom.

"Sorry, Mama T." As always, her sugary sweet smile didn't fool anyone who knew her. Paula was too much of a badass for that to fly.

"If anyone needs to use the restrooms, now's the time."

My lips twitched at Mom, and I flicked a glance at Dylan, who openly grinned.

It didn't matter that Dylan was less than three months away from being twenty-one and two days away from leaving to head to Virginia for the start of his police academy training—knowledge that made it difficult for me to breathe if I thought too long and hard about it. Nor did it matter that by the end of the night, I'd be playing professionally and have a contract earning me the big bucks. For sure, none of that mattered to Mom, who still liked to remind us to pee while we could.

"You need to go potty, Dyl? Need me to hold your hand?"

Without speaking, Dylan stared at me, silently telling me to fuck off. We didn't need to exchange words for me to know what he wanted to say.

It was all I could do to not burst into laughter and drift into hysteria. With my emotions high and close to the surface, it wouldn't take much to push me over the edge.

Rather than visiting the little boys' room, I tried to relax, focusing on Colton telling a very different version of a story of when we were at the training academy together and I'd "accidentally" mistaken Byron Dexter's dick for the hoop.

My bad.

The guy was a homophobic fuckwit and had deserved to be walking with a grimace and an ice pack pressed to his balls for the rest of the afternoon.

"How the hell you didn't get kicked out of the academy I'll never know." Despite his words, there was a proud gleam in Dylan's gaze.

"Seriously, is there even a tiny part of you that could underestimate me?" I cocked my brow at my best friend, earning me an eye roll.

"I have no idea of underestimations," Colton butted in with a grin. "I seriously just think Dylan here deserves a medal for putting up with your ass over the years."

Dylan bobbed his head, feigning seriousness. "Thanks, Colton. It's nice to feel appreciated."

"Whatever, assholes. I know love and worship when I see it."

Neither of my friends had the chance to flip me off as Mom cleared her throat.

I quieted down, my nerves once more sparking to life when I noticed the number of film crew taking up their positions. They'd been milling around since before we got here, but with the bustle of activity and more people taking their seats, including the specta-tors at the back, it was clear it was almost showtime.

Falling to the hotel mattress with a grunt, I grinned at the ceiling.

The mattress dipped beside me when Dylan followed suit. At the touch of his arm against mine, I turned my head, our gazes clashing, the grin on his lips matching my own.

"I need to keep pinching myself."

"If you need a hand with that…." He lifted his arm and reached for me, humor in his expression. I stopped him short of pinching my side and instead clasped his hand.

"LA Tritons." I squeezed his palm. "As long as I get through training camp, I'm going to be playing alongside Phelps." For real, there were so many players who were incredible. It just happened that Eddie Phelps was fucking phenomenal. He'd been in the League for a few years now but was nowhere close to retirement.

"You'll dominate camp."

The conviction in Dylan's tone caught my attention. I flushed at his belief, at the gentle yet somehow fierce way he stared at me.

"You think?" While I quite liked an ego boost every once in a while, right now, this was more than that.

The names drawn today reminded me that I'd be going up against the best the country had to offer.

And once I was at training camp, I'd be legit competing against some of the best players in the world for a starting spot.

Talk about intimidating.

"I know." Dylan brushed his thumb over my skin, the touch centering. "You'll push yourself and find your place in no time."

As reassuring as his words were, they were an unwelcome reminder of the new distance between us. Just over two and a half thousand miles, in fact.

I'd been holding out hope for a southeast team, just so I could be closer, not only to Dylan with his move but also not quite as far away from home.

"Hey, stop with the pouty lip."

I huffed out a laugh and straightened my features, not realizing I was being quite so obvious.

"I know there's a bit of a distance, but I won't be in Virginia forever."

He wouldn't be. I knew that.

While he could have applied to a police academy closer to home, apparently Virginia offered hard-core training and was recognized countrywide as one of the best training institutes. It meant he'd also need to police there for a couple years or so before even looking at returning home. The whole decision hadn't been made lightly, especially because of his sister.

But with Paula living with my folks and with her own plans for a scholarship at pretty much any college of her choice, she'd convinced him she'd be fine and he should follow his dreams.

So he had. And I was so damn proud of him.

But the reality of the miles between us was a shit of a thing.

It also made me feel even needier than normal.

We'd always half jested about Dylan being the cuddler of the two of us. Him initiating contact. We both knew the truth. It was bullshit.

While Dylan enjoyed affection, having been pretty touch starved at home, I'd been the one to latch on, embracing the cuddle monster title with pride.

I turned on my side, angled my thigh on top of his, and pressed my cheek against his chest.

"Nothing between us will change, yeah?"

Believing him, I bobbed my head and closed my eyes.

Tonight we'd had a few drinks in my parents' room, but we were far from drunk. Just enough to help us celebrate and make us a little rowdier than normal.

In the hotel room we shared, though, it was easy to embrace the comfortable quiet. Relax into the way

Dylan stroked my hair, his nails every now and then scratching lightly over my scalp.

Content, not only with Dylan's affection but also by his reassurance that we had this, I sighed into his touch, letting the effects of the alcohol swim through me and relax me even more.

My dick twinged, not a surprise considering the gentle caresses or the fact that I tended to get horny when I'd had a few drinks. I suspected most people did.

With each touch, I sank deeper into the sensation, luxuriating in the tenderness.

This year had been full-on in school, leaving little room for any real connection.

It was difficult to open up when I questioned every hookup. Were they in it just for the spotlight? Was getting in my pants a chance to get knocked up? Paranoia was rife in the sporting world—something I'd experienced firsthand last year when one girl "swore on her life" she was on the pill.

Like fuck I'd fall for that.

It was shit feeling that way. Thinking that way.

Doubting women seemed especially unfair. I knew it. No doubt I was preventing any real connection with my paranoia. Not that I was looking for a relationship anytime soon.

And guys?

Fuck. Just the thought of sinking into a man's ass thickened my cock. But I hadn't been able to get over what happened last year and my irrational freak-out. Dylan had been incredible when he'd flown out to me, helping to draw me out of my funk and get me out of my head. His insistence that I'd been traumatized rather than irrational had been kind too.

Did I want to believe that? Reluctantly, I supposed so.

But trauma?

I continued to roll my eyes whenever I thought that.

It seemed a little excessive.

And didn't it belittle those who experienced real, honest-to-god trauma?

When I'd said as much to Dylan, he called bullshit and reminded me that trauma wasn't a competition.

Regardless, sinking my cock into a tight channel remained central to so many fantasies.

That would not happen. Not unless I could do so with someone I trusted implicitly. Someone I knew I could fall apart in front of and not want to disappear. Someone who I trusted to get squeaky clean and not laugh or destroy my usually big ego if I panicked.

In this, my ego shrank to the size of a walnut. Hell, maybe a shriveled peanut.

But fuck, how I wanted it.

Want turned my dick to steel. Want had me forgetting who the fuck I was with when I angled my hips, brushing my straining cock against Dylan's thigh.

Dylan's fingers froze in my hair, stopping me immediately.

"Fuck. Sorry." I tilted away as I spoke and started to pull back fully. *The hell is wrong with me?*

"Hey."

I paused when his hand moved to my shoulder.

"Get your ass back here." He tugged me toward him, my face settling once more on his chest.

"Fine, but still. Sorry." I ignored the heat filling my cheeks. I just wished I could ignore my aching cock. Even the awkwardness of rubbing up against Dylan hadn't done a thing to make me deflate.

"S'all good. It happens."

Hearing his words, I sagged into his touch, knowing Dylan never lied to me.

"Happens all the fucking time these days when I'm not getting any."

At my words, the pounding of Dylan's heart, loud against my ear, picked up speed. And while his movements in my hair faltered, it was for barely a couple of seconds.

He didn't say anything for a beat, the room quiet,

though the thumping of his pulse filled me. When he finally asked, "There a reason you're not getting any?" I didn't hesitate in angling to see a glimpse of his face.

Truth was, Dylan knew all my reasons.

"Same old. Trusting is virtually impossible."

Despite his wince, he smiled down at me. It was a little sad and filled with understanding.

"I get it. For different reasons, but I do get it," he said softly.

Being gay in a small town could be tough. Dylan being at college had made things a little easier, but letting down your guard and sharing your sexuality always came with risks. I felt like I only knew or at least experienced a fraction of what he did.

Don't get me wrong—I was regularly frustrated that the B in LGBTQ seemed to be ignored or brushed aside, but Dylan had a couple of quite shitty reactions over the past couple of years.

Honestly, I dreaded him joining the police force. Worrying about his safety for simply being a cop was one thing. Worrying about his safety and well-being because he was a gay cop added a whole new level to my fear.

The last thing I wanted to think about was Dylan at risk. Though my dick flagged a little, so there was that.

"This is going to sound all 'woe is me' or something, so tell me to get over myself, but it's going to get even harder, right?" I shifted, moving more fully on him so half my body pressed against his front. He scooted up a little as I did so, leaning against the headboard so he wouldn't be in such an awkward position to be able to see my face.

It was a dance we were used to.

When comfortable, I pressed my hands against his chest and rested my chin on top. Peering up at him, our gazes catching, I waited for him to answer.

"More difficult knowing who to trust?"

I bobbed my head.

Sending a tender smile my way, Dylan reached for my face. A gentle stroke followed before he dropped his hand. "I hope you can trust your team."

I hoped for that too.

"You'll find your place and settle into it. Make friends. No doubt there'll be a bigger circle of friends there in the process. You'll learn how to trust them."

What he didn't mention was my decision to stay in the closet. Or maybe with my door slightly ajar.

There were no out queer players in the League. I hoped there would be some day soon.

Sure, I was comfortable in my own skin and with my sexuality. Lots of my teammates at college knew, but it wasn't public knowledge; I kept things on the down-low.

It was *that* reality that sucked.

It was also *that* reality that would mean I'd have to be even more careful. The press were everywhere, and when I did choose to come out, it would be on my terms.

At least that was the plan.

It meant hooking up with a guy now that my contract was signed would be even trickier. I needed someone I could really trust so I knew they wouldn't kiss and tell and could help me get past my fear.

Dylan knew all this. Respected it even.

Now, with just two days before he packed up and left for Virginia, we'd had a similar conversation. I didn't know whether it was ironic or simply funny, but I'd always been the loud and proud bi and was now stepping into the shadows.

Dylan, though, had come out later and was always a little hesitant and nervous—understandable considering his upbringing.

Though he'd decided to no longer hide away, even when at the academy and when he was working in the force. After being taught to feel shame, he refused to conceal this part of him any longer.

Jesus, he was strong and brave. Stronger and braver than I ever was.

"What's that smile for?" He tilted his head, searching my gaze.

I hadn't even realized I'd been smiling, lost in thought about how proud of Dylan I was.

"Just thinking how awesome you are."

The pink in his cheeks made me grin. His pale skin always highlighted his feelings, drawing them front and center.

"It's about time you recognized how phenomenal I am." He hid his embarrassment well with his teasing words.

"I've always known how phenomenal you are." I arched a brow, saying, "You had a good mentor, someone to aspire to be like." By the time I managed to say, "You're welcome," I huffed out a loud laugh as he grabbed hold of me and managed to wrangle me so I was on my back, Dylan between my legs, his weight pushing against me.

He snagged my hands, shoving them above my head, holding them with one hand.

"Fuck no." Laughter had me wheezing, knowing the asshole was going to go for my ribs and tickle me.

I bucked against him. All that did was make him push harder against me, a wide grin on his lips and a flush in his cheeks. His eyes virtually sparkled with amusement.

By the time his fingers danced across my flesh, his hands under my shirt, I was bucking like a fucking bronco.

One jolt forced his hand high, his fingers trailing against my nipple.

Goose bumps broke out across my skin, and my breath caught.

Two hip jolts and his grip tightened around my wrists. And why the fuck was I beginning to like the idea of him holding me down like this and doing all manner of sinful things to my body?

One more thrust had him locking his feet around my calves. I hadn't even noticed him straddling me rather than being between my thighs.

My eyes glazed over.

His dick was hard.

There was no mistaking the thick, solid appendage against my stomach. My dick throbbed, the sound of our combined heavy breaths doing nothing to calm my racing pulse or the awareness sweeping through me.

Our gazes locked, and it was impossible to look away.

This was Dylan. *My* Dylan.

The fuck was happening?

His tongue darted out, and I tracked the movement as it swiped over his bottom lip.

My dick jerked. At the movement, my gaze flicked up, meeting his.

Did I say anything? Did I want this?

Did he?

Never, not once, had we gotten close to doing anything like this.

Almost fifteen years of knowing the man, and not even once had my awareness of him turned my dick to steel.

Dylan parted his lips, and I held my breath, waiting, wondering what he was going to say.

Nothing. No words followed. But I saw his struggle, his confusion. I felt it bone-deep and saw it mirrored in the reflection of his eyes.

Could we do this and not have it ruin everything?

Could we do this so I could selfishly have my first taste of something I'd been desperate for? Something I'd been craving?

Trust.

I trusted Dylan more than I trusted myself.

Did that mean—

Fuck it.

Consequences be damned, I angled up and pressed my mouth against his.

Heat, perfection, and awareness all slammed into me as we kissed. Our touch was tentative, exploring.

Until it wasn't.

Until Dylan ground against me.

A strangled moan punched out of my lungs, which Dylan caught with his mouth. He pressed harder, chased my tongue, dominating my mouth and surprising the fuck out of me with the strength of his kisses.

I should have questioned it. Probably should have pulled away.

But with the intensity of how he fucked my mouth with his tongue, how he punched his hips against mine as he gave me his whole weight, nothing short of someone dragging me away by my feet could have stopped me.

With his hand already on my chest, he caressed my flesh, fingers swiping over my nipple. A shudder barreled through me, making me cling on for dear life, chasing this moment.

His kisses. His touches.

But fuck did I want it.

Want more.

Want everything.

The realization snapped into me with the force of a tidal wave. I pulled back, our lips parting.

Our breathing heavy, the warmth pressing against my lips, I opened my eyes.

Already peering down at me with half-lidded eyes surrounded by flushed skin, Dylan looked as fucked as I felt.

It should have been the moment to stop, the time to chuckle this off and scramble away. But with my dick harder than it had ever been before and liquid courage in my veins, I didn't want to. Wasn't even sure I could if I tried.

The only thing stopping this would be Dylan.

And while his eyes were a little glazed and I was pretty sure he was as bewildered as I was, he remained atop me, weight still on me as his gaze roamed my face.

Somehow I managed to form words. They were shaky as hell as the reality of the moment, the possibility, slotted into place. "You're the only person I trust. I think the only person I can ever truly trust."

The hitch in his breath and the flare in his eyes let me know he understood where I was going with this.

"We don't have to, but fuck, Dyl, if there's ever going to be a man who I felt I could do this with, it's you. It will always be you."

The words were out there, snapped taut between us.

This was my best friend. Our friendship was

everything. The last thing I wanted to do was mess with that.

"What if it fucks everything up?"

His words may as well have been tugged from my heart.

I swallowed and took a steadying breath, still holding on to him. It should have been strange, clinging to Dylan like this after the kiss that I suspected would be scored into my memory forever.

"We won't let it." I believed it, trusted it. Trusted us to have this. The voice in my brain told me I was a selfish dick for wanting this, but it didn't stop me from saying, "Just this once, and then we shake it off, talk about it if we want to or never mention it again. You're my best friend, Dyl. That'll never change."

I didn't mention that he was leaving anyway, and I'd soon be heading out in a whole new direction. There was no need. He knew our story as well as I did.

"And you want to fuck me?" Intensity filled his voice as his focus zeroed in completely on my reaction.

"Yeah." The click of my swallow was impossible to not hear. "If you'll let me." Heat flooded my cheeks. "If I don't freak the hell out."

With a soft gaze, Dylan moved his hand and cupped my cheek. It was a gesture he'd done a million times, but not quite like this, and definitely not with his hard dick pushed against my own.

"You're safe with me. If you change your mind, you can. If you want to stop, that's okay. If you want to close your eyes, that's okay too."

Jesus. Emotion rushed into my chest.

This right here was why he had to be the one.

How could I even begin to trust someone so implicitly? It wasn't possible.

Allowing his words to settle in my chest, I took a fortifying breath and tried to shrug off the nerves and the intensity that was serious and so not us.

I kicked my lips up into a smile, relaxing into the gesture, taking comfort that, between the unexpected reality I found myself in, this was Dylan. The guy who'd thought it was an awesome idea to stick a french fry up his nose when he was seven, only for it to get stuck.

"Just to make it clear, there's not a chance I'm going to be closing my eyes. If I'm getting the opportunity to see your asshole, no way am I missing it."

His laughter was loud and abrupt. "Fuck off. Don't make this weird."

Relief swept through me, amusement thick and heavy in its wake. "There's something weird about your asshole? I think I might change my mind," I teased.

"Fucking hell."

He made to fall off me, but I held on tight.

"You're impossible."

I rolled my hips, reveling in the hitch in his breath and just how hard he still was. "And you're just as horny."

He groaned in a "you're fucking impossible" way and collapsed on me, burying his head next to the crook of my neck. "It's only because no one has touched my cock in six months."

Surprised, I pushed his chest a little to see his face.

"What?" he said, a little defensively. "I've been busy finishing my associate's degree and working all the hours at the diner."

"And you couldn't squirrel in ten minutes for a bj? Dude, no wonder you're so hard. You're going to go off like a rocket." Not clamping down on my excitement, I wriggled my eyebrows, my smile broad. Fuck, I so wanted to see him shoot his load and lose his mind.

Something I'd never truly considered wanting to see before.

But right here, right now, I was so up for it.

"You think you've got what it takes to make me come that hard?" The challenge was there, his smirk all amusement.

"Dyl, it's like you don't know me at all." I squeezed his ass for good measure, liking a little too much the darkening of his eyes and the way his gaze dipped to my mouth.

"Let me get my toiletry bag and head to the bathroom."

And he was gone, and this was really fucking happening.

Holy shit.

As soon as the bathroom door closed, I was on my feet. Nerves skated across my skin as I undressed, trying not to think too long and hard about what was about to happen.

I attempted to push the doubt and worry aside, reminding myself of all the reasons why this wasn't the worst idea in the world. Hell, maybe it was something I should have considered the first time I realized I had an issue.

Dylan always made everything better.

Just being in his orbit was usually enough to settle whatever bugged me.

He could make me laugh and relax. The asshole could even make me cry. He could help make my worries disappear.

And apparently, he could make me come.

Hopefully.

It was a mindfuck, but back to not thinking about

that, I snatched my discarded towel from earlier and spread it on the bed. Then I settled on it and paid attention to my dick.

Still hard, my cock jerked.

That was something. My cock being on board helped settle some of the buzzing in my brain.

Supplies. I needed supplies.

Butt naked, I jumped off the mattress and went to my bag. I rummaged around for the lube and the condoms and smiled in triumph. I'd nearly not packed these, but it was actually Dylan's voice in my head that had made me grab them last minute.

The asshole was an unofficial Boy Scout. His mantra of "being prepared" had long ago been drilled into me. My cock jerked and precum glistened despite the direction of my thoughts when I considered the contents of his toiletry bag.

Without needing confirmation, I had no doubt that Dylan had a douche stowed away. The thought made me smile, and the precum beading had me chuckling, relieved that the thought of a douche didn't make my dick droop.

Supplies in hand, I went back to the bed, leaving the covers pushed to the end.

Not a chance I wanted either of us covered up.

This was a onetime deal. That was a discussion we didn't need to have.

And I wasn't lying about wanting to see his asshole.

Stroking my cock, I took a steadying breath.

I had this. I wouldn't freak. Wouldn't get caught up in my head.

And if there was any mess—I swallowed hard— I'd be fine. I'd get out of my head and man the fuck up.

I grinned as I thought those words, knowing Dylan would slap me around the head at the phrase that, in truth, we both thought was bullshit.

But I did like getting a rise out of Dylan. That would never stop.

The door opening grabbed my attention. My hand froze.

I was here. Spread out on the bed. Naked. Jacking myself off. In front of my friend.

Holy fucking shit.

Any self-doubt flew out the window as soon as I met his gaze and saw the heat in his eyes. Taking in my fill, eating up his exposed skin, I licked my suddenly dry lips.

His cock stood to attention. And unlike me, he was cut, his bulbous head on display, smooth and a deep pink, and looking so fucking lickable.

"Fuck." I grabbed the root of my cock, surprised by the rush of need.

Immediately, a smirk tilted Dylan's lips.

"Yeah, yeah." I rolled my eyes and still held on to my throbbing cock. "Just get your ass over here."

When the fuck did Dylan get so sexy? Like, holy fuck.

That his abs weren't as defined as mine, I liked a whole lot. That his milky skin was scattered with dark blond hair made it impossible not to eat him up. His chest wasn't quite smooth—he didn't wax like I did. The scratch of his light fur would feel so fucking hot brushing against my chest.

It didn't escape my attention that Dylan took his fill of me either.

It was the first time we'd seen each other this way.

My pecs jerked when his gaze roamed my chest, and his smirk deepened. When his gaze traveled to my hand, still gripping my cock, my breathing turned ragged.

His tongue dipped out and swiped lightly at his bottom lip. Just remembering how he'd fucked my mouth with it had me trembling with need.

His attention landed on the supplies before we finally made eye contact.

Despite the heat in his gaze threatening to set me on fire, his voice was gentle as he settled on the bed, saying, "Anytime you want to stop, just say, okay?"

Fucking hell.

I launched, tugging him toward me while managing to slot him beneath my limbs as I scrambled on top. He reacted with a laugh and an "*Oomph*." The latter I caught in a searing kiss.

Hot need, the brushing of lips, the caress of a tongue, and I glided my hands down his body. Mapping his curves and ridges, I drank in his shuddery gasps. By the time I reached his cock, the both of us panted.

Unsure of who groaned first when I gripped his warm skin wrapped around steel, I focused instead on the weight in my hand. And still our lips pressed against each other's, the movements sloppy and urgent and oh so bone melting.

I jolted abruptly when he palmed my cock. The touch was unexpected, which was ridiculous considering my hand worked him over. Peering down at him, I captured his gaze, getting lost for a moment in the hunger staring up at me.

"I need you inside me."

The words, quiet and desperate, tore through the last threads of my control.

I wanted that too. More than I thought would ever be possible.

In barely a blink, I slipped on the condom, slathered lube on my cock and my fingers, and knelt before him. I risked a glance down, swallowing hard when he parted his thighs even wider. As he grabbed a pillow and shoved it beneath his ass, I couldn't do anything but stare and exhale shaky breaths.

"You okay?"

At his question, my head snapped up. Concerned eyes looked back at me.

I nodded. "Yeah. Just…." My words struggled to form. This was a lot.

"Too much?"

And just like that, I smiled, losing some of the growing tension swirling in my gut.

Dylan knew me. Could read me. Hell, the man understood me at a level that sometimes blew my mind.

"I want to do this." Proud as fuck that my voice sounded strong, I reached out my slippery fingers and first swept them over his balls.

His shuddery breath was everything.

Trailing my fingers lower, across his taint, I didn't stop my descent, needing to do this. Wanting it so bad.

As I edged closer, he lifted his hips. I snapped my attention to his face. Dylan bit his bottom lip. His pale skin was dusted with a sweet pink, and while I could see his nerves, I knew he wanted this. Knew this wasn't simply about helping me out, allowing me to get past my fucked-up overthinking and fears.

At the expression on his face, I stopped just shy of his pucker. When I did, his breath hitched, and fuck if his whimper didn't twist something up deep inside me.

Voice tight, I asked, "I know you said six months, but when was the last time someone was in here?" Color me curious, but I wanted to know. It didn't matter the answer, not really, but still, I was interested.

All flushed skin and heavy breaths, Dylan stared at me. For a moment I didn't think he would answer. Maybe he wouldn't, but when I finally, slowly traced my finger over the delicate skin of his opening, he answered, "Never. I've always topped."

Surprise widened my eyes. Eagerness had me gently easing a finger inside.

The whole time, I kept my gaze locked to his, not yet ready to look down.

With my pulse loud in my ears, the pounding almost erratic in its intensity, all I could do was focus on his expression. Focus on breathing. Focus on the sensation rather than the bubble of uncertainty threatening to rise and—

"That feels so good."

I latched on to his words of praise, shoving down the voices in my head tempting me to listen.

"So fucking amazing."

From his blissed-out expression, I believed it. It gave me the courage I needed to pull out and insert a second finger.

This time I focused on the feeling, the tightness.

Lust bolted through me just thinking about how he'd feel around my cock.

"Oh, fucking hell." A deep groan chased his gurgled words, and he bore down against me.

A beat of panic thudded against my rib cage, only to stop when Dylan opened his eyes, ordering, "Give me your mouth."

I went willingly, refusing to stop working my fingers in and out of him as I angled down and pressed my lips to his.

A new tenderness slowed this kiss down. Different from what we'd shared so far. With each gentle brush of his lips and careful stroke of his tongue, my thumping heart quietened.

I leaned into the sensation, taking advantage of the moment of calm to push three fingers carefully inside him.

Lips parting in a gasp, Dylan tilted his head back. A loud moan followed.

"You okay?"

"Don't stop," he answered quickly, responding to my still fingers. "So fucking good."

"Yeah?"

"Feel like I'm going to blow."

A rush of relief pulsed through my veins, clearing my mind of everything but Dylan. His pleasure. Him being okay and not hurting.

This was a first for both of us.

"So fucking hard."

Unable to resist, I finally glanced down, taking in his weeping cock. Red and angry, he seriously did look ready to explode. Emboldened, I took a shaky breath and focused on my fingers.

"Holy fuck." He gripped them, the sight so erotic, so fucking everything, that my dick wept.

Nothing but lube coated my fingers, and what a visual as they pushed in and out with increasing ease as he loosened around me.

"Okay?"

Despite the strain in that one word, Dylan's concern was obvious.

I didn't want to look away, but he deserved to see the truth for himself.

Making eye contact, I nodded, swallowing thickly. "Fucking amazing."

He beamed at me, an honest-to-god beam of relief and pleasure, and I was sure pride stared back at me too.

Feeling nothing short of joyous, I grinned back. "Are you ready? Can I...?" Words were difficult, barely comprehending what we were doing. What we were about to do.

"Please, yeah… inside…." His gaze still intense, he whispered, "Just go slow, yeah?"

It was a reminder of the gift he was giving me.

Releasing my fingers, I leaned close to him, feeling heady as I offered what he'd previously given me. "I promise. Either of us wants to stop, we stop, okay?"

"Okay."

Pecking a kiss to his mouth, I gathered some more lube and placed it on my covered cock. I repositioned myself, my attention drifting between his ass and his expression.

While I trusted that he'd tell me what he needed, I had to see for myself.

"Do it."

My lips tipped high, despite barely being able to think of anything but being inside him. "Still bossy. I think there's a name for that."

His narrowed gaze shifted immediately as I pressed against his opening and eased inside an inch. Eyelids slamming closed, Dylan's breath hitched.

I waited, my muscles vibrating with restraint. Just the inch of heat and the iron grip around me threatened to unravel me.

Like fuck I'd come. Not with just an inch in. Not

after all this time of waiting and wishing and worrying this would never happen.

"More."

"Thank fuck."

A huff of a laugh jolted out of him. It quickly turned into a deep groan as I pushed in deeper, farther. Inch by inch, I pressed inside until I bottomed out, fully seated and wrapped up in mind-blowing heat.

There was no time to think about my fears. No time to even consider the what-ifs.

All that mattered was Dylan and me and our pleasure.

His order to "Move" had me driving into him.

Each glide, every sensation, all of it sent a flurry of heat to the space deep in my gut. It zipped around my body, catching my breath, threatening to unravel me, but still I moved.

Short gasps spilled from Dylan's parted lips. His eyes were half lidded, his gaze fixed on me.

Like this, all lust and passion, I'd never imagined, couldn't even fathom I'd ever see Dylan this way. Nor him me.

A deep groan echoed around the room as I shifted my hips, chasing my desire, speeding toward the moment I would spill and become lost. But fuck if it wasn't Dylan's gruff moans that spurred me on.

I wanted his gasping breaths, wanted to peg his prostate and make him come his brains out.

Moving as fluidly as possible, which was pretty damn difficult when I felt like I was unraveling, I kept the same angle.

"Holy. Fuck." His eyes widened. His stuttered breaths were better than any sound I'd heard before.

"There?" I punctuated my question with another deep thrust.

He grabbed onto me in response, his grip tight, blunt fingers pressing into my skin. "Yes. Right there."

A man on a mission, I focused on his soft pleas tangled with his eager groans.

Every sound had my toes curling, my balls tightening.

"Fuck. Touch yourself. Get yourself off," I demanded through gritted teeth, my tone desperate.

He did so immediately, a sultry smile spreading across his lips. Another thrust and I lost his smirk, and fuck if it wasn't a heady win, earning each breathless request for more.

Lifting fully, arms straight, weight on my palms at either side of his head, I glanced at his fast-moving hand.

The grip on his cock tightened, movement going out of sync a little.

"Jesus, yeah, like that. Just like that," he breathed.

He went fast, and try as I might, I pushed harder, went deeper, needing the rush of release, desperate to see him spilling onto his hand, squirting onto his stomach.

"Fucking give it to me."

My demand called forth the first shot of cum. Thick and white, and holy shit, I wanted to taste it. Taste Dylan. Savor this moment.

With jerking hips, I pounded into him, watching him spill the last drops of his release, and then I was gone. Flying. Charging through the stratosphere as my orgasm tore through me.

Shuddering jerks followed as I collapsed, feeling his heat and the sticky cum spreading on my stomach.

I wanted to groan, thinking once more about tasting it, but I held back, instead focusing on drawing in ragged breaths.

"You okay?" I finally whispered, not yet moving to look at him. My limbs were jelly, boneless as my adrenaline crashed.

"Yeah."

Hearing the tightness in his voice, I pushed myself up. Immediately, he dragged in a fresh breath.

"When the fuck did you get so heavy?"

I chuckled, relief capturing the sound and passing between us.

That I still had my cock buried in his ass wouldn't make this weird. Change things. I had to believe that. And from his amused smile, I hoped to hell I was right.

He shifted a little and winced. My gut clenched, knowing I needed to move. Needed to pull out.

Unwanted anxiety skittered across my skin as I thought about the action.

Fuck.

How fucking ludicrous. Planted inside him after having hands down the best sex of my life, and now my brain started to catch up.

It could fuck right off.

I didn't want the irrational thoughts. Didn't want the—

"Hey, breathe for me."

The soothing tone, Dylan's familiar voice, pierced my growing panic.

Taking a deep breath in, I held it before slowly exhaling.

"Another one for me."

I did as he directed, breathing with him, trying not to let the threatening embarrassment crawl along my skin and take me under, send me spiraling.

"Okay, that's good."

Concerned eyes met mine. I took solace in them, grateful Dylan was in this with me.

"Okay, now I want you to ease out. Slowly," he tagged on, and I frowned, my worry for him cutting through my looming freak-out.

"Are you okay? In pain?"

A soft smile lifted his lips. "Tender. Think I'll be walking bowlegged for a while," he teased, loosening some of the hovering panic in my chest. "But I'll be fine."

I nodded and eased out of him, focusing on the sensation of his tight channel and how perfectly I fit inside him. The thought was so much better than worrying about dealing with the cleanup.

And didn't I feel like a fucking dick for even thinking that right now.

His wince was thankfully short-lived. Once his features smoothed out, he reached up and squeezed my shoulder.

"You want to lean back and let me deal with the condom?"

Jesus, he was too good to me.

I took a deep, steady breath and shook my head. Putting more bravado than I truly felt into my words, I said, "Sex is messy right?" My smile tightened. "If I can't handle a little mess with the cleanup, I shouldn't be fucking."

A deep frown sliced across his features. "Fuck that, Cass. No bullshit. Not with me."

Emotion. Unwanted, foolish emotion squirreled its way into my chest.

Dylan had taken it up the ass for me. We smashed down all the "don't even think about it" rules between best friends, jumped over that invisible line without looking back.

His dick said he'd wanted it. As had his mouth.

And I knew I'd made his body sing.

But still, he'd done it for me.

Because of my fucking ridiculous, irrational issues.

I hated them. Hated that I felt this way. Hated that my reactions and fears took the lead.

Taking a deep breath, I loosened my limbs, saying, "Let me try."

Eyeing me carefully, he nodded.

I loved him for it. For everything.

I just wished it didn't make me feel like a prize dick.

Grabbing the root of my cock first, I slowly looked down.

A rush of breath escaped me. There was no hiding my relief.

My dick was half hard, the condom slippery.

Evidence of my own release was the only thing capturing my attention.

Jesus. There was nothing like turning sexy times into dread thinking about what else I could have spotted. A romance novel this would never be. How the fuck could it if I was the main man and too scared to look at the evidence of my lovemaking?

I stumbled at the thought.

Both at the ridiculousness and the "lovemaking."

It was sex. Hot, mind-blowing sex.

I looked down at Dylan, his uneasy gaze on me, and I smiled. It was all I could do to share my relief and hide the sting of knowing that I could never put him through this again.

Honestly, I didn't think I could to anyone else either.

Swallowing the realization down, I eased back fully and carefully removed the condom. "I'm just going to clean up and then grab a shower." My gaze drifted around his body as he lay exposed and vulnerable before me. Heat filled my belly, and I cleared my throat and smiled a little shiftily at him. "How about I clean up and turn the shower on for you first?"

Somehow, I tore my attention away from the drying cum on his stomach and made eye contact.

His smile was tentative, though it held a hint of amusement that I grabbed onto with both hands.

"I should write a damn book. *Magnanimous 101 with Cassius Britton.*"

Dylan snorted and sat up. "Uh-huh. A bestseller right there."

Once off the bed, I headed for the bathroom. "Right. Global sensation. League star."

Fuck, I was officially in the League. The jolt of reality shot excitement to my chest.

"I'm sure your fans will lap that right up," he tossed out at me, humor in every word. "It's your humility that makes you so endearing."

Grinning, I spun to look at him, my hand on the door handle. "One of my better qualities." I followed up with a wink and stared at Dylan, who'd since pulled the towel across his lap. My amusement faded away as I took him in, my grin softening to a gentle smile. "Thanks, Dyl. For everything."

If he was surprised by my words, he didn't show it. He stared at me hard for a beat. Wordlessly, he nodded, tenderness coloring his features.

I turned away and escaped into the bathroom.

Tonight had been unexpected. Incredible.

But from that one look, I knew we'd never talk about it again.

I winced at the pang in my heart and rubbed my chest.

There was only space for one kind of love for Dylan, and that was as my best friend, the man who selflessly gave me everything.

NOW....

CHAPTER 7

CASSIUS

EIGHT YEARS LATER

"EAT A BAG OF DICKS." NOT THE MOST ORIGINAL comeback, but with the speed Dexter turned red, I figured it hit the mark.

"And time to get off the court." Ollie gripped the back of my neck, just firm enough to get me moving. I expected it stopped me from getting into trouble too. Receiving a fine for talking shit to Dexter, the bigoted prick from the Bobcats, would have caused Coach Jenkins to have an aneurysm.

While I was used to him being pissed off with me, he usually did it with a "Jesus, I can't believe this asshole kid's an Eagle, but he is and he's kinda great" sigh. But a big fine and bad press would have meant

I'd be subjected to a "come to Jesus" moment with him.

"Cool it, yeah?"

"What?" I grinned widely and shrugged casually as my captain finally released me. "I'm so cool I'm like that ice character in *Batman*. Mr. Ice."

"That's not his name." Ollie ushered me toward where Coach and our team were waiting. The game was over, our team kicking the Bobcats' asses with a ten-point lead.

"Sure it is. He's all icy and frosty." I paused just as we reached hearing distance of Coach talking to Lintman. "Is it Mr. Frost?"

"Mr. Freeze."

I didn't have the chance to respond to Ollie, not sure he was right about the name—wasn't that an ice cream or something—before I stopped in front of Coach.

His narrowed gaze landed on me. "There a problem, Britton?"

"Absolutely not, Coach. Just giving Dexter some suggestions about what's good to eat in town."

Out of the corner of my eye, Ollie's whole body became taut. This usually meant he was reining himself in, and I expected working hard at not laughing. That or calling me out.

"Uh-huh. Well, in the future, get your ass off the court and back to your team."

"You got it, Coach."

He stared at me for a few more seconds, almost as if he expected me to say something else.

While I could, so very *very* easily, I had little doubt he'd overheard Dexter's ridiculous slur. And because he had, I expected he'd already made a formal complaint. That meant if I got caught up in it, Coach would be steam-out-the-ears mad.

I'd been playing for the Minnesota Eagles, returning to my home state, for five years now. It had been the best move ever, and I was grateful as hell.

It also meant I knew just how far to push Coach without him losing his shit and threatening to transfer me. If that happened, who the hell knew what I'd do.

Sure, I had a no-transfer contract, but if I pissed the man off, he'd find a way. That or he'd bench me.

I focused back on Coach as he told us to get our asses into the locker room. We did so quickly, the few on-court interviews having been wrapped up. Once inside our home locker room, he called for our attention. "Right. Monday morning, team breakfast, and then we're flying out to Louisville."

A collection of hollers went around the room.

The Roosters were always fun to play, especially

close to the end of the season. Without the pressure of being in the running for the championship—our season had been decent but not great—it meant we could let loose.

That didn't mean it wasn't shit that we couldn't make the playoffs.

"All right, all right." Coach rolled his eyes and shook his head, following up with a slight frown from something Finnegan, our strength coach, said too quietly for me to hear. "Tomorrow, you need to be in at ten, reviewing footage."

We all bobbed our heads, relieved he was giving us a break and not dragging us in at the butt-crack of dawn.

"Just three games left, Eagles. How you played tonight is what I expect from you for the final games."

We'd played our asses off. The Bobcats having so many players who were prize pricks had been a good motivator for all of us. There was nothing quite like giving dickwads the proverbial middle finger—and maybe a verbal slam or two as well—by taking the win.

Especially Dexter, who hadn't changed a bit since our days back in the academy.

But Coach was also right about our less-than-stellar season as a whole. Not that he verbalized it quite like that. While we were nowhere near useless, with more wins than losses, it was only by a pinch.

Coach continued giving us his end-of-game pep talk. I nodded in the right places, ribbed my teammates with sly looks, mouthed words, and hidden hand gestures. I could be subtle as fuck when the time called for it.

"Cassius."

My gaze snapped to Coach, and I dropped my hand from the jacking-off motion I directed at Joel. It was our love language. "Yeah, Coach?"

I kept my face relaxed, ignoring Joel's snicker.

"A word," he said pointedly before telling the rest of the team to get showered.

Ollie nudged me as he passed by, shooting me a meaningful look to keep my mouth shut and out of trouble. It wasn't like I was completely without a filter. I could, when I chose, do exactly that, but telling the truth and calling people out on bullshit—myself included—was kind of my thing.

But there was something in Coach's gaze that seemed a little off. He didn't seem pissed off or even frustrated.

"In my office."

Ah, fuck. Maybe I'd completely misread his tone.

I followed him in, shooting Marlow a middle

finger on the side of my face as he jeered and made kissing noises.

"Take a seat."

My eyebrows drew together. Usually, he called me out as soon as the door closed. This was different.

Unease settled in my gut as I sat.

He didn't look angry.

"Everything okay, Coach?"

His expression turned solemn as he lifted his finger before picking up his phone.

A slither of unease unfurled in my gut as he spoke into his phone. "Yeah, I'm in my office with Britton now."

My brows shot high. With my brain going a mile a minute, I thought back over the last week. I'd done nothing particularly bad. Hell, I hadn't even been out for drinks, so it wasn't like the cops could be showing up due to post-drinking stupidity.

This week, I'd even been catching a ride in with Miles, as my car was in the shop receiving a pretty slick paint job. So not even a traffic violation could be coming my way. Not that I expected cops. It had been a long-ass time since I'd gotten into any kind of trouble with the law. And even then, it was so not my fault.

A knock at the door had me angling around, trying to see who Coach had summoned. Rather than hollering like he usually did, Coach continued to pull the rug from under my feet by racing to the door. One tentative look in my direction, sending a fresh wave of alarm through me, and he opened the door.

I frowned. My brain took a second to catch up.

"Dylan?" The word finally broke free as my best friend stepped fully into the room. "The hell?" A grin split my face, and I shot up out of my seat.

On the first step toward him, I faltered.

Something was wrong. Off.

It wasn't even the fact that he was in his police uniform, his chest proudly displaying his Zumbrota PD badge.

This man had been my best friend since day one of kindergarten when I'd shared my gummy bears with him. We'd been through everything together. Coming out. Losing family. Ditching school and a hundred million other moments.

His eyes, the way he stepped into the room, the harsh swallow as he finally stopped, gaze on me, screamed something bad had happened.

"What's wrong?" I was in his space in the next second.

And then he did something I hadn't seen him do since almost three years ago when we were at his sister's funeral. He cried.

Big, fat tears rolled down his face.

"The fuck?" The words spilled out of me, even as I wrapped him up in my arms.

I vaguely heard Coach leaving the room, but with my heart pounding loudly in my ears, it was difficult to focus on anything beyond the man gripping me and hugging me hard.

"Hey," I whispered, still holding him. He clung to me, head pressed against my chest, our seven-inch height difference perfect for me to rest my chin on the top of his head. "You want to sit down?"

A shuddery breath left Dylan.

"Come on." I all but dragged him to the small couch, needing the support of the seat to stop the shake in my body as worry clawed at me.

By the time we sat, he'd stopped crying. I took in his expression, the shell-shocked look peering back at me.

Dylan swiped a hand over his face and shook his head. "Fuck, I'm sorry." He cleared his throat. "I shouldn't be here. Shouldn't have come here like this." When his gaze dropped to my Eagles uniform, his frown deepened. "Fuck, your game."

"Already finished, and we kicked ass."

A hollow laugh spilled from him. "I can't stay long. Fuck." The rough word sounded scratchy. "I've got to get back to Mikey."

Alarm tightened my chest, my heart thudding

heavily. "Who's looking after him?" It was late. Two-year-olds should be fast asleep at this time of night. At least, I assumed as much.

"Helen's at my place babysitting. He's fast asleep."

Some of the anxiety loosened in my chest. "Okay, so Mikey's fine…." I petered out, waiting for him to fill in the gap. When he swallowed hard and tears welled in his eyes, I reached out for him, taking his hand. "Dylan, you're killing me here. You're an hour away from home, still in your blues. The hell is going on?"

Expelling a slow, shaky breath, he angled to look at me. His eyes were wide. Fuck, he looked terrified.

"Mom and Dad are trying to take him."

"What?" I shook my head, my brows bunching. "Take Mikey?"

He was already nodding before I finished. "Yeah. They're spouting shit about grandparents' rights, saying that as a single, working parent, they've got a case for full custody. Saying shit like my work hours mean I'm neglecting him. That and using his broken arm as ammo." Pink colored his cheeks, his voice turning hard.

And thank fuck. A pissed-off Dylan I could get a better handle on rather than a defeated one.

"The fuck! That was at a playground. Kids break

shit all the time. And Jesus, you're a cop. A fucking sergeant." I legit didn't understand. How his asshole parents would think they had a case against Dylan blew my fucking mind.

Hell, they hadn't even attended Paula's funeral.

The familiar bitterness and hatred I had for his folks clawed at my throat, but I pushed it down.

"Like they give a shit about that." He shook his head. "Mom said she's reached out to their lawyer, said they're going to say Paula's last wishes are worth shit as she was high."

"The fuck they are. As if Paula would ever be on anything." Hell, I'd known Paula almost as well as I knew Dylan. As his little sister, Paula had spent many hours following us around and annoying us. And as we'd grown, she'd become a friend, especially when she'd moved out of their childhood home as soon as she was able to.

Their parents were fuckheads. Super conservative and sat happily on their backward moral high grounds.

Hell, it had been one thing for Dylan to become best friends with me, a gangly Black kid—a handsome splash of color in their whitewashed world. Add in them finding out Dylan was gay, and their daughter following suit at sixteen, and they'd practically had heart attacks.

"I know, but fuck, what if they do?"

A holler from outside Coach's office startled us both.

"I'm so sorry to come here. I just panicked. I should have just called."

"Screw that. You did the right thing. If you were so worked up, it was better to come here, get your Cassius fix. That way, when you get home, you can focus on being the best dad to that crazy-ass kid of yours." I smiled softly, even as my heart squeezed. It did every single time I thought about Mikey.

"Let me call my lawyer," I continued, my brain already going into planning mode. "We'll get this fixed so your parents can't come anywhere near him."

Nodding a little numbly, Dylan stared back at me.

"No one is taking Mikey from you, okay?" I forced seriousness into my tone, something I rarely did. "Paula wanted you to be her kid's dad, and you're fucking amazing at it."

His eyes closed at my words, a single tear dripping down his cheek. "Thanks, Cass. It's just shit, you know?"

I bobbed my head. I was all too aware that in four weeks, it was Mikey's third birthday, which would also be the anniversary of his sister's death. This time of year was always hard.

"Do you believe me when I say Mikey's yours and always will be?" I tilted my head and smiled.

He studied me a beat, softness entering his gaze, and his shoulders relaxed. "Yeah, Cass. Just let me know how much your lawy—"

"Fuck no. I said I've got this, yeah?"

As always whenever anything related to money came up, Dylan's jaw tightened. It was never my intention to shove my earnings in his face. He worked his ass off in a profession that took so much bravery and dedication, and damn if he didn't deserve to earn a lot more than he did. But not a chance would I have him worrying about paying for a lawyer.

This was my responsibility as his friend. I shoved the other reasons way down below into the darkness of my conscience, like I always did. I didn't have the capacity to deal with the dump of guilt that sat heavily on my chest if I didn't.

"You need me to make the drive home with you?" I offered. While I was tired from the game, if Dylan needed the company to get home safely, I'd do so in a heartbeat.

"No, man. I'm good." He huffed out a heavy breath. "I heard from my mom at the end of work, so I just drove straight here after talking to Helen about taking care of Mikey. I just couldn't go home and let my kid see me wrecked, you know?"

"I know. Like I said, you're a kick-ass dad."

My words pulled a small smile to his mouth. "Thanks, Cass." He stood, and I followed suit.

"Just let me know when you're home, okay?"

"Will do," he answered.

"I'll talk to Granger, my lawyer, and let you know what he says. Then three more games and I'll be over for a long-ass stay, yeah?"

A genuine smile split his lips. "You planning on hanging around for a while? You know my spare room's always made up for you for as long as you want."

Fuck, I loved this guy. Our friendship had gotten me through so much shit over the years—including coming out to the public, not long after League superstar Ryan Broadwater—and barely a day went by without us making some sort of contact with each other. But a visit longer than a couple of nights was a luxury we usually had to wait until offseason for—ridiculous since he didn't live that far away.

But this visit looked like it had come at a perfect time since he was dealing with his hateful parents.

I was just so damn grateful he'd moved back home to be near my folks when he became Mikey's guardian.

"I'll be there and hang around for as long as you want me. I've no plans to rush off." Sure, since he'd taken custody of Mikey on the day he was born, our downtime together didn't look like it once had, but that was more than okay. Mikey was amazing. It had only been four days since I'd last seen him in the flesh—and that was literally for an afternoon—and I was keen to see how much more he'd grown and changed.

I swore the kid grew faster than a weed.

"Okay, thanks, Cass. I best get back on the road, get some sleep before my shift tomorrow."

"Just stay safe, okay?"

"Always," he said.

With a bob of my head, I embraced him, relishing just how awesome his hugs were. "I've got your back," I reassured him as he pulled out of my hold.

"I know you do." He smirked this time, and I grinned, knowing full well he had mine too.

I walked him out, taking him as far as I could go without venturing into the public areas. By the time I made it back to the locker room, most of the guys had already left. Ollie, though, was dressed and waiting for me next to my locker.

"You good?" His brows were drawn together, and concern laced his words.

"Yeah." I expelled a heavy breath.

"Was that Dylan?"

I bobbed my head. Before Dylan became a dad to his nephew, he'd been a frequent-ish face in the crowd and on nights out—when his work shifts allowed, as he had to fly out back then. "It was. He's just heading back home now."

"I didn't know he was coming to watch the game."

I scrunched my nose and tugged off my basketball jersey, needing to get my sweaty ass showered. "He didn't. He just needed to see me in person."

"Okay, well, if you need anything, you just let me know, yeah?"

I smiled, grateful Ollie was such a good guy. "Thanks, Ollie. Will do. You heading out for a beer?"

"Not tonight. I've got some stuff to do at home. I'll see you in the morning, though."

"Yeah, will do. See you tomorrow."

Ollie stepped away, leaving me to get showered.

I'd been planning on going to our local bar to have a few drinks and kick back after the game, but after seeing Dylan, it was the last thing I wanted to do.

His parents would take Mikey over my dead body. Dylan had already lost so much, and I'd do whatever it took to make sure he retained custody. His parents needed to back the fuck off.

CHAPTER 8

DYLAN

THE PAST WEEK HAD ME ON EDGE. BETWEEN CRAPTASTIC shifts, Mikey's potty training, the BS with my parents, all while feeling guilty for pulling Cass into this mountain of drama when he was finishing up the season, I wanted nothing more than to disappear into a bottle of Jack.

Since that wasn't possible, I didn't stop bouncing my knee, even though the action pissed me off.

A bouncing knee was better than me losing my shit.

"I'm here."

I jolted out of the seat when Cass barreled through the waiting room door of the lawyer's reception area.

"The traffic was a nightmare. Whoever thought it was a great idea to start all this roadwork now must have been a sadistic genius. I bet for shits and giggles they simply thought, 'You know what'd be hilarious? Closing every major road, at the same time, and seeing how long it takes for drivers to lose their shit.' Like, I get the need to fix gigantic potholes, but man, they had to pick the moment I was in the city. I reckon they have an evil underground network of roadworkers monitoring our schedules, and when it's going to piss folks off more, they're like 'Bam, move, move, move, Cass has a meeting. Let's lock that shit down.'"

I didn't have time to respond before Cass was in my space and had his arms folded around me. As always, I sighed into the touch, hugging him back.

Was I touch deprived? Quite possibly. Being a single dad didn't give me much opportunity to get up close and personal with another adult. Nor did it have a lot of my old friends hanging around.

These days, the most physical contact I got—beyond cuddles with Mikey—was when I was wrestling an asshole to the ground who was resisting arrest. It was not a kink I was a fan of.

Plus, this was Cass. I craved his touch more than I craved a quiet shift.

"Thanks for coming." I pulled away, a real smile finally forming. God, it was good to see him. Last week when I'd spiraled and reacted, I'd been in full-on panic mode. The news from my mom came at the worst time. That day I'd been involved in a situation with Maryann, a social worker I saw more often than I liked—especially considering how small our town was—removing two kids from a home.

Sure, it had been the right thing to do, but the kids' mom had been jacked up at the time and hadn't allowed her kids to go quietly. And I got it. Fuck, did I get it. But between the screaming, the devastated kids, the mom who I had to convince to calm down as I didn't want to arrest her, and my own mom's shitty phone call, in that moment, I'd needed Cass.

My rock.

My sanity.

And he'd come through, because of course he did. He was the king of managing shit in an emergency, and he also took organization to a level that Marie Kondo would be envious of.

"As if I wouldn't be here." He rolled his eyes at me before angling to look around the reception area. "Let's get this bullshit nipped in the bud." With a wink, he sauntered up to the desk, and I just knew he had that ridiculously sexy smirk on his face.

The man had a talent. He could woo men and women alike with that butter-wouldn't-melt-unless-I-licked-it-off-you smile he directed their way. I'd seen him in action more times than I'd written a speeding ticket.

"Hey there, beautiful Miranda. The old man in?"

Miranda, the middle-aged receptionist, blushed even as she rolled her eyes. "Mr. Lisle is waiting for you in conference room three. Do you need a bitter coffee to tamp down all that sweetness?" She arched a brow, and I snorted. Just how much time did Cass spend in this office for her to know how much shade to throw his way?

"Uff da, Miranda." Cass clutched his chest in that ridiculous way he did when being dramatic and hoping for a laugh. "You wound me."

I shook my head at his drawl. Since we were both Minnesota boys, born and bred, his thickening up his accent didn't take too much work.

"Uh-huh. I'll bring your coffee right on in." Miranda turned her attention to me, an amused, almost fond smile on her lips. "Would you like a drink, Sergeant Turner?"

I returned her smile. "A water would be great, thanks."

"In that case, you both can head on in. I put fresh water out five minutes ago." She focused on Cass. "Off you go before you're any later." With that, she walked away—I assumed to go get Cass a coffee.

"Jesus, Cass. Just how often do you come here?"

"What?" Wide-eyed, he turned to me and shrugged. "I've no idea what you're talking about. I'm the motherducking picture of virtue and innocence." He fell into step beside me, and just like that, the tight coil of fear that had been wrapped around me all week snapped.

Cass never failed to break through my walls, obliterating tension and fear like my very being was made out of putty or something, just waiting to be molded by him.

Grinning, I peered at him, angling up to catch his gaze. "Virtue and innocence, huh?"

"Yeah. You know it. Dictionary definitions that include examples have my handsome mugshot right there under it."

"Picture book dictionaries… sounds legit."

With twitching lips, Cass's gaze roamed my face. I knew damn well what he was searching for. We'd spoken every day this week, and he'd managed a quick visit. Just like he could tear through my worry, he was the only person in the world who could read me like a book.

He knew my tells. Knew my heart. Well, most of it. There was the slightest sliver that I kept to myself.

"I'm okay," I promised, responding to his silent question.

"Yeah, you are. How could you not be when I'm

the best fucking friend ever? It means you're always okay." He nudged me, shooting me a wink.

"Yeah, because I'm nothing without you and you complete me or something, right?"

Smirking at me, Cass paused at a closed door. "And that is why you'll always be okay. Your acceptance matters." He wiped at a pretend tear and sniffed ridiculously. "You make me so proud."

I shook my head. There was no point calling bullshit. Not only because he was right—which I'd never admit as his ego was already giant-sized—but because this was Cassius. In all his full-on, unapologetic, in-your-face glory.

And damn if I didn't love him for it. I never wanted him to change.

I didn't get the chance to respond before he was pushing open the door and entering the room.

"Granger." Cass walked in with a big grin and a loud voice. "Good to see you again."

Granger Lisle was up out of his chair and shaking Cass's hand before they patted at each other's backs like they were old-time friends. I scrunched my brow, wondering if that was the case, how come I'd never heard Cass mention the man before.

"Good to see you, Cassius." Granger pulled away, all six-foot slickness and ridiculously handsome. The lawyer also had probably twenty years on us, and since I was fairly sure none of Cass's conquests had been an older guy—and Granger screamed daddy—something in my chest loosened. "And you must be Sergeant Turner." He shot me a bright, genuine smile. "It's good to meet you."

Shaking his hand, appreciating his firm, friendly grip, I finally smiled. "Thanks, and it's Dylan."

"Right. Dylan it is." Granger stepped away and indicated toward the table. "Shall we take a seat?"

"Sounds good, thanks," I responded, sitting down and settling even more when Cass sat next to me.

"You take in the game last night?" Smugness filled Cass's tone. They'd obliterated the Wolverines, so the smugness was warranted.

"You know it. Good game." Granger flicked his gaze to me. "Perhaps we can talk B-ball after this meeting." His tone turned serious, but his expression remained open.

Cass must have noticed, too, as he straightened in his chair. For all his shit-stirring ways, Cass was levelheaded and could step up. It was something I was sure not many people knew about him.

When I nodded and Cass bobbed his head, giving his go-ahead, Granger picked up a file from next to his laptop.

"I've been in contact with Mr. and Mrs. Turner's lawyer."

Surprise rippled through me. Nothing had come through the mail. I'd received no official petition. Heck, I wasn't even sure if they still used the same law firm from when I was a kid.

"It wasn't hard to track down who their regular lawyer is."

"It wasn't?" I asked.

"Cassius told me something of your history."

I bobbed my head, more than okay with that. The more information Granger had, the better. Especially if he could shut down this nonsense.

"Grandparents do have rights here in Minnesota. They have a case to file for visitation rights at the minimum."

While I knew that, it was something I'd been actively ignoring. My parents made it easier by not even trying to get access to Mikey before.

"They've never even met him. Not once." My throat felt scratchy, emotion catching my voice.

"That has to prevent them from getting access, right?" Cass asked, tone hard. "Why the hell do they want to see Mikey now?"

Exactly what I was thinking.

"That they haven't seen Mikey before or even tried for access is good for you. The law surrounding this is very clear with the focus being on the best interests of the child."

"So this is case closed, then, right?" Cass asked. Thank Christ he responded because my mind was reeling. "They're the shittiest parents in the state of Minnesota. Hell, they tried to send Dylan to conversion therapy when he was seventeen fucking years old." Venom all but dripped from his tone. It always did whenever he spoke about my parents and the time when he'd appeared at my door, his car still running, to take me in and get my belongings.

Granger angled his head, gaze on mine. "Is that true?"

I nodded. "Yeah. My folks didn't much appreciate having a gay son."

"Fuck, you should have seen their asshole faces when Paula packed her bags and left home when she was sixteen, shouting she was a lesbian." A chuckle followed, but the sound was tense, something it often was whenever he talked about Paula.

"And she went and lived with your parents?" Granger pressed.

While Cass nodded, I said, "Mama T and Pop took us in, supported us with everything. When I turned eighteen, my small inheritance from my grandaddy was released. Cass's folks refused to take anything, so I used it to help complete my associate's degree and law enforcement training. The rest I gave to Paula to help with community college."

Granger jotted down notes and asked, "So your parents didn't provide any financial support or contribute in any way once you left home at what… seventeen?"

I shook my head. "No, sir. I worked at a local diner after school and on weekends, and other than my inheritance, which helped a little with college fees, Cass's parents took care of the rest."

"Okay, that's shitty, but it's good for this situation."

Relaxing at his words, feeling like he really did think this whole thing was indeed shitty, I exhaled.

We spent the next forty minutes going through my history, Paula's, when I'd moved back to Minneapolis—or more specifically Zumbrota—and everything I knew about my parents. Granger spouted legalese, most of which I understood thanks to working in the system and attending court more times than I liked over the years, especially when I used to be based in Detroit.

"I have a copy of Paula's will." Granger displayed it on the screen for all three of us to see. "She had this created when she was eight months pregnant."

"Yeah. She was organized as hell." My lips twitched in fondness at the memory of my sister, despite the shroud of sadness that came whenever I thought of her. I didn't add that she'd also written me a letter after that. Though I hadn't received it until long after her death. "She asked me to take on guardianship for Mikey if anything was to happen to her."

"And Mikey's birth certificate indicates no father's name. Records show she used a donor."

I looked dead ahead and stopped myself from shifting uncomfortably. "That's right. She was inseminated at a clinic."

"And she was single. No partner to ask for custody?"

"That's right. My sister was always fiercely independent. She would have been a great mom." I swallowed hard, the dry click in my throat sounding loud in the meeting room.

Cass's hand appeared on my shoulder, offering a firm squeeze.

"She would have been amazing," he said at my side. "But you're an incredible dad."

I angled to look at him. Our gazes connected, and I drew strength from the familiar eyes, the certainty staring back at me. I bobbed my head.

"Okay, this is all good."

Granger's words drew my attention back. "Yeah?"

"Absolutely. From what I see here, your parents

have no real chance at custody. Your sister's wishes were clear, but we do need to look at visitation."

Panic shot through me, making my shoulders stiffen. "I don't want them anywhere near Mikey."

Understanding morphed Granger's features.

"They're nasty pieces of work, Granger. They wrap their hate in Christian scripture, and while they've since moved out to Owatonna, my mom's heard talk of more than a few anti-LGBTQ groups the Turners have been active in."

I watched Cass as he spoke, his jaw tensing, distaste and anger in every word.

"Now, my mom and pop are God-loving Christians. Attend chapel every Sunday. The difference here being the focus on love and not the hate the Turners spew. What do we need to do to make sure they don't have any rights? That they stay as far away from Mikey and Dylan as possible?"

The tripping of my heart didn't surprise me. It never did when it came to Cass and how fiercely he loved and protected me. It had always been this way between us, and I was grateful for his love of green gummy bears and my obsession with red every damn day.

I reached out and squeezed Cass's forearm, drawing his attention to me. In response, he winked, letting me know we had this. Together and always.

Granger leaning forward in his chair, his elbows resting on the table, drew both our attention.

His gaze was laser-focused, dancing between me and Cass, studying us intently. A beat later, he nodded.

"What?" Cass asked. "You've thought of something."

Granger's brow quirked. "Mikey needs grand-parents."

I parted my lips to argue, but Granger's raised hand stopped me.

"He needs a support system, extended family so he's clearly not 'missing out on anything,'" he said, complete with air quotes. "Your history, your estrangement, already puts you in good stead. What we don't want is a sympathetic judge. Fighting visitation rights will be easier if you do two things."

I was already nodding, my pulse accelerating. Anything for Mikey. And anything to keep my asshole parents out of our world.

Cass's "Name it and we'll do it" had me squeezing his arm once again.

"The two of you get married and adopt Mikey. Make him yours officially and become a family."

CHAPTER 9

CASSIUS

"Done." My response was immediate, the galloping of my heart easy to ignore.

"Wh-What?"

I peered at Dylan just as he snapped his head in my direction.

"What do you mean, 'what'?" I shrugged, nonplussed by his question and the way his features blanched.

"What do you mean by 'done'?" he fired back. Wide-eyed, Dylan's reaction appeared more than simply confused. Something else twitched in his gaze that I couldn't get a read on.

"I mean, let's get the paperwork needed, marriage license or whatever. Get this done today. That means we can get the adoption application sorted immediately after."

I shrugged again and looked at Granger, the epitome of collected. Remaining quiet, the man studied us.

"You can do that, right? Get this ball rolling?" At his nod, I angled back to Dylan, grateful he couldn't hear the frantic beating of my heart. "I've got a game tomorrow, so it can't be then, but the sooner we get this done, the better, yeah?"

Once more, I focused on Granger, looking for confirmation. He offered it with the barest of nods, but his gaze darted to Dylan.

Dylan's "Don't you think we need to stop and talk about this?" grabbed my attention.

I took him in, the pink crawling up his neck snagging my focus. *Shit.* The pink combined with his still-wide eyes was a tell if ever I saw one, and since I knew this man almost as well as I knew myself, I reached out and squeezed his shoulder.

"This isn't me railroading you."

At my words, his lips twitched. The panic also began to disappear out of his eyes.

"It's not, but—" I smirked. "—I reckon I'm quite a catch."

The teasing earned me a snort, and I relaxed into the sound.

Granger cleared his throat. "How about I give you guys the room? Just hit the buzzer on the side panel when you're ready for me." Standing, he smiled over at us. "This isn't time sensitive, and as your lawyer, I wouldn't recommend you rushing into anything." A pointed look was sent my way.

"Me, rash?" I quirked my brow.

"Uh-huh." Granger shook his head, only stopping and offering a kind smile before he said, "From everything I know and have seen, you two have an excellent relationship and have been friends for seemingly forever."

Damn straight we did.

"You both want what's best for Mikey, so every decision you make, he needs to be at the center of it."

I nodded, in complete agreement, but once again, the pointed look he shot my way didn't go unnoticed. This time, there was so much more behind it. The implication made me shift uncomfortably.

Not that he officially knew anything. But considering I'd changed my will to include significant assets to be left to Mikey, it was obvious he suspected.

Beyond Paula and the clinic, no one else knew my full involvement with Paula's journey to become a mom. That my best friend remained in the dark never sat right. An understatement if anything, since the secret between us hurt my heart. But I took every promise I made seriously.

That included the one I made Paula.

Once alone, I angled my chair, my knees brushing against Dylan's thigh. "What are you thinking?" I studied his pink cheeks, trying to figure out why he wasn't jumping all over this and trying to get us before a judge.

"I could ask you the same question." A hitch of emotion, quite possibly panic, pitched his voice high.

"I'm thinking about Mikey and what's best for him."

His gaze softened at the mention of his son. "And what do you think is best for him?"

"That he never has to be in breathing distance of your parents. That I've witnessed up close the sort of hatred they can spout, and if there's anything I can do to make sure that never touches Mikey, I'll do it in a heartbeat."

His pink was back, as was the widening of his eyes as he studied my expression intently. "Even marriage?"

I nodded quickly. "Especially marriage." At the pursing of his lips, I took a breath. "I know you said you never wanted to get married." It was a conversation we'd had countless times over the years. "But this is different, right?"

"Because it's you?"

My grin was immediate. I arched a brow,

throwing some extra cockiness in that one move. "Hell yes because it's me."

His snort loosened something tight in my chest.

I sobered a little before saying, "But yes, because it's me. You're the person I trust most in the world."

"I trust you the most too."

I reached out and took his hand. "Getting married makes so much sense if it helps stop any petition your parents make."

Two lines appeared between his brows. "So say that we do. We make it legal."

My heart jumped a little at his words.

"What do we tell Mikey? Sure, he won't quite understand yet, but give it time and he will. And how long do we stay married for? Do we change anything? Live together?" He shook his head, something close to panic appearing on his face. "What about Mama T and Pop?"

My jumping heart did a little stutter. "Hell, my parents will be over the moon. They already think of you as theirs and Mikey as their grandkid."

"Exactly." His "exactly" sounded more rattled rather than happy confirmation.

"So what's the issue?" This whole arrangement made so much sense to me. Sure, Dylan's questions bounced around my brain, but every single one wasn't insurmountable.

Dylan's brows shot high, and his breathing seemed to cut off. Surprise slammed into me, his reaction not making any sense. This was legit the perfect solution. I loved and trusted him. Loved Mikey. Hell, the more I thought about it, if I was going to get married to anyone, Dylan was the perfect and obvious choice.

One, he wasn't a gold digger. Heck, I wouldn't even have to worry about a prenup or such shit, as I trusted the man more than I trusted myself. Two, hanging out with the guy, even living with him… there was zero problem with that. As my best friend, every chance I got to spend with him was a win.

"The issue?" He shook his head, and the gleam in his eyes told me exactly what he was thinking. Admittedly, I sometimes acted without thought to the consequences, but that wasn't now. Okay, maybe it was a little, but I'd already rationalized two solid reasons on top of doing this for Mikey. "Marriage is one thing, but Granger said adoption."

My pulse thundered. I'd heard every word Granger had said. Making Mikey mine and in a way that wouldn't destroy my relationship with Dylan…. I swallowed hard. It was something I'd never dared contemplate.

My promise to Paula to not tell Dylan festered in my gut. But fuck if she hadn't made one hell of an argument four years back when she'd first asked me to be the donor.

And that was what I'd always intended to be. The silent donor. I'd made peace with that.

Had I wobbled when Mikey was born and Dylan became his dad?

Only in the unease of keeping a secret from Dylan. Because fuck if he wasn't an amazing dad. Even from day one, I'd known he'd be incredible, and he'd loved Mikey like he was his own.

I just hadn't been ready—too unprepared to deal with any possible "claiming." Jesus, even the thought that Dylan would think I was trying to take Mikey away from him made me want to crumple.

It still did.

"I know."

"Marriage can be fixed with a quickie divorce. Adoption…." Emotion filled his eyes. "That's not something you can sign away. It'll be it, for life. He'll be yours."

My stomach swooped, fear and excitement battling it out in my gut. Taking a deep breath, I squeezed his hand and palmed the back of his neck. "I would never do anything to hurt Mikey. I love him. That will never change."

How could I tell him that Mikey was my biological kid now? Jesus, everywhere I turned I felt like I was an inch away from manipulating him. This situation.

I didn't want that. But fuck, was that what I was doing?

Unable to bear the thought of hurting Dylan and losing him, I shoved my secret away. Banished it as best as I could.

It took two heartbeats before the tension drained from him, a softness replacing his features. "I know you love him. It's never something I'll ever worry about."

The conviction in his voice was a hell of a thing.

"So what is it you *are* worried about?" I trapped the teasing words I wanted to add to make him smile and cut through the tension. While this wasn't how I expected any of today to go down, I could commit. I also knew this was some serious shit we were talking about.

"Everything." Honesty rang through that one word and vibrated in my brain. "All the questions already said. Your folks, our friends. Fuck… the media." He winced at that. "You want to drag Mikey into that? Him getting his photo taken? People commenting on our lives? Then, when you find someone who you actually want to marry for real, the fallout from that?"

Stopping his spiral with a soft "Hey," I shook my

head. "Who's to say I want a divorce or want to marry someone else?" At the roll of his eyes, I continued, "No, I'm serious. You know how I am." He was the only person who knew the real me.

Hookups with guys had always been brief. While they were fun, I'd never done more than exchange hot bjs and hand jobs. Not for a lack of wanting more but because of that damn fear that had never disappeared.

There hadn't been a man I'd hooked up with who I trusted enough to even contemplate going further. Not since Dylan. And that wasn't a memory I allowed myself to think about often.

It was too dangerous to recall all the ways he'd made me come undone.

The only times I had no control were in the brief moments of waking from a dream when I'd remember all too clearly the touch and feel of him.

Shaking the thoughts aside, I tried to get back on track.

Sure, there were women. But fuck if the horror stories of jersey-chasers hadn't left their mark.

I didn't have time for that level of bullshit.

Since Dylan still hadn't responded, I continued, "Hell, *you've* got a better chance of meeting a guy who you want to get serious with." I ignored the bitter taste the words left in my mouth. It was always there whenever we talked about him hooking up.

Add in the thought of another man coming into his life and being around Mikey and a flash of pain barreled into me. I wrangled that beast, shoving it deep into my gut. Focusing on Dylan rather than Mikey was easier.

Of course my friend needed cock in his life, but I was nothing if not a needy fucker filled with double standards.

At his snort, I raised my brows. "What?"

"That's not likely."

Rather than pressing, I sighed. "Either way, I'm not worried about that. But you're right about Mikey."

Perplexed, his eyebrows dipped. "In what way?"

"That he'll get confused. Sure, I come and go all the time now, but I suppose this is all about real stability, right?"

Genuine shock registered on his expression, making me tut.

"No, no," Dylan said immediately, no doubt reading my unspoken reaction. "I'm not surprised you feel this way about Mikey. I suppose I just…." He huffed out a breath. "I suppose I'm just wondering what you're thinking and what that means to you. 'Mikey's stability.' If we go ahead—"

At my huge grin, he narrowed his eyes at me. "That's not me agreeing. I'm just asking what Mikey's stability means to you. I know that ridiculous brain of yours is working overtime."

I held back my laugh, but only because I didn't want him freaking out or punching me in the arm. The fact that he asked the question meant he was taking my words seriously. *Holy shit*. And they were serious. I was totally on board with marrying him.

But he was also right—as was Granger—that I had to think logistics.

"So, we tell my family the truth. No chance I can lie to my folks about this."

"Agreed."

My lips twitched at his acknowledgment, earning me a stink eye. "As for the media, they can have an announcement, and we'll make sure Mikey is protected. Hell, his dad being a police sergeant has to come in handy for that, right?"

"And," he started, looking decidedly uncomfortable—something I wasn't used to seeing from Dylan. "Fuck, I can't believe I'm going to say this, but what happens when photos of your latest conquest appear online?"

"I'm not that bad." When his eyebrows darted high, I amended, "Anymore. I'm more discreet. Plus, it's been fucking ages since I hooked up.

These days, during the season especially, you know I'm usually hanging out at my apartment or with one of the guys. If not them, I'm with you and Mikey." Truth was, partying didn't have the same excitement or pull it once had. Nor did casual hookups.

And since I had hang-ups about dating, it meant most action tended to be with my hand or my Fleshlight.

Dylan's searching gaze compelled me to say, "I promise not to do anything that fucks things up for you or Mikey. That includes me humiliating you by 'stepping out on you.'" Even as I said the words, meaning every syllable, I wondered where my head was at.

The fuck was I saying? That I was going to be celibate?

But looking at Dylan's worried expression, the concern easy for me to read in his gaze, I couldn't take it back. Just like I wouldn't let him down.

There was little doubt in my mind that I wasn't truly thinking about the ramifications of this, but the alternative of messing this up for my best friend and for Mikey would be worth it all. If there was anyone in this world I'd sacrifice for, hands down it was Dylan.

Mikey went without saying.

"I promise you we've got this and will figure everything out."

"Okay."

A flutter of relief tickled my chest. "So what do y—"

"I said okay."

"Okay as in…?"

"Fuck it. Let's get married."

CHAPTER 10
DYLAN

A QUICKIE WEDDING BEFORE A JUDGE TURNED OUT TO BE a more elaborate gathering before an officiant two days after Cassius's final game of the season. And in true Cassius style, he'd managed to organize access to a private lakeside location—his teammate Jerome Miles's kick-ass second home—just south of my house in Zumbrota.

This meant we'd have servers for our late supper after our early-evening ceremony, as apparently, the sunset would make for killer photos. In attendance was his family, my colleagues—though only four could make it since we were a tiny station consisting of eight officers and two admin staff—and practically the whole basketball team who hadn't already had end-of-season plans.

"Man, I can't believe you're doing this." Suzie,

my beat partner when I wasn't chained to my desk, passed me a shot glass.

Eyeballing the liquid, I shook my head. I refused to get wasted, despite wanting the extra courage. "It'll be fine." I huffed out a breath, wondering where Mama T had taken off to with my son. I could have done with a cuddle right about now.

"Riiight," she replied before knocking back the liquid. Not even a wince. Not that I was surprised. Suzie could drink everyone under the table.

Ignoring her sarcasm, I peered at myself in the full-length mirror. With a shaky hand that I refused to dwell on, I fixed my collar and flattened down the designer jacket Cassius had given me yesterday.

I could do this.

It was for Mikey.

Plus, Cassius wasn't wrong. As my best friend, being married to the guy wouldn't exactly be a hardship. Not only did we speak to each other, or at least communicate, every day, but we rarely went longer than a week without seeing each other in the flesh, especially since Mikey was born.

We had lots to talk about for sure, but he'd told me we had this, and he'd never given me a single reason to doubt him before.

Mikey loved him. Hell, "Cass" had been one of his first words. The possibility of the three of us spending more time together was something I could get behind. As for Paula, it went without saying that she'd approve and be actively cheering for this to happen.

Logistics and reality could wait.

I huffed out a calming breath and cracked my neck.

"You sure you don't want a shot?" Suzie held out another glass of clear liquid.

"No." With one last glance in the mirror, I nodded at my reflection and turned toward her. "Will I do?"

"You look hot. You know, in that 'Theo James wearing a three-piece suit' way. Do that smolder thing." Suzie bounced her eyebrows up and down.

"I don't do a smolder thing." I rolled my eyes, refusing to give in to temptation and peek into the mirror. Theo James was smoking hot. I thought I scrubbed up okay—and the suit was the nicest thing I'd ever worn—but since Suzie made it her mission to fuck with me, I wasn't buying it.

"You so do. Tilly in administration talks about it all the time. Let me grab a photo to send to her."

"Do not send a photo." I shook my head, my lips twitching at her ridiculousness. "And since when have you been spending time gossiping with Tilly?"

A salacious grin curled her lips. "Since Emily Garrot joined the admin staff."

I snorted out a laugh. "You are just continuing to ask for trouble. You know who her dad is, right?"

A shrug preceded her "I don't give a shit" expression. "I'm not trying to date her dad. She's sweet."

From what I knew about Emily, Suzie was right: Emily was sweet. And so not Suzie's usual type.

But what the hell did I know since, in five minutes, I'd be exchanging vows with my best friend? A guy who remained my constant. Was officially my soul mate.

And yeah, who I happened to share the hottest night of my life with and was the only man I'd ever given my ass to.

I was just asking for trouble.

"Anyway, it's time to go, lover boy." I didn't even bother correcting her, especially when I knew she was genuinely concerned. "That pain-in-the-ass fiancé is waiting for you." She knocked back another shot. "The cheese head has more money than sense that he was able to throw together a whole fucking wedding in a week."

"Leave him alone and stop being a miserable dick."

Suzie had something of a love-hate relationship going on with Cass. She refused to believe it was because they were alike and had perfected being fun-loving assholes with an unhealthy side of sarcasm.

Though, while she was all strong, bitter black coffee, Cass was an extra-shot, extra-sweet, fluffy foam latte with rainbow sprinkles and a cocktail umbrella.

She arched a brow at me. "*You're* going to have a miserable dick since you're never going to have sex again unless you start fucking your 'husband.'" There was no malice in her words, but fuck if they didn't smack me in the face.

What on earth was I doing?

I'd be a celibate married man who one day would look down to realize my dick had shriveled up from lack of use.

"Jesus. Are you going to puke?" My gaze snapped to Suzie's. Her eyes widened, and a flash of regret, something I rarely saw, appeared. "Dylan, I'm just messing with you. It'll be fine. You know I can't not fuck with you, and especially Cassius."

A trickle of sweat rolled down my back. *Shit, am I going to pass out?*

"Listen." Moving to stand in front of me, she latched on to my sweaty palms and didn't even wince. Hell, I must have looked like I was going to lose it if she didn't say anything. "Cassius is your best friend, right?"

I nodded mutely.

"You can tell him anything and everything, right?"

With only the slightest hesitation, I bobbed my head. I'd never told Cass about the time I hooked up with John Harris when he'd left town to go to college. Cass had hated the football player something fierce. Plus, John had been a lousy lay and an asshole, and I didn't want an "I told you so" from my best friend.

The inability to erase the night I'd shared with Cass years back was also something I kept secret. More specifically how I'd struggled to form any type of real attachment with a man since. Let alone allow anyone even close to my ass.

My feelings for him, the thought of what could have been, I pushed way, way down into the dark void of "shit you don't share." Years had passed since then. As far as I was concerned, it was a night we'd never repeat.

I didn't think I could make myself vulnerable like that again. Not without it destroying everything.

"In that case, I can reluctantly admit that the two of you getting hitched isn't the most ridiculous thing I've ever heard."

Her words were so unexpected, it did the trick of slicing through my meltdown. "Really?"

"Yes, really." She released my hands and scrunched her nose as she stared at her palms. "You're both good guys," she started, her begrudging sigh tugging a smile from me. "You both love that cute kid of yours. That, after all these years —you know, since you were fetuses or whatever— you're still so close has to mean that you'll be fine. Plus, have you actually seen the two of you together?"

It wasn't necessary to ask for clarification, but I still rolled my eyes anyway.

Everyone at the station, my friends, his friends, hell, anyone who'd seen us together at one point or another had asked if we were a couple. Cassius being tactile was something I loved about him. We cuddled, still shared a bed every now and then, and shared food. I enjoyed every moment.

Receiving his attention and being able to give it back so openly made me feel good. It always had.

Every time and without hesitation he gave it to me in spades, though it never escaped my notice that he was only like that with me.

"So," Suzie said as she rubbed her hands with an antibacterial wipe she'd pulled out of her bag, "clean your gross palms with one of these"—she passed me the packet—"and let's get to it."

Tugging out a sheet, I cleaned my hands. "Okay. I've got this."

"You sure as shit do." A wide grin formed. "I'm so fucking awesome at pep talks. You think I should go for the promotion at work for the public liaison officer?"

I snorted as I threw the wipe away, knowing she was fucking with me. The thought of Suzie in any sort of PR role was terrifying. "Why don't you ask Chief Nelson that? Just let me be there."

Flipping me off, she headed toward the door of one of the bedrooms we'd commandeered. "Whatever. Come on. Let's get you hitched."

She left me to it, and I took the moment to take some centering breaths.

When the door opened again, I smiled. Pop, Cass's dad, stood in the doorway with Mikey in his arms.

"Looking good there, son."

Emotion smacked me square in the chest. *The hell is going on with me?* I cleared my throat as he shot me a soft, fatherly smile. Pop had called me "son" for pretty much all my life. That the words hit me with emotion now didn't make sense.

"Thanks, Pop," I managed and accepted his hug, Mikey squealing between us. Pulling away, I chuckled, looking at my little guy. "Did you not like your suit that Cass got you?"

He scrunched his nose tightly, his brow pulling low. "No. Stinky."

"Well, I'm not sure stinky is the right word. Do

you not think I look handsome?"

His deep brown eyes roamed over me. "Youse looks hamsome, Dada."

The tightening in my chest had me releasing a shaky breath. No word of a lie, becoming this kid's father was the best thing to ever happen to me. Losing Paula was hell. It still was. But her entrusting me with her son, the boy who had the same shaped eyes as his mom, was a gift I'd be forever grateful for.

"I think you look like the best B-ball player in the League." Because of course Mikey was wearing his favorite full basketball uniform Cass had gifted him at the start of season. Complete with Cass's number 12 and *Britton* etched on the back.

Fitting, I supposed.

"I ams, Dada. Cass pway B-ball."

I chuckled and reached out for him. He settled on my hip, something he only tended to do these days when he was tired. Since he'd found his feet when he was fourteen months old, he'd turned into a wriggle monster whenever anyone tried to carry him. "A very quick game of B-ball before bath and bed sounds awesome. Nana and Papa are going to put you in bed tonight, though, so just one game, okay?"

His pouty bottom lip puffed out.

"We'll have a great time, won't we, Mikey?" Pop tickled Mikey's tummy. The giggle spilled from my boy, wonderful and contagious. "Maybe we can read one of your basketball stories for bedtime. How's that sound?"

At the mention of story time, Mikey's eyes lit up. "Cass weads me."

"Hmm, you know your dad and Cass have a big party to get to, right, Mikey?" Pop smiled at me, shooting me a wink. His ease settled a tightness in my chest I'd been actively ignoring. While he and Cass's mom had been surprised at our announcement, they'd also been supportive, Mama T joining Cass in the hectic last-minute planning.

But still, I was marrying their son.

While they treated me like one of their own, it hadn't stopped the nerves from forming, wondering how they'd react and take the news.

"'Kay." Mikey bobbed his head, then wriggled in my arms, making it clear he wanted to be put down.

Pop's "Mikey" grabbed his attention. He peered up at the man who was the closest thing to a grandfather he'd ever had. The thought had my eyes widening. Once Cass and I married, it would make that connection finally official.

Fresh emotion bloomed in my chest. This was what I'd always wanted for Mikey. Today, I'd be giving it to him.

"Remember your super important job, Mikey?"

Confusion scrunched my kid's forehead.

"The ribbon on your wrist." Pop indicated to the yellow-and-blue ribbon—the Eagles' colors—tied to Mikey's wrist.

"Yes!" Mikey bounced up and down, excitement pitching his voice loud and high. "I's gots wings for Dada and Cass."

"Good job. And you're going to hold your dad's hand all the way until you reach Cass. Then you can come and sit with me and Nana, okay?"

"'Kay, Papa."

My heart squeezed, and I took a deep breath. I turned my attention to my soon-to-be father-in-law. "Thanks, Pop."

"Anytime, son. You know how much Mama T and I love you."

I nodded, not trusting myself to speak.

"You sure you don't want me to walk on down that aisle with you? Nothing would make me prouder." He chuckled. "Just don't tell Cass that."

I appreciated his soft laughter. It helped cut through the emotion clogging my throat.

This day was turning out to be a lot. I hadn't expected the swirl of sadness from losing my sister, even though the feeling was never far away. I certainly hadn't expected the pain whenever thoughts of my own parents tried to sneak in.

Not a chance that I'd let them steal any more energy or happiness from me, though.

"Thanks, Pop," I finally managed. "Mikey and I have got this."

In fact, Cass had already said he'd wait for me and the three of us would walk together. Damn him for his thoughtfulness. Maybe he had an inkling I'd lose my nerve and not make my way down the aisle by myself.

"Sounds good. In that case, I best get to that son of mine. Check he's all right, then find my seat." He leaned forward, hugging me hard. "I'm proud of you, Dylan." With that, he pulled away and left me alone with Mikey.

I was pretty sure I was running late, but I needed a moment. Just me and my boy.

"Hey, Mikey." I crouched down, not too worried about wrinkling the pristine suit. "You doing okay?"

"Yeah." He bobbed his head.

"And you know that Cass and I are getting married?" I'd discussed it with him a few times, but honestly, Mikey wasn't even three, so who the hell knew how much he really understood.

"Yeah. We's famwy." He shrugged, his telltale nose-scrunching action quickly following. "But we's famwy now."

"I know we are. Just think about this as a way for

us to have fun and tell everyone what a great family we are, okay?"

"'Kay. We go?"

My lips twitched. "I think that's a great idea."

With every step I took, I focused on Mikey. Focused on the way I felt about Cass. How I cared about him. How we always—through sickness and in health, apparently—would have each other's backs.

The dozens of strings of lights caught my attention first. A quiet chuckle spilled from me as, hand in hand with Mikey, we followed the twinkling pathway, complete with pink and cream flowers that I had no idea the name of, toward the beginning of the aisle where our fifty or so guests stood.

This was real.

My pulse spiked, fast and loud, filling up my ears.

Then there was Cass, a huge-ass grin aimed my way. He winked as I stopped beside him, and he reached for Mikey's hand. The three of us walked past our guests toward where the officiant waited for us.

"You okay?" His voice was quiet, words just for me.

"Yeah," I croaked. "Not sure why I feel so nervous," I admitted, just as we stopped at the front before Leroy, a friend of Cass's folks who was a registered officiant. I turned to look at Cass, still holding Mikey's hand.

A soft smile played on his lips, completely at odds with his whispered "Don't panic about our wedding night. I got you."

The bastard. A snort shot out of me, loud and inappropriate considering where we were. Amusement filled me, warmth spilling into my chest as I grinned at Cass.

One thing was for sure: my best friend knew exactly what to say to get me to relax. I loved the asshole for it.

Mikey's bobbing up and down drew my attention. "You okay, bud?"

"Needs potty."

Laughter rippled around the group, and I grinned down at my boy. I knew better than asking him if he could wait. We were in the middle of potty training, so the fact that he remembered to ask was a win.

"I've got him." Pop was there before I even had to ask.

I grinned at him. "Thanks, Pop."

"We won't be but a tick."

The chuckle around our small group continued, and I peered back at Cass. "So, looks like we need to wait a few."

"Just adds to the memory of the day, right?" He

followed up with a wink, his wide smile revealing his pearly white teeth. The man could have made a killing in Colgate ads. Maybe they didn't pay as much as Under Armour, and considering I knew the millions Cass made from an endorsement deal with the brand, Colgate would have needed to pay the big bucks.

"Right. I think this day's going to be pretty memorable already," I deadpanned, not even joking, let alone exaggerating. "Mikey doing a wild pee behind the big bush is barely going to register." There was no disguising the quiet uncertainty in my low voice.

Concern appeared in Cass's expression. "You still want to do this, right?"

My gaze roamed his face, landing briefly on the small scar above his right eyebrow that was a few shades lighter than his dark skin. He'd done that falling from a tree when we were seven, which he'd originally climbed because my ass had frozen in fear when I'd gone too high.

Unsurprisingly, Cass falling and landing with a thud had gotten me moving so damn fast, I'd been by his side a stumbling heartbeat later. The asshole had grinned at me, blood covering his face, saying, "See, I said you could do it by yourself. You can do anything, Dyl."

And fuck if he didn't make me believe it.

For a man who was known as a joker and a pain in the ass, he made the best cheerleader.

"Yeah, I want to do this." Honesty clamped down tightly on my whispered words. I meant them. Amusement tangled with surprise in my gut, wondering exactly when it was that I'd decided getting married to my best friend was the greatest thing ever.

"There's no backing down after this, right?"

I startled at the vulnerability in his gaze.

Did Cass want this as much as I did? If he did, I had no idea what that really meant. But I couldn't leave him hanging.

I reached for him, clasping his shoulder, blocking out the murmuring of quiet conversation while we waited for Mikey to return. "You know I love you, man," I whispered. "You're my best friend, and I don't want to back out."

His reaction was immediate: the great big grin I was used to seeing aimed my way. "Fucking A. Let's get this done."

And damn if his joy wasn't contagious. My heart flipped as fluttering wings took flight in my stomach.

It looked like we were really doing this.

As soon as Mikey returned with Pop, announcing to everyone that he'd peed on the lemon tree, we got started. Leroy kept the whole affair light and quick, with an added bit of sweetness as he told a couple of stories of me and Cass as kids.

We repeated our vows, going with the standard words. Though, honestly, I could have been saying anything. With my heart once again thudding loudly, it was all I could do to hold on to Cass's hands as I said, "I do"—and thank god he didn't let go.

That I was certain about this exchange made everything more real, but there remained a haze of "holy fucking shit, I can't believe this is really happening" at the edge of my mind.

At Cass's "I do," I swallowed hard, my eyes straining with how intently I stared at him. Blinking proved difficult, too wrapped up in the significance of those words.

"Wonderful," Leroy said, his voice bright and loud, but still, I didn't pull my gaze away from Cass. "In that case, thanks to the great state of Minnesota, I have the pleasure of announcing you married, and you can go ahead and kiss as husbands."

The words jolted a reaction from me.

We had not discussed this. Hell, I hadn't even thought through anything about this moment beyond saying "I do." Figuring out what to do next had been a future Dylan problem.

We should have gone to city hall. It would have

prevented all manner of awk—

My thoughts were cut off by Cass's lips pressing against mine.

My brows shot high, a gasp shooting from my lungs. The action parted my lips. At the movement, Cass's eyelids dipped closed, and he brushed his lips more firmly against mine. But it was when his tongue swept across my bottom lip that my own eyelids fluttered shut.

The buzz in my brain stopped me thinking. All I could focus on was the flick of his tongue, the slight hitch in his breath, and the strength of his fingers against my back.

When did he hold on to me?

Awareness stuttered to life, the fluttering wings taking flight for a whole new reason as desire ignited in my belly. This kiss, his touch… combined they turned my limbs to jelly and my brain to mush.

It had been eight long years since I'd felt his mouth on mine. Eight long years since my heart had behaved this way.

The memory hadn't done it justice.

And then he pulled away, bringing with it the loud clapping and cheering.

Wide-eyed, I stared at Cass. With glazed eyes, he appeared as bewildered as I felt. *Thank fuck. Because holy shit. What the hell just happened?*

CHAPTER 11
CASSIUS

As we waved off my parents, who'd dropped us off at Dylan's place while they headed home with a sleeping Mikey, I side-eyed Dylan. "Shouldn't we be carrying each other over the threshold or something?"

"Each other, huh? How'd you expect that to work exactly?"

Armed with a smirk, I angled fully toward my best friend. Scratch that. My husband. The thought, let alone the reality, was fucking weird, but we'd had a blast tonight, so I rolled with it. "You can just piggyback me if you want." I bounced my brows for good measure. Not to say I wasn't totally up for clambering on Dylan's back.

Pausing from unlocking his front door, he glanced

over at me, a smirk already forming. "As long as you're not expecting bridal style, we can do that."

"Fuck yeah." I jumped onto his back before he could change his mind.

"*Oomph…* fuck, Cass. How much are you pressing these days? Or is that extra slice of cake I saw you inhale to blame?"

Chuckling, I clung on, wrapping my arms around his broad shoulders. While Dylan wasn't as tall or as toned as I was, his chest was broader. He could most definitely handle my weight without breaking a sweat.

That and clinging onto Dylan in any way was never a hardship. Not with the familiar traces of the aftershave he used still lingering, and the light hint of his natural scent that I'd easily recognize in a crowded room.

It was all comfort and eased the part in me that usually felt a little antsy.

"Stop your complaining," I sassed, planting a kiss on his cheek for good measure, ignoring how the kiss was nothing like the one we'd shared after our "I dos."

He huffed out a laugh as he stepped into his home, a modest three-bedroom town house on a quiet street near a couple of great walking tracks.

Once in the hallway, he tilted his head to peer back at me. "Comfortable there?"

"You betcha."

He grunted, his grip on my thighs firm as he hitched me up a little. Settling my chin on his head, I yawned, ridiculously at ease in Dylan's familiar home and surrounded by his calming scent.

"I'm beat." Another yawn tore free. It had been a bizarre, long, but strangely incredible day. Between a ceremony that had made me more emotional than I expected and partying hard while not drinking myself silly, I was beyond ready for bed. "Can we go straight to sleep?"

Still holding me tightly, Dylan nodded. "Let me just lock the front door." He turned and flicked the lock. The click echoed around the unusually quiet house.

"It's odd Mikey not being here," I whispered, for no other reason but feeling like I needed to be quiet.

"Yeah. Mama T and Pop insisted on having him overnight."

I nodded, knowing this. Just like I knew Dylan had balked a little, not a fan of spending too much time away from Mikey.

"It's weird now, but I know I'll appreciate it when he's not throwing himself on my bed at five in the morning." He took steps toward the staircase, but my huff stopped him. Once again, he peered back at me. "Really?" Amusement laced his tone.

"Just get to it and stop behaving like you're even a little surprised."

After spending so many years sharing a room and often a bed with Dylan, I was the first to admit that I slept a whole lot better when I shared Dylan's space. I wasn't the slightest bit apologetic. His sleep noises were familiar and calming.

Without a word, he bypassed the staircase that led to two upstairs bedrooms and a bathroom and headed down the hallway, past the sitting area and the kitchen/dining room, and through the door to the master bedroom.

Backing up to his bed, he released me, dumping me on his mattress. I landed with a chuckle and a happy sigh. "You have the best mattress ever."

"It's exactly the same as yours." He shook his head and went to his side of the bed, because after twenty-plus years, of course we had dedicated sides of a mattress.

He also spoke the truth.

I'd deliberately bought the exact same mattress as Dylan's. "It doesn't feel the same," I complained. It seriously didn't. As he pulled off his jacket and reached for a coat hanger, I turned on my side and watched him. "You looked great today, in the suit."

Dylan paused his movements. "Thanks?" He arched his eyebrow, the word lifting into a clear question. His gaze dipped to my chest for a moment before our eyes met. "You looked great too."

"I think the photos are going to look fucking awesome."

While his lips twitched, he didn't respond, focusing instead on undressing. I couldn't look away, even knowing I was being fucking weird.

In the process of tugging off his slacks, Dylan paused, the lack of movement tearing my gaze away from his hands to his face. His brows almost touched his hairline as he asked, "You okay?"

"Uhm—" I cleared my throat. "Yeah. Just zoned out." Angling away, I sat and clambered off the bed, wondering what the hell my problem was. Seeing Dylan in any stage of undress was nothing new. But the moment he'd lowered his zipper, a swirl of awareness had caught me by surprise.

Those sorts of reactions needed to remain locked away in the box I'd shoved them into all those years ago.

"How come?"

The creak of the floorboard pulled my attention to him.

When we made eye contact, I released a shaky breath, reassured by the familiar look staring back at me. Curiosity and concern. I knew the signs well. With my shoulders relaxing, I admitted, "Just thinking about today and what it means."

He nodded and sat on the mattress. "It was a lot."

"Yeah, but it's also, I don't know, fucking great."

Dylan huffed out a laugh. "Yeah, it was a good night." A soft smile settled on his mouth, drawing my attention to his lips.

I struggled to pull my gaze away, remembering the kiss we'd shared. Remembering seemed like an understatement. Hell, I still felt the pressure and warmth.

Still tasted him.

"You've zoned out again." This time his Adam's apple bobbed after speaking.

Flicking my gaze up to make eye contact, I parted my lips to tell him exactly what was on my mind. Secrets between us were the worst. I hated the couple I had with a vengeance. It didn't help that they were so huge. We always talked shit out. Shared so much of ourselves with each other. "I'm going to grab a bottle of water. You want one?"

I couldn't do it. The words refused to tumble free.

"Yeah, thanks. I'm going to brush my teeth."

I hightailed it from the room, my brain a jumbled mess. The fuck was my problem? So what if I thought the kiss was hot. He'd kissed me back. I didn't imagine his tongue tangled with mine. Beyond the almost silent exchange and agreement we'd had on draft night, we'd always been able to talk about stuff like this.

Were probably a little too vocal at times with our oversharing.

Today had pissed all over our silent agreement. Though officially it was what I'd promised myself: to not go there again and definitely not do anything to mess up our relationship.

It was the most important one I had, and I valued it more than anything.

But to be fair, our getting married had made the promise a little blurry. It wasn't like we couldn't share a kiss to seal the deal.

But you didn't need to shove your tongue in his mouth or cling on for dear life.

That was also ignoring how he would react if he knew the truth about Paula's and my agreement.

Fuck.

I shook my head, trying to untangle my thoughts and stop the way my dick kept twitching. You'd have thought my swirling thoughts and the twist of guilt in my gut would be enough to calm me down and get my head out of the gutter. But kissing Dylan had been necessary and admittedly hot. That didn't mean it would or could happen again.

Getting married was an arrangement and all about Mikey.

Not only that, but kissing could also lead to more complicated developments. Sure, Dylan knew my hang-ups. He was the only person who truly did. No way would I subject him to that.

Not again.

I wasn't convinced I hadn't traumatized him the first time around.

I tugged open the refrigerator and grabbed a couple bottles of water.

I'd drink this, brush my teeth, and get my tired ass to sleep.

Between the high emotions of the day, it was understandable that I was overthinking.

I took a gulp of water, letting the cold liquid calm me. After a good night's sleep, life would make sense again. Just the thought made me breathe a little easier.

Dylan and I had been through everything together. Of course we could make this work without entangling our feelings, all while making sure Mikey always saw the best of us.

I woke with Dylan's arm draped around me and his face buried in the crook of my neck. Smiling at the familiar position we tended to be in when sharing a bed, I closed my eyes, luxuriating in how well rested I felt.

No doubt I slept so much better not only when at Dylan's place but also when we snuggled against each other. It had always been this way.

My heart panged for Dylan. His fuckheads of parents had done a number on him over the years. The man being touch starved was just one of the many reasons I hated them.

The moment Dylan stirred, his breathing changed, letting me know he was awake.

"Morning, husband." For sure, it still sounded weird. Even more reason to lean into it.

He grunted in response, still tangled around me. That he didn't scramble away, despite this not being how we'd first drifted to sleep, settled something in my gut. Left me feeling perfectly content.

"You sleep okay?" I hadn't budged once, not even when at some point in the night, he'd plastered himself to me.

"Yeah." His mumbled answer against my neck sent warm breath over my skin. The sensation tickled, and goose bumps pebbled. "It's not time to get up, right?"

Shifting my arm to get in a better position, I combed my fingers through his light brown strands, enjoying the softness and how they slipped easily through my digits. His hair was so different to mine. Where mine was thick and had tight, coarse curls—a real balance between my pop's thick, tightly cropped waves and my mom's softer coils—his was a little longer on top, a style he wore messy when not in uniform and slicked neatly when on the job.

"Not yet. The sun's not long been up." I didn't want to move to check the actual time. "Mom and Pop won't be bringing Mikey home till after lunch. They want to take him to the park first."

"And that's why my in-laws are the best ever."

I snorted out a laugh, a little surprised at how casually he'd said "in-laws." And hella relieved too. This relationship status was on paper only—apart from a few teasing word changes. Neither of us wanted it to change things between us.

With the exception of…

"You've got three more days before your next shift, right?" Dylan worked a four-day-shift roster usually, but he'd managed to swing a couple of extra days from accrued overtime.

"Yeah. Cap said I could have more for a honeymoon period, but I'd prefer to leave it for another time."

"Makes sense," I agreed. In fact, perhaps the three of us could head to the coast for a beach break or something soon. I wanted to make the most of the offseason. "I thought tomorrow we could go to my place, and we could pack some shit up to move here."

When Dylan stopped breathing, I frowned, trying to angle so I could see his face. His breathing restarted when I moved, and by the time his head was on the pillow rather than on my arm, whatever I'd expected to see on his face wasn't there.

With a quirked brow, this was very much my amused best friend peering back at me. "There something you need to tell me?"

"Thought it made sense for me to spend the offseason here, which means I'm going to need my stuff."

His brow furrowed. "Well, you usually spend two or three weeks…." He trailed off, and while there was no question in his words, it was evident on his face.

"But we're married now, yeah, so it makes sense I move here for now, and maybe we look at buying a new place somewhere between the arena and here. That way we can both do a bit of a commute to work."

It made sense. On a good run, the trip between

the city and town took an hour. If we bought a place in Cannon Falls, or somewhere similar, it would mean just twenty minutes for Dylan. I could handle a longer commute. Plus, on late game nights, I could always stay at my condo near the arena.

Though, an hour's drive was not a hardship.

I rambled on, sharing my thoughts, only to stop short at Dylan's expression.

Huffing out a breath, I shook my head. "This isn't me railroading you."

It was a phrase I found myself saying a lot. In my defense, I had the best ideas.

"It isn't, huh?" Amused disbelief stared back at me.

Dipping my voice low and into a question, I scrunched my nose, saying, "No…?"

That quirked brow of his, which was pretty spectacular since half his face was pressed to his pillow, called bullshit.

Thinking over my words, I settled on "Me saying it makes sense means 'what do you think?'" I tagged on a shit-eating grin.

"I think this is too much talk when I haven't had coffee."

"True. I knew we should have stayed in a hotel. Room service would be fucking awesome right about now."

"Hey, I'm still down for breakfast in bed if you want to go put the coffee on and make one of your kick-ass breakfast omelets."

"Fuck. I walked into that."

"You know you make the best omelets."

The asshole knew how to push my ego buttons. "Fine. But if I'm cooking breakfast, you make coffee," I challenged.

"Deal." Dylan lifted up on his elbows. The sheet pooled around his waist, revealing his broad chest. There was no stopping my gaze from dipping down as I took in the scattering of light brown hair covering his pecs, leading all the way down to his happy trail.

It was everything I'd seen a million times. And even once up close and super personal. The twitch of my softening morning wood, though, was awkward as hell.

"Right, uhm, yeah." My gaze snapped to his. Seeing his bemused expression had me relaxing. "Omelet it is." I reached out, pinched his nipple—as hello, it was just there, practically winking at me.

"Ouch, fucker."

I jumped out of bed, the pillow missing me as Dylan swung it at my head. I barked out a laugh, happy for the break in my weirdness. "Ass up, husband."

I grinned all the way to the bathroom, ignoring the double entendre and the visuals, and instead delighted in Dylan's grumble and his "The fuck have we gone and done?" The smirk on his lips and the shake of his head as he pulled on a pair of sweat-pants made it clear—he wasn't that cut up about saying "I do."

Neither was I.

My only concern was getting out of my head and the strange compulsion I had to see Dylan as some-thing different than my best friend. Something more. That road would only lead to frustration and upset.

His and Mikey's happiness meant everything to me. Not a chance I'd mess with the dynamics of that.

CHAPTER 12
DYLAN

WHEN CASS SAID HE WANTED TO MOVE SOME OF HIS things over, I'd thought a couple of suitcases of clothes. I peered around my spare room that was apparently now Cass's training room, wondering why I was actually surprised.

This was Cass, the man who never did anything by halves.

The spare bed and furniture had been dismantled and stored in the garage, and Cass's bulging cases were shoved in my bedroom, ready for him to unpack and stow things away in my—or apparently *our*—closet.

"Perfect."

At Cass's holler, I marked the wall, then passed down the hoop. By this point, I'd given up on rolling my eyes or even attempting to question what was going on.

Steamrolling was Cass's thing. Even though he'd deny it. And most of the time—like now—I let him get away with it. That didn't mean I didn't fight the good fight and shut down his eagerness when the situation called for it. But this, I'd given him.

How could I not when he was in golden retriever mode?

Add in Mikey—when he was home (I'd organized childcare for a few hours this morning)—following him around, loving the changes and Cass's attention, and this was one I'd lose.

Not that I truly wanted to stop him.

Having Cass in my space was not a hardship. Hanging out with him, living with him, I was here for it all. The man was my favorite person—barring my devotion to Mikey. And that he'd gone all in with this marriage thing we were navigating, hell, I couldn't find fault in his commitment.

That didn't mean that if he said I'd not leveled the hoop correctly again I wasn't going to cause him some serious pain.

"Drill." I held out my hand, latching on when he passed it to me. I held eye contact, saying, "You're sure this time?"

"Yeah. It's right."

I raised my brows in challenge. He'd said that for the last three marks, which I'd gone ahead and drilled holes into, only for him to say the hoop wasn't level.

"It is, definitely."

"Fine, but if it's not, tough shit. Up here's looking like a pincushion."

"Nope, it's good."

I huffed out a breath and angled to face the garage wall. The ladder wobbled.

"Shit, sorry. I let go."

"If I fall, you'll be waiting on me hand and foot, and I'll kick your ass."

"Uh-huh. Not sure you're fast enough to catch me."

"You may be quick, but I've got stamina. Your itty-bitty short bursts of speed would get you nowhere in a chase."

"You get in any awesome Hollywood police chases recently in our bumfuck-nowhere town?"

I didn't need to look at him to know he was grinning widely. *Asshole.* "I'm totally flipping you off right now," I muttered, trying to control my lip twitch.

"You're so talented. Racing for donuts, defeating bad guys, all while being an ace at drilling."

My "Fuck off" earned me a loud laugh.

Trying not to snicker, I made the hole, then passed him the drill before taking the hoop back off him. "You got the electric screwdriver?"

"Yeah." He stood on the bottom rung of the ladder and angled up to pass it to me, his head all but pressed to my ass. "I swear, if you let one rip…."

A grin split my lips. It would be oh so tempting. But this was also Cass, and honestly, when it came to asses and, specifically, their bodily functions, I never quite knew how he'd react. While we could joke about it—often with him leading the way—there'd be times it would be too much for him to handle.

I loved and respected him too much to put him in that position.

Sure, he acted like the joker jock and played up the whole aversion to literal shit and bodily functions with his teammates and other friends, but I knew the truth. I understood how, despite the laughing, his heart would be going a million miles a minute and how close he would be to feeling nauseous.

Phobias were a hell of a thing. Cassius's was just more complicated and personal than most.

"You're safe. Promise," I offered, pushing sincerity into my voice.

"I'll just admire from up close, knowing I'm safe," he teased.

I snorted out a laugh. "You do that."

I focused on fixing the hoop into position. Once the screw was tight, I passed the screwdriver back to him.

"All done."

Seeing Cass move off the ladder, I stepped down and away, the two of us backing up to see my handiwork.

"Good job."

I side-eyed him, my movement pulling his attention to me.

"It is." He raised his hands as I turned toward him.

"No corrections? No getting out the level?"

"Nope. You nailed it. Well, screwed it to perfection."

I rolled my eyes but didn't hold back my grin. Cass happy was one of my favorite things.

"Right, so all done. That it, or…?" I left the question hanging.

Since he'd moved in yesterday—I was still unsure if that was official or not—he'd been a man on a mission, getting his belongings set up and in place.

Sure, I was still tripping over boxes and cases, but I could handle it. It had been years since we'd lived together or spent longer than three weeks living side by side. It would be an adjustment, but difficult? Never.

"I've still got the closet to organize, but the gym's all set up. I don't need to sort anything now if you want to do something together."

I checked the time. It was coming up to lunch. Mikey was in childcare this morning. I usually pulled him out when not on shift, but getting Cass settled needed our focus, and chasing an almost three-year-old around would have made that impossible.

"Lunch out, and then we can collect Mikey?"

He stayed with a registered at-home childminder when I worked, though occasionally, Mama T and Pop would look after him. While Mama T took early retirement—thanks to a demanding Cass—Pop ran stock portfolios from home. That they insisted—and loved—taking care of Mikey was incredible. I was hella grateful for their love and support.

"Sounds good."

Even though I suggested lunch, I also kinda dreaded whenever I was out with Cass. Not only was he a successful basketball player, nationally recognized, but that he was local meant extra attention.

Eagles fans could be hard-core at the best of times. I was sure Zumbrota residents felt like they owned a piece of Cass. That he was one of theirs. One of their own.

It meant a meal out could go one of two ways. Either locals would leave him alone with a smile and a nod or they'd be clambering for a selfie or auto-graph and usually a long conversation. I suspected that was the same for most professional athletes and their fans, but in the past, folks around here tended to feel like they knew him personally. That Cass was their friend.

"You sure you want to go out?"

Cass's question snapped my attention to him. "Why'd you ask?"

He shot a quirked brow and an "are you serious, I know all your expressions" look at me.

Since he really did, I huffed out a breath. "I just hate the touching and folks feeling like they can get all up in your business."

His features softened. "I like when you get protective."

I tutted and rolled my eyes for good measure. "Excuse me for not wanting grabby assholes trying to wrap around you to get a photo."

His sweet smile morphed into a self-satisfied smirk. "It's a good thing I have my cop husband with me, then. You've always been like my own personal bodyguard. Now you have the added status of husbutt."

"Husbutt? Really?"

"Yep." A cheesy wink was shot my way. "Let's just head to the Coffee Mill."

When I hung my head in defeat, Cass chuckled and slung his arm around my shoulders. "Dude, there's what? Four thousand residents or something who live here? Three-quarters of those have to be at work or school. Plus, it's not like everyone doesn't know who *you* are, Sarge. What exactly do you think's going to happen?"

Was I being a reluctant asshole? Most definitely. But it was all those reasons that made me hesitate.

Likely every single busybody in town would know we were married by now. Cass's agent had also organized a press release, which I'd approved of with a grunt, that was published yesterday.

Not that I wasn't grateful that we'd managed to keep the wedding under the radar, which meant we hadn't been hounded by paps.

Us stepping out together in my town made the marital status between us real. This was our first time going public.

I had expectations that our heading out for lunch would turn more than a few heads.

"Fine, but if I have to call in Jack—or worse, Chief Nelson—for crowd control, I'm taking away your gummy bear privileges."

For real, the cops at my station were all good people, but they'd never let me live it down if they were called in to save the day.

I HELD BACK MY SIGH, BUT THERE WAS NOTHING I COULD do about the tightness of my false smile.

It was great that everyone and their dog were congratulating us on our marriage, especially considering when growing up, our community wasn't quite as progressive as now. But still, I only managed two interruption-free bites through the entire meal.

"Thanks, Mrs. Maldone." Gracious as ever, Cass was all smiles as he spoke to our old second-grade teacher. "I can promise you I'm the lucky one." After shooting her a charming smile, he winked at me, his eyes practically twinkling in pleased amusement.

"To think you boys are finally a family. It's just wonderful," she gushed.

My heart fluttered at her words.

Not only was it impossible to be resentful when she was being so genuine and kind, but also the meaning behind her words hit their mark.

Cass had always been my family, and now that we officially were was a hell of a thing.

The bell above the coffee shop door tinkled, drawing Mrs. Maldone's attention away. I took the moment to stare at Cass. Wide-eyed, I looked at his plate, urging him to hurry up. A small group was entering, which would mean even more residents stopping by our table.

While I was aware that it made me sound ungrateful and like a grumpy asshole, especially since the positive response was so incredible, I just wanted a semblance of normality. With only two more days before I was back at work, which would put me front and center of the public, a need to hide away with Cass and Mikey was a siren call I couldn't and didn't want to ignore.

"Ooh, it's Leanna. She—"

"I'm so sorry, Mrs. M. We have to get going to collect Mikey. We can't be late." Cass shot me a "see, I've totally got this" look and then Mrs. Maldone a charming smile, one he saved for folks he wanted to win over.

It worked. It did every time.

Pink-cheeked, Mrs. Maldone smiled and nodded. "Of course. You two go and get that precious boy of yours."

Grateful she gave us a free pass to escape, we stood quickly and headed on out, saying goodbye to so many residents, I gave up registering exactly who was around.

Once outside with the light breeze brushing against my skin, I inhaled deeply.

I loved our small town. There was a real sense of

community that I appreciated. When I moved back here after Paula's passing, it had felt right. Almost serendipitous that a job position became vacant. It helped that my asshole parents had moved fifty minutes west a few years back. While still a little too close for my liking, at least they weren't in my immediate jurisdiction.

Cassius's strong hand gripped my shoulder as he wrapped his arm around me. "You doing okay?"

I bobbed my head, trying to get my thoughts and feelings under control.

"It's not like you to want to flee like that." His voice was soft, a thread of concern weaving through his words.

It wasn't.

I chose to come home. Chose to be in an environment where folks had an opinion about your life. And between Cass being a star athlete and me being one of the two town police sergeants, it made us prime targets to gossip.

Considering all that, I couldn't quite grasp what my issue was. Why I felt the need to hide away with Cass and Mikey.

Aware Cass was side-eyeing me, waiting for my response as we headed to his SUV, I offered, "Let's just get Mikey and head home."

Half expecting Cass to call me out, I exhaled in

relief when he nodded, saying, "Okay. We can do that."

As he dotted a soft kiss on my temple, my pulse spiked. The gesture was something Cass had done a million times, but with the pounding in my ears and hitch of my breath, any doctor would have been concerned for my health, worried about imminent heart failure.

Me? I wondered why I was behaving so ridiculously.

Stepping away from me—and thank god unaware of my meltdown—Cass headed to the driver door. The locks disengaged. I focused on the click and the sound of Cass opening and closing his door, taking the time to shake myself out of my reaction and the thoughts trying to crawl into my mind.

Not a chance in hell that I'd think back to that kiss. The one following "I do." The one that made my head spin and left me wondering, *What if?*

I was not living in a fucking *Avengers* movie, for Christ's sake.

Getting myself under control and giving myself a stern "stop being a fucking dramatic dick" talking-to, I tugged open the door, deliberately making eye contact with Cass.

I ignored how he looked at me like I had two heads and instead focused on how much the man at

my side was my best friend. Late-night talks, whispered and sometimes hollered conversations, and
above all else, love where it mattered. My relationship with Cass was all that and more.

"Now that the hoop's up, you want to play
around when we've got Mikey?"

If Cass was surprised by my question after how
I'd quietly studied him, he didn't show it. Instead, a
happy smile formed quickly. "Absolutely."

He put the SUV into Drive and pulled away,
heading toward the babysitter's house.

The closer we got, the more I relaxed.

It was this, hanging out, being with my two
favorite people, that helped everything make sense.
Playing B-ball, spending time with Mikey, maybe
starting up the grill tonight and having a couple of
beers—yeah, all my favorite things.

CHAPTER 13

CASSIUS

"Are you sure you've got this?"

There was no disguising the uncertainty in Dylan's tone. Between that and the way he hesitated at the door *and* asked me the same question for the fifth time, maybe I should have been rethinking this whole thing. Sure, I'd never looked after Mikey by myself for longer than thirty minutes before, but I could do this.

What kind of parent would I be if I couldn't handle twelve hours with my kid—something I'd actually insisted on rather than sending him to Mom and Pop?

"We'll be fine. I've got a plan. Plus, Mom and Pop are less than a ten-minute drive away." Because yeah, I wasn't completely naive. While I wanted to handle the whole day without interference, I wouldn't hesitate to reach out to my backup plan. That being Mom and Pop. "Mikey loves me. We've got this."

Dylan pursed his lips, studying me carefully. Ensuring I gave off my usual cocky, confident vibe, I smiled. His gaze softened as he peered at the quiet staircase, up where Mikey was miraculously sleeping in. Shifting his attention back to me, he bobbed his head.

"Mikey does love you, and I'm sure you've got this."

I was pretty certain there was a silent "think you've got this," but I let him say his piece.

"Just reach out to me or your folks if you need anything."

Quick to reassure him, I said, "I will."

When his brow dipped, I wasn't sure he was buying it. While I understood his hesitation, it didn't mean his uncertainty didn't sting.

"I promise. I'm not going to screw this up."

"It's not that."

My shoulders relaxed at the speed of his reassurance.

"I just know Cassius Britton isn't synonymous with failure."

I winced, feeling my cheeks heat.

"And I don't want you to think asking for help

and not handling the whole day by yourself is failure, because it's not."

Since I'd already planned to not be a hero and ask for help, I agreed with him. But again, the bite of a sting that he expected me to need help didn't exactly feel great.

Rather than reassuring him again or attempting to challenge him or even letting him know the impact of his words, I instead leaned against the newel and folded my arms. With a smile, I said, "You're going to be late."

With a flick of his eyes to the hallway wall clock, Dylan blanched. "Fuck." He tightened his hand on the bag on his shoulder, gaze roaming over me one last time.

And hell if I didn't do the same. In his dark blue uniform, he looked hot as hell. Not for the first time, I appreciated how well his shirt stretched over his broad chest, and once he spun around, that ass would inevitably draw my attention.

Admiring my husband without wanting to fuck him into the mattress was totally a thing.

Thankfully, his "Okay. I'll call you a little later and will keep my cell on" tugged me away from my bad, bad thoughts.

"Uh-huh. Ass out the door."

With a roll of his eyes, Dylan smirked. The sight relaxed something further in my gut.

"I'm going. I'm going." With that, he hightailed it out of the house, the sound of the engine starting a few seconds later.

I huffed out a shaky breath, not feeling half as confident as I'd tried to convince Dylan I was. The skittish nerves dancing through my system needed to take a hike.

Parenting Mikey, finally being able to step up, was everything I didn't even realize I wanted or was able to do.

My promise to Paula had been all that had held the possibility of being a parent back. Okay, maybe not quite all. The fear of Dylan's reaction, the absolute terror of my best friend losing his shit and me losing him, remained a huge factor.

But this way, we could be a family, and I could be the dad I never dared to dream I could be when Paula had been pregnant. Hell, or even after.

The first time I considered the alternative was that time in the lawyer's office.

Dylan not discovering I was Mikey's biological father weighed down on me every breathing minute. But my promise to Paula when she'd asked me, practically begged me to be her donor for her insemination had outranked all the promises of not keeping secrets from my best friend.

And in some ways, she'd been right. Maybe.

She'd convinced me this was about her and having the "best" genes for her child. Yeah, there'd been a bit of ego when I'd first contemplated saying yes. That she loved me and her child being part of me helped her argument. Then it had become about speed—a willing donor—and supporting Paula's dream.

Being told this was her one shot had convinced me.

I'd argued at the time to let me talk it through with Dylan. She'd been convinced he wouldn't be supportive, especially with my tendency to react first, consequences be damned. That would have made it awkward, hell, maybe impossible for me to go ahead without his blessing, knowing it could have possibly destroyed our friendship.

And I'd wanted to do it. Wanted to support Paula. Give her the child she craved.

That I'd never given Dylan a chance to have an opinion was shit. I'd never know how he would have reacted.

But along with that, it was my decision. And Paula's.

The truth was, I hadn't wanted him to be rational

and talk me out of it. I also didn't want to go against him if he'd point-blank told me he didn't want me to follow through.

There'd been no backing down when I'd handed over the cup. And honestly, at the time, I'd handled it fine. Even when Paula had been eight months pregnant, I'd managed to compartmentalize, knowing I'd be competing for best uncle status.

Losing Paula during childbirth and not revealing the truth had been the hardest thing I'd ever done. The white lie bled deep shades of gray every day that passed by. Right along with my aching heart and my battered soul.

This was my chance to make things right for Mikey.

That I deceived my friend every fucking day… Jesus, that was a stain I didn't want to think too deeply about.

But fuck, I wasn't perfect. I was flawed. Made huge, gigantic mistakes.

I should have told him then, in the hospital. But how could I when he'd just lost his sister and become a dad? He'd needed me to step up and be his best friend. If I'd told him the truth, it would have made the most difficult time in his life infinitely worse.

I believed that with everything inside me.

Burying my unraveling thoughts as deep as possible, I pushed away from the doorframe and headed into the kitchen. No way would Mikey stay asleep much longer. It was close to six thirty, and usually he'd already be racing around the house.

Being an early riser myself, I could appreciate his morning energy. Dylan thought we were spawned from some sort of morning devil, since the man couldn't truly function without two cups of coffee.

Me? I liked a decent cup of coffee, but my energy levels tended to be high at the best of times.

Add caffeine to the mix and overly enthusiastic and I became friends.

I peered around the kitchen. With Mikey's booster seat permanently strapped to one of the chairs around the small kitchen table and his cereal bowl already out, I had no idea what the hell I did next.

Talk about being out of my depth.

I had to handle this. Had to be able to cope.

I wasn't usually this clueless. Whenever I stayed in the past—and most definitely over the last few days—it wasn't like I sat on my ass. While I'd been following Dylan's lead, I was a capable human being, fuck you very much.

Taking a calming breath, I reminded myself of that.

Laundry. That was just one of the domestic tasks Dylan seemed to do daily since Mikey was born.

With a plan, and after checking the mobile unit was switched on so I'd hear Mikey wake, I stepped into the small laundry room.

Splitting the load, I organized a dark wash. When the machine was on, the water rushing in, I returned to the kitchen. I filled the dishwasher, then went about cleaning the countertop.

The rest of the house was tidy, something we did last night.

Picking up after Mikey after a hard day of playing was a daily task and for good reason. There wouldn't be a spare patch of floor space if we didn't. The kid really liked to spread out.

A thump, the pattering of feet, and my heart bloomed in my chest.

Mikey was awake.

I headed out to the hallway, spotting him when he reached the top landing of the staircase.

He looked disheveled and ridiculously adorable in his Spider-Man jammies.

"Morning, Mikey. Good sleep, little man?"

Beaming at me with his wide grin that I was convinced was identical to mine, he bobbed his head and bounced up and down on his feet. As I headed up the stairs, my nose twitched, the scent hitting me.

But I had this.

Wet bedsheets weren't a big deal, and the kid was

still three weeks away from his third birthday. It wasn't like he still wouldn't be having accidents.

"Shall we go and get you washed up before breakfast?" I stopped on the staircase when I was only a little higher than him. It was easier to meet his gaze this way.

With a nod, he tugged at his pj bottoms, pulling a face. My lips twitched at the movement. The gesture was all Dylan.

"Pee-pee bed."

While he didn't seem happy about the revelation, he wasn't hung up on the accident either.

"Not a worry. Let's get you into the shower, huh."

"'Kay."

And then he raced away into the family bathroom.

By the time I'd entered, the kid was butt naked and searching through a small toy basket kept in the bathroom. While he grabbed a couple of superhero action figures, I turned on the shower and waited to get the temperature right.

In no time at all, I hosed Mikey down and was treated to a battle between Wolverine and Superman. I didn't dare tell the kid they weren't in the same universe. After getting him dressed and stripping his sheets, we headed downstairs for his breakfast.

I sat with him, ignoring the new chores of making

his bed and washing his sheets. Sitting here, having breakfast with the kid, or in my case a second bowl of cereal, was a treat.

And to think I'd be getting this as often as my schedule allowed.

Breakfast was a blast and messy.

And the morning pretty much continued like that.

A swirl of chaos that left the place looking like a tornado had whizzed through. And that was okay. I'd learned that picking up just one collection of toys and making it a game was the thing to do and that it was okay to ignore the mountain of mess behind us.

That was a "when Mikey napped" problem.

Mom called once, and I received a text from Dylan. Both simply asked if we were having a good day. I liked a lot that they didn't come right out and ask if I was coping.

After an early lunch, we headed to the playground.

Knowing Mikey tended to have a nap between one and two, it made sense to walk the short distance. I'd swiped the back carrier should he need a lift, and from the way he tore around the playground that looked more like a kick-ass fort than any sort of playground I had access to as a kid, I figured he'd be needing that ride when we headed home.

"Hey, Mikey." I managed to swipe him up in my

arms as he attempted to zoom past. He squealed and laughed. "It's time to get going, bud."

"No." He squirmed, legit turned into a slippery wriggle monster as he fought to get to the ground.

"'Fraid so, little guy. Home, and then we can play some hoops later."

Pausing in my arms, Mikey tilted his face to look at me. With his gaze intense and, I was sure, studying me to see if I was bullshitting him, he pursed his lips. Jesus, this kid was the cutest.

"B-ball?"

"Yup. You and me. You can even get your special jersey on."

Short of offering him candy, only because I'd learned that lesson the hard way, I was absolutely open to bargaining and a little manipulation.

"'Kay."

Huh. I grinned, proud as punch that it was that easy.

No tantrums. No drama. No blackmail.

I was nailing this parenting gig.

"Let's get you on my back."

Not a chance that he'd make the walk back home. It wasn't a long trip. By myself I could have done it in maybe fifteen minutes. It took us over thirty to get here.

"No baby." His pouty lip was back.

I held back a grin, saying, "You're definitely not a baby. That's the reason why you're allowed in the carrier. Only big boys can. It's too high for babies."

The way he eyed me let me know he wasn't convinced. Hell if it wasn't almost identical to the look I received far too often from Dylan.

"You know, from up here, you're that much closer to the sky. It wouldn't take much to stretch out and feel the clouds."

He angled back in my arms to peer up at the blue, practically cloudless sky. I held tight, my heart jolting with how far he threw himself back.

The way he did such things, with no care or thought of consequence, knowing instinctively I wouldn't let him fall, clenched my gut. It was a hell of a thing, and something I promised to never take for granted.

Returning his gaze to me, he yawned, a big, adorable yawn that reminded me so much of when he was a baby rather than this walking, talking, adventurous toddler.

"Come on, Mikey. Let's get you strapped in."

I got to work securing Mikey into the carrier, ensuring the backrest was lifted up as napping was imminent. Once safe, I hauled the carrier carefully onto my back, secured the waist strap, and tightened the arm straps too.

"Ready?" I could just about see his face if I angled my head far enough.

Another yawn and half-lidded eyes. Mikey wouldn't make it out of the playground before he was snoozing.

The fact that he didn't answer was another pretty big giveaway.

We weren't far from the police station—just over the river, in fact. It was tempting to walk in that direction, just to stop by to say hi.

It was kinda weird being back in my hometown and not being with Dylan.

These past few days especially had been incredible, relaxing in a way that I hadn't felt since I probably last called Zumbrota home.

There was nothing different about our days together, beyond me moving some of my belongings in. It was the normality of it all that made Dylan and I work. It was us being together that settled a deep ache in my gut that I always ignored.

We just fit.

It felt like I was finally home.

Ignoring the fact that this place was where I spent the first eighteen years of my life and was a town I'd visited regularly since I'd been transferred to Minneapolis, each visit had felt odd during those years that Dylan was in Virginia.

My trips here had vastly improved since he'd moved back three years ago. Seeing Dylan so regularly, being able to touch him, laugh and joke face-to-face, bury my nose against his neck and inhale deeply to take his scent with me when I left again, made my world infinitely better.

But under the heavy heartache of losing Paula and all of our struggles dealing with her loss while caring for Mikey, it never quite felt like I was coming home.

There'd been something missing.

And apparently, that was a marriage certificate and the wedding ring I found myself twirling often, usually with a beaming smile.

Walking past the covered bridge, I grinned, thinking of all the times we'd been run off by the police when we were kids.

Too many times to count, a group of us attempted to claim the old bridge for a hangout spot, but we'd never been successful. Since it pulled the tourists into town, now more than ever it seemed, it wasn't that much of a surprise that we'd failed. Instead, we'd headed out to the west of town to sneak in a few beers while playing loud music in our cars.

The spot by the river, though, that had been for just me and Dylan.

Tugging my cap lower and putting my sunglasses

on as I stepped closer to the main road and off the park lane, I peeked at Mikey. He was out for the count.

It made sense to head home rather than taking him to see his dad, as much as I missed him. Fully aware I'd made that all about me and how needy I was, I traveled north toward the softball fields instead of spinning on my heels and heading across the bridge.

The quiet road was peaceful. Just the occasional trundling pickup went by. I suspected most folks would be tucked away having their lunch around this time of day. And heading home meant I only passed one person, someone I didn't recognize.

Though, the more time I spent in Zumbrota, I suspected I would be familiar with most local faces.

By the time I passed the softball field, I slowed my gait. My legs were so long, I'd be back home in no time at all. That would mean Mikey would wake up when I tried to get him out of the carrier.

Only having a fifteen-minute nap wouldn't cut it.

While this was my first time flying solo, I'd witnessed a couple of times the reality of a tired, grouchy Mikey. The horror stories were aplenty too.

Aware that forty minutes was the glorious sweet spot to make sure he was refreshed and made it to dinner and bath time without melting down, instead of crossing the road, I headed inside the park toward the softball field.

A few young kids raced around the place with their parents in tow, but with school in session, it was quiet. It made walking the field without interruption easy. I grinned at a girl who was probably the same age as Mikey as she sped ahead of her mom, dragging a leash wrapped around a football behind her.

"Interesting pet."

The kid slammed to a stop, grinning as she peered up at me.

"Bertie."

"Bertie the ball?" I flashed a smile at the amused-looking woman who reached us.

The brunette smirked at her daughter, then at me. "Much safer option than her doing this to a poor dog."

Amused, I snorted. "Makes sense."

"I'm hoping she gets all this energy out her system so she crashes like your little one."

It was on my lips to say I wasn't his dad. With a flip of my heart, I stopped.

For almost three years, I'd refused to allow myself to think I was anything more than a donor, and nothing more than an uncle. The reality of the moment, the shift, crashed into me.

Somehow I kept my smile light despite the

pounding of my heart. "If she keeps racing like she is, it shouldn't take long. Stops them being cranky and wanting to pass out by five."

That I knew such things eased some of the tension in my chest, the worried voice that kept telling me I was a fraud.

"Right!" The woman chuckled as her daughter picked up her pet ball and hugged it. "Then awake at 2:00 a.m. thinking it's playtime."

"Fetch." The kid threw her ball with an impressive arm.

My brows shot high. "Damn, definitely not ready for a four-legged pet."

The kid raced off, and the woman shook her head in amusement. "I best go and catch up before she thinks Bertie needs a bath in the river."

We said goodbye, and I continued walking toward the river.

The warm late-spring sun pressed on my skin along with a gentle breeze. Life back home, the temperature, the quiet calm of the town, was a million miles away from what it was like when I lived in LA.

Fast and manic had been my constant then. Not only the city but my life.

It had been easy to get pulled into the party scene and the expected lifestyle of a pro athlete. Not going to lie, I'd loved every moment. Lapped up the attention, dove right into every opportunity being a celebrity afforded me.

But glancing at the river ahead, the steady flow of water and the soothing sounds that always calmed something in my chest as I reached the edged, I smiled.

This right here worked for me.

Eight years in the League meant I was blessed.

Over the eight years of playing pro B-ball, I'd been in the starting five almost every single game. My shooting average was high, my rebound count pretty fucking spectacular.

All of that had been made even sweeter when the Minnesota Eagles picked me up. Sure, Dylan had still been in another state, but Paula and my folks had been close by.

Returning to my state had changed everything.

Okay, not quite everything.

I still liked to cause chaos and have fun every now and then, but I'd spent more time hanging out with friends and making trips back to my hometown.

It was how I'd really connected with Paula and formed a stronger friendship with her.

Sorrow bloomed to life in my chest once again. Losing her hurt, left a rawness behind I wasn't sure would ever fully heal.

She'd been a good friend. A sister.

When she'd first spoken to me about insemination, no doubt about it, I'd freaked. My instinct had been to balk and say no.

In fact, that's exactly what I'd said.

It was only when she'd told me about her medical conditions that would impact her ability to have a kid, and the docs telling her that it would be likely she'd need a hysterectomy before she reached twenty-four that I'd relented.

Fuck, she'd been young.

Stubborn too.

And so damn determined and passionate.

Mikey stirred behind me. A quick check on him and his scrunched-up face, and a rush of emotion swept through me.

Mikey was never meant to be mine.

A burning stab clenched my heart at the thought of never having this.

The thought dragged guilt with it, thick and fast, knowing the only reason we were here together was because of Paula's death.

I exhaled a shuddery breath, trying to release the conflicted emotions constantly dragging me down. The what-ifs, the should've, could've, would've had no place in my headspace, or my heart, not if I wanted to pave this future for myself.

And fuck me did I want that.

I wanted it all.

Wanted Mikey to call me his dad. Wanted Dylan to always be at my side. Wanted more kisses, more—

The thought smacked me in my face before sucker punching me in the gut.

When the fuck did I start wanting more?

Mikey stirring had me moving. I welcomed the interruption. Clung to the escape he offered.

My thoughts were dangerous.

But not completely unexpected.

I'd bullshitted myself a lot over the years. Ensured my brain overruled the want in my heart.

Now? I wasn't sure I could keep denying myself. This pull.

Maybe this what-if was something I could chase and make happen?

The fizz in my gut had me pausing. I latched on to the feeling, questioning it. Examining it.

Was Dylan the only person to ever make me feel this way? A kick of my pulse and I felt giddy with possibility.

Stirring again, Mikey grunted in his sleep, shifting around in the carrier. It got me moving as I headed back the way I came.

Halfway through the softball field, Mikey woke with a startled cry.

"Hey, there." I peered over my shoulder, seeing his red face and his out-of-focus eyes. "You're okay, Mikey."

He just cried harder.

"Five minutes and we'll be home." It was closer to ten, but he wouldn't know the difference.

"Out."

I paused. Maybe it would be best to get him out. Every tear he spilled I hated. A hug could fix everything, right?

"Sure thing, kiddo. Give me a second."

Before I could move, before I could even grab the straps to remove the carrier, his face turned beet red and a fresh sob started, right alongside the stench of my worst nightmare.

No, no, no. Not now.

Panicked, I removed the carrier as quickly as possible, trying to hush Mikey and not let my horror show. Once on the ground, I unbuckled him and lifted him out, my hands underneath his armpits.

Wide-eyed, I swallowed hard and held my breath.

No, no, no.

An explosion had detonated in his pants. A shit-bomb so extreme, my brain short-circuited.

Meanwhile, I stood with Mikey held away from my body, the poor kid still wailing while I was in a nightmare.

I also needed to get my brain to work, keep my fear in check, and care for my kid.

Taking a deep breath through my mouth, I focused on his face, his bright red cheeks, and his distraught eyes.

"Hey." I placed him on his feet on the ground, kneeling before him. "You're okay, Mikey. We'll get this fixed right up."

I touched his face, concern making my heart trip at the heat of his skin.

Fucking hell, my first day as a solo parent and I'd made my kid ill.

I tugged him toward me, wrapping him in my arms and dotting a kiss on his sweaty forehead. "Hush, baby boy. I've got you."

A stuttering breath and his crying fractured a little as he clung to me.

"That's it." I hushed him again, focusing on taking slow, even breaths.

While I had no idea what to do next, comfort Mikey I could do.

I didn't have a spare change of clothes or anything. A rookie mistake.

"Hey, you need some wet wipes?"

The question took me by surprise, having not heard anyone approach. It was the brunette with the kid who had the pet ball.

"God, yes, please."

A smile of understanding slipped onto her lips. She crouched down, her daughter at her side, and opened the small backpack. "Here, grab these as well."

Gratitude crashed into me as I took the offered pack of wipes, a small plastic bag, and a pair of shorts. "This is amazing, thank you."

"It's all good. There's never an ideal time for a diarrhea explosion. Parents of toddlers have to stick together."

I chuckled. "I really appreciate it. Thank you."

A changing mat appeared next, and I placed Mikey down for the first time, taking in the horror of the explosion. My breathing was choppy, but I had this.

Mikey needed me. Plus, I had an audience.

For years I'd bullshitted my way through my adverse reaction to shit—usually making a joke of it —no one beyond Dylan knowing the truth. What was one more incident and moment of me faking it?

I got him cleaned up with almost mechanical precision. Focusing on his calming whimpers helped. Knowing he wasn't so upset and must be feeling better not being in soiled clothes kept me going.

By the time he was clean and wearing the borrowed shorts, I breathed easier. My hands were as clean as I could get them—though I seriously appreciated the antibacterial gel Kelsey handed me. And yes, we were on first-name basis now.

How could I not be when she'd saved the day?

"You are a lifesaver," I said as I stood, holding Mikey on my hip.

"Not a worry." Her gaze drifted to Mikey. "Perhaps check his temperature when you get back."

I nodded and looked at my boy. "He's warm."

"Have you got some Tylenol at home?"

I wasn't a hundred percent sure. "Maybe?" When Mikey was teething, Dylan gave him meds to help him. I couldn't imagine something like that not being stored in the medicine cabinet. "We're bound to have some."

I shot off a quick text to Dylan, letting him know where I was and asking if we had meds. If we didn't, I'd need to head to the pharmacy to pick some up.

Together, we walked to the park entrance. Millie was being carried by her mom, finally flagging, and Mikey's face pressed against my chest.

The poor kid.

I held the carrier, complete with soiled clothes, in my hand, wanting to hurry up and get home. Getting Mikey cleaned up properly and checking his temperature was my priority. Though damn if I didn't want to get in the shower and scrub myself down.

Reaching the entrance, we paused.

"So, thanks again."

"Honestly, it's not a problem." Kelsey shifted Millie a little higher on her hip.

"Is there a way to get the shorts back to you?" Maybe I should just give her some cash so she could buy a new pair.

"No need. We've got at least ten at home. Keep them as spare when you're out and about." Humor laced her words.

I chuckled lightly, not wanting to jolt Mikey. "I hear you. Point taken."

"Millie's available for playdates if Mikey's ever in need of company."

"Yeah," I answered immediately. Millie seemed like a cool kid and just the right kind of hyper to be entertaining to be around. "That sounds good. Mikey spends some time in childcare, but I'm home pretty much all summer and will be looking after him. I'll talk to Dyl about it."

Her brows pulled together at the mention of Dylan's name. A moment later, her eyes widened in recognition, her gaze settling on Mikey.

"Sergeant Turner?"

"Yeah." I studied her carefully, wondering if I'd been wrong to even attempt to be friendly with this woman. "My husband."

Kelsey seemed nice enough. Having already clocked her wedding ring, I had no issues with giving her my number, reassured there'd be no mistaking this was about the kids.

"Oh my. Right." A tentative smile lifted her lips, and a light blush colored her cheeks. "I heard he'd gotten married. Congratulations."

My smile was real, relieved she wasn't a dick-head. "Thanks," I said before giving her my number and asking her to text me hers so I didn't have to juggle with my hands full.

I heard the message alert and smiled. "Great. I best get going and…." I trailed off at the sound of a car pulling up beside us.

Taking in the unfamiliar pickup, I waited, wondering why it had stopped right here. A glance at Kelsey and my brow furrowed.

Her face had paled, eyes widening with what I thought looked like fear.

I peered again at the truck.

A guy stepped out with a face of thunder and a scowl firmly in place. He was thick-set, I supposed tall, relatively speaking. Around me, the majority of the population were pocket-sized.

"Nolan."

The quiet voice threaded with panic caught my attention. I snapped my gaze back to Kelsey.

"I was just on my way home right now." A subtle shift in her body and Kelsey held tighter to her sleeping daughter as she spoke.

Nolan stepped around the vehicle, his fierce gaze moving to me. The widening of his eyes as he took me in would have been amusing if I wasn't so concerned about Kelsey's reaction.

Then he recognized me.

His eyebrows darted up, and a grin that didn't do a thing to make me like him any more was shot my way.

"Cassius Britton." He shook his head. "Holy shit. I'd heard you were from around these parts."

A tight smile formed on my lips. "Born and bred," I answered. It didn't take a genius to figure out this was Kelsey's husband. I could be polite and not create shit when I wanted to. But fuck, I was glad I had my hands full and couldn't shake his hand.

"Fucking A."

I winced at his cussing, hating that he was doing it around Mikey. Sure, I slipped up every now and then, but I tried to rein it in.

"Not the best season you guys had," the fucker said.

I quirked my brow, wishing I was surprised he was *that* sort of fan who'd say such shit to my face. Assuming he *was* a fan, of course.

"Some good games. Just hope that coach of yours makes a few changes next season. Heard he's after Blake Henderson in the draft."

"That right?" Rumors were always entertaining and usually bullshit.

"It would be good to get some more Minnesota blood on the team. Better than some of the shit overseas assholes who think they can come in and take over."

I ground my teeth together. If he started talking shit about immigrants next, I didn't think I'd be able to walk away without saying anything.

"Nolan, honey, do you mind taking Millie? She's getting a little heavy," Kelsey asked quietly, preventing me from having to respond to Nolan.

A flash of annoyance appeared on Nolan's face as he looked at his wife. It disappeared when he returned his focus to me and rolled his eyes. "Fucking women." Stepping to Kelsey's side, he took Millie from her, surprisingly gently.

As he got about putting Millie in her car seat, Kelsey turned to me. A tentative smile was sent my way before she said, "Nice meeting you, Cassius."

"Yeah, you too. I'll let you know about a playdate."

As soon as the words were out of my mouth, I knew I'd said the wrong thing.

Her paling face was the first indicator. Her wide, worried eyes was the second.

The third was Nolan snapping his attention in our direction, an expression on his face I couldn't quite read.

And then a second vehicle pulled up. The markings I recognized. The man stepping out with a frown I wasn't used to seeing on his handsome face, my best friend.

Eyes just for me, Dylan asked, "Everything okay here?"

Before I could answer, Nolan slammed the pickup's door, startling Mikey in my arms. Immediately after, the sound of Millie's cries breached the closed door.

"Nolan, you've—"

A fierce look from her husband stopped Kelsey in her tracks as she reached for the door.

"Get in the damn truck."

When she hesitated at Nolan's order, my gut clenched, and I took a step forward. Before I could move again, Dylan was before me, hands on his belt, his back to me as I looked on. With Nolan now looking his way, I expected Dylan eyeballed him right back.

"Kelsey, you okay?"

While Dylan's tone was soft, tension all but

vibrated from him. With the speck of distance between us, I felt the heat, felt his carefully controlled frustration.

Apparently, he knew exactly who Kelsey and Nolan were.

"Kelsey," Dylan said again when she didn't respond.

"Just get in the fucking truck, Kelsey." Nolan's voice was low, holding a bite that sent alarm spiraling through me.

Who the fuck was this asshat?

Without a backward glance, Kelsey fumbled her way into the seat of the pickup truck.

While I didn't hear Dylan's sigh, I saw how his shoulders sagged.

"Nolan, I don't want to be called out to any disturbances at your place tonight."

Jesus.

The stark reality of what kind of man Nolan was made my gut clench. How the hell did Dylan do this? Deal with this kind of shit day in, day out?

"Why don't you keep your nose out of my business, *Sergeant*." The word was a sneer.

Not liking his tone one bit, I shifted in frustration behind Dylan. Sure, I'd keep my mouth shut. That didn't mean I fucking liked this situation one bit.

At my movement, Nolan's gaze shifted to mine.

The questioning glance disappeared in the time it took for me to blink and for Dylan's shoulders to tense.

"Jesus fucking Christ. You?" Venom sliced through the words Nolan spat at me. He looked me up and down, disgust morphing his features. "Fucking knew there was a reason the Eagles went to shit. The number of butt f—"

"Don't."

The ice in that one word should have chilled me to the bone, but fuck if Dylan in protective cop mode wasn't ridiculously sexy. Damn, maybe it was protective husband mode that was getting my engine revved.

Either way, my dick perked up, taking me by surprise. It was so not the moment for this.

Not only was I sure I had shit on the back of my tee, but Mikey was unwell. Then there was the dickwad before us.

A sly smile filled with malice slashed across Nolan's face. "Sure thing, *Sergeant*." He turned his back on us, got in his truck, slammed the door shut, and sped away with a squeal of tires.

A shaky breath rushed out of me, and I brushed a kiss on the top of Mikey's head.

Turning on his heel, Dylan took the two of us in. His worried gaze settled on Mikey, then on me. "You okay?" Concern tightened his voice. He stepped closer, placing his hand on Mikey's back.

At the touch, Mikey shifted and peered over at his dad.

I expected him to lunge out of my hold to get into the safety of Dylan's arms. That he didn't, instead snuggling further into my chest, caught my breath.

"We're fine. A little thrown by whatever that was," I admitted. "I need to get this guy back to the house and washed up. Get some meds into him."

"What happened? You said he wasn't well?" Dylan stroked Mikey's back.

I lifted the carrier, complete with the bag. Wrinkling my nose, I explained the explosion, still proud that I managed to rein in my desire to gag.

"Damn. Are *you* okay?"

The fluttering in my chest that I usually ignored when Dylan proved he knew me so well and cared for me took a life of its own. "Yeah." I huffed out a quiet, self-deprecating laugh. "Will be even better when we've both showered, and I'm telling you right now, this bag is going in the trash."

No way would I be washing the clothes. I didn't want to look at them again.

I had half a mind to throw out the carrier too. If I ordered the exact same one, I could probably get away with it.

"How about I meet you at home, and I'll take care of Mikey while you focus on getting cleaned up?"

Was it wrong that I wanted to kiss the hell out of him for offering?

The truth was, between the disaster of getting Mikey changed and my worry for his health, my nerves had already been fried. Add in the crazy confrontation with the thug Nolan, how unsettled I felt with how he treated his wife, and his clear opinion of Dylan, and I was grateful for any help I could get.

"Aren't you on shift?"

"Let's call it my lunch break." A warm smile tilted his lips.

"You have lunch breaks? Since when?" Sure, I took on a teasing tone, but with such a small department, I knew lunchtimes at the station weren't a real thing.

Not that our town was a hive of activity, but there was a sizable area in our county needing to be covered, and Dylan was as much about the preventative side of policing as he was about dealing with the aftermath of callouts.

"I've got my radio. We'll be fine." He glanced at his son. "You okay to walk since I don't have his seat?"

"Of course."

Dylan took the carrier off me, his nose twitching as, between the movement and the breeze, the scent of his son's accident lifted.

"I'll put this in the trunk. See you in a few."

With a smile, I held Mikey closely, dotting another kiss to his head. He'd been worryingly quiet through the whole exchange. But nothing some medicine, a bath, and sleep couldn't cure. At least, that's what my folks had always told me, and they'd never given me a reason to doubt them.

CHAPTER 14

DYLAN

While the bath ran, I pulled out the Tylenol, then a soft pair of pj's.

I carried out the tasks methodically, focusing on making sure that when Cass arrived with Mikey, I could take over and look after the both of them. Concentrating on them helped keep my anger in check. Prevented me from stewing over Nolan and going over and over in my head what a nasty piece of shit he was.

Taking a steady breath, I went back to the bathroom, throwing in a few bubbles. Not that I expected Mikey to play, but the lavender scent would hopefully calm him a little, too, and help him settle.

Sleep would help him heal.

The front door opening and closing caught my attention. The sound of footsteps on the staircase followed, and Cass appeared in the open bathroom doorway.

A tentative smile sat on his lips as he eyed me carefully.

"I'm okay."

He didn't need to ask me; I knew he was concerned. Cass was smart enough to have read what went down with Nolan.

He bobbed his head and stepped farther into the room. "Okay. You still good to bathe Mikey?"

"Yeah, of course." I took Mikey from him and frowned at the pink in his cheeks. "When did he start getting hot?"

"He was fine all morning. We went to the playground, and there was no sign of him being ill. Raced around like the Road Runner. He hit his wall and fell asleep as soon as he was in the carrier, and then he woke up ill."

I winced, imagining just how rotten that was for the both of them. The stench coming from the plastic bag I'd shoved in the outside trash told me how bad it had been.

"These shorts?" I already had an idea of what else had gone down.

"Yeah, Kelsey saw what happened, gave me what I needed to clean up, and those."

I nodded. From what I knew about Kelsey, she

was a kind, good woman. A good mom. This confirmed it even more, helping Mikey and Cass out like that. The fuck she was still doing with Nolan, though, just brought me to new levels of frustration.

Not that I didn't recognize that leaving was a hard choice. Hell, an impossible choice sometimes. Domestic violence was a hell of a thing.

It had only taken the first year on the job for all the bullshit, preconceived ideas of "surely the victim can just leave" to fly out the window. Experience had told me there was nothing easy or straightforward about DV incidents.

"That was kind of her."

I just hoped the next time I saw her, she wouldn't be wearing a bruise for her kindness. It wasn't even like I could do a welfare check without just cause. Those only made things worse for her.

Though the next time I saw Nolan's pickup outside his preferred bar, which would likely be in a few hours, it would be safe to stop by to check in.

"It was. Said we'd let the kids have a playdate."

My frown was immediate.

"That not okay?"

I sighed and turned the faucet off. Aware little ears could be listening, I said, "Let's chat later, yeah?"

"Sure."

Worried eyes took me in. They also had me moving into his space and drawing him into a gentle hug, Mikey sandwiched between us.

The dot of a kiss to my neck did the trick of smoothing out the tension between my shoulder blades. My pulse shot high, though.

"I was worried about Mikey," I said, pulling away, "but I knew he was in the best possible hands."

My words hit their mark as Cass swallowed hard and emotion settled in his gaze. And I felt it. Lived it and breathed it. Cass and Mikey meant everything to me.

"But finding the two of you how I did…." I shook my head, absorbing the heat of Cassius's hand that had found its way to my forearm.

Truthfully, I'd seen red when I'd pulled up to Nolan around the two most important people in my life. No good would ever come from them in the same breathing space as the abusive bastard.

"We're okay too." Cass squeezed my arm, not needing me to finish my sentence.

I nodded. "I know."

"Right." Cass stepped away. "It's time to get cleaned up. Holler if you need me."

I watched him go before turning my full attention to my boy, who was worryingly quiet in my arms. A quick check and I was surprised he was still awake.

"Come on, Mikey. Let's get you some medicine and cleaned up."

It didn't take long to bathe Mikey, but he wasn't having any of it when I tried to put him to bed, despite clearly needing to sleep.

His temperature was elevated but not worryingly high. So that was something.

It meant I lay on my bed, Mikey cuddled up at my side by the time Cass stepped out of the en suite in nothing more than a towel around his waist.

Surprise flooded his features as he took us in, his gaze softening when he saw Mikey fighting sleep at my side. I focused on his reaction rather than the trail of water dripping down his chiseled chest.

"Let me just put some boxers on and I'll take over."

His ability to read the situation and what Mikey needed made my heart squeeze. The throb of my heart changed dramatically and traveled south when he turned and dropped his towel to tug on a pair of boxers, revealing a luscious ass that I had no right to be mesmerized by.

Fuck. Why the hell was Cassius getting to me like this?

And now? After all these years?

And it wasn't just when I saw his delectable ass either. This was so much more than thinking he was hot. But that didn't stop my dick thickening at the expanse of perfect, dark skin on display.

I partially blamed my sister for her not so stealthily putting ideas into my head in that damn letter of hers.

My stare jerked north when he turned, revealing his sizable package.

The asshole smirked, all knowingly and shit.

I narrowed my eyes at him, Mikey still awake next to me preventing me from telling him to fuck off.

A twitch of his lips, and then he peered at Mikey. "How's he doing?"

"Tired but fighting it." I trailed my fingers through Mikey's hair. "He's had five milliliters of Tylenol. If you give him another dose at five o'clock, that'd be great. Hopefully I'll be home on time tonight."

By the time I finished speaking, Cass was on the mattress beside Mikey.

"And he's okay if he sleeps? I don't need to wake him?" Concern colored his words as he maneuvered Mikey to his side. I smiled, happy Mikey went willingly.

"If he's unwell, he'll sleep as long as he needs. I'm not making promises that tonight will be great for any of us." I tilted my lips up.

"We'll be fine."

There was no doubt in my mind that they would. It made me feel a little like an asshole when I said, "There may be more explosions."

The wince was immediate, but Cass bobbed his head. "I kind of figured."

"You going to be okay?"

In truth, I was so fucking proud of Cass and how he'd handled the whole mishap. Explosions were the worst at the best of times, but out in public and with no backup, well, that was a nightmare. Add in Cass's struggles, and I was legit proud of him.

Determination formed on his features. A confident nod followed. "Absolutely."

Warmth wrapped around me. While it was a sensation I was used to when being with Mikey and Cassius, there was a stark difference that threatened to have me unraveling.

For the first time since being a dad, I didn't feel like I was going this alone.

Needing to leave before I quite possibly lost it as I examined those feelings more closely, I eased off the bed. With my focus on pulling my service belt on, I took a cleansing breath.

I totally had this.

Familiar deep brown eyes filled with questions stared back at me when I peered at Cass. This was something I couldn't unpack right now. So with a smile and a wink, I said goodbye and got my ass out of there and back on duty.

———

SOMETIMES I HAD SECOND THOUGHTS ABOUT THE wisdom of moving back to the small town I grew up in. Last week's bullshit with Nolan was just one of several reasons for the doubt.

As were the couple of run-ins I'd had with him since the altercation by the softball grounds.

The world was full of assholes like Nolan. I was sure there were several just like him in every town. Small-town living came with its own kind of challenges, though. Not escaping scrutiny was one of several.

It would take just one question for someone to discover where I lived. Who my child was. Who my husband was. There was a semblance of safety in that, being in a largely supportive community, though.

Folks around here tended to look after their own. While I'd left town for a few years, that I'd come back had been enough for me to be brought back into the fold.

With the exception of assholes like Nolan.

In truth, me being a cop remained at the center of his hatred. His mistrust.

That I was a gay cop simply fed that disgust.

That I was a dad to a biracial kid and the more recent development of me being married to a Black man, hell, I was surprised his head hadn't exploded with hatred overload.

That would have been paperwork I would have happily given up an evening filling in.

But today, at the playground with the picnic table covered with balloons and a bunch of toddlers racing around, playing and celebrating Mikey's third birthday, it reminded me why I'd chosen to come home.

"Dylan, honey, do you want to attempt to gather the kids for a photo?"

I peered over at Mama T and smiled. She lived for this stuff, totally in her element hosting and keeping friends and family—ones who I'd chosen rather than blood—happy and their sodas topped up. That and every other loop around the park, Mikey would hug her legs hard before giggling and racing away.

"I sure can. Not sure my odds are great, though." I chuckled as Cassius picked up Mikey and Tahlia—one under each of his arms—and pretended to be an ogre as he tried to capture the rest of the kids. "You're best off asking that growly son of yours. He seems to have it handled."

And like his mom, Cass lapped this up—playtime with Mikey. Not only that, he was amazing with him, stepping into parenting Mikey in a way that shouldn't have surprised me.

It had been foolish of me to underestimate Cassius, but after being by myself for three years and having sole responsibility for Mikey, it had been hard to let go.

Sure, Cass had made it clear his job wasn't babysitting, a conversation that had left me wide-eyed and my heart beating a little too fast. He'd promised he was in this with me and with Mikey.

I believed him. I did. But that hadn't stopped me waiting for... hell, maybe for him to get a wake-up call and question his life decisions.

Just thinking that made me feel like a piece of shit. Cass was not like that. Ever. He'd never given me a reason to believe for one moment he'd do that. If anything, that made me feel even more guilty about my irrational thoughts.

But seriously, he was my husband.

What the hell was rational about that?

Not that being married to Cass was a hardship. In truth, everything had been perfect. Worryingly so.

Before we'd exchanged vows, I would have told anyone, hand on heart, I knew Cass inside and out. But over the past few weeks, he was so much more than my best friend and the man who I'd known for over twenty years.

Yes, he'd always been thoughtful. But the man legit made me meals for when I got home from work and ate with me. But because this was Cassius Britton, the man who never did anything by halves, he also made sure he had a tiny version of Mikey's dinner, so every night when I was at work and missed Mikey's early dinnertime, they ate together. Cass's "No one should eat alone if there's an opportunity to have company" was now a mantra our little unit lived by.

Considering all that, I didn't truly expect the other shoe to drop. Not really.

Two kids ran past me, pulling me away from staring at the ogre I quite happily called husband.

"I think it's cake time," I hollered, stepping into the fray of squealing kids. "Hey, ogre."

Cass cut off midroar and peered over at me. While half of his face was hidden by a Shrek mask, his expressive eyes made it clear what an amazing time he was having. I suspected that had everything to do with Mikey's huge grin.

"You want to bring those offerings you have so we can get a group photo and cut the cake?"

"Can do, my fair and handsome prince."

I snorted at his god-awful attempt at a Scottish

accent, then managed to capture a couple more kids and shepherd them closer to the picnic table.

The cake sporting Donkey's cheesy grin was pretty epic. And while I was sure none of the other kids here knew who the characters were and likely hadn't watched the older film, I was grateful that Mikey's fixation was on *Shrek* rather than a lame movie.

Appearing at my side after dropping the kids next to the table where Pop and Mama T were herding them, Cass wrapped his arm around my shoulders.

I sighed into his touch, always appreciating his closeness. And days like these, his comfort too.

The day would always be bittersweet.

As always, my heart overflowed with joy and happiness that Mikey was in our lives, but I didn't know if a birthday would pass without the pain of losing Paula.

A kiss was pressed against my temple, and I blinked back the tears as I watched Mikey standing with his arm around his best friend, Tahlia. That Cass knew I needed his touch made me lean into his side a little closer.

"Do you remember when Paula hid your fishing line and you found it later wrapped around those Disney prince dolls?"

I snorted out a laugh, the sound abrupt. Before I

answered, I turned my head a little and dotted a kiss on his shoulder.

And then Cass did things like this. On every one of Mikey's birthdays, he stood by my side, wrapping me in love, and told stories about my sister.

"She said that she had no interest in the princes, and they weren't cut out to save the day."

Cass's chuckle was deep.

"How the hell my parents didn't figure out she was a lesbian until she came out to them and left home boggles my brain." Though I expected, after I left and the humiliation of that, they buried their heads even further in the sand.

Paula had been trying to stick it out at home until she left for college, but in the end, our parents had pushed her too far. And thank goodness they had. Knowing she was with Mama T and Pop had made it easier to head to a different state for the police academy. Even more than that, Paula had been happy and loved living with them.

"Mom's eyeing us."

I peered over and took in Mama T's tender expression. A flutter of wings paid attention, too, and I couldn't help but wonder what she really thought about me and Cass.

We'd told them the truth, like Cass and I discussed.

But still, was she disappointed that Cass hadn't married the love of his life?

Discomfort pressed against my chest at the thought, and not because of Mama T's possible disappointment. Cass marrying someone else? Fuck, my heart pinched at the mere idea.

Clearing my throat and trying to shake free of my negative emotions, I stepped away from Cassius. A disgruntled "Hey" left him when we no longer made contact. With a smirk and an eye roll, I reached for him, took hold of his hand, and led him toward Mikey.

"It's time we light the candles and get those wishes nailed down," I said, tugging on his hand.

He came willingly, and I couldn't help but make a wish of my own. *I wish he always does.* Come willingly that was. Not having this with Cass, this life we'd started building together, regardless of how it started with that meeting with his lawyer, I didn't want to imagine what my world would look like.

"YOU SURE YOU'RE OKAY?"

Having not heard Cassius enter the room, I jolted. Rather than laughing at his ability to take me by surprise, his frown deepened.

"Just tired." And I was.

The last four-day roster had been long and busier than usual. With the annual Covered Bridge Half Marathon taking place yesterday, more visitors had been in town. While it was great for our small businesses, inevitably there were more issues, more patrols needed, more idiots drinking too much last night.

Yesterday, my twelve-hour shift ended up being fifteen hours.

The overtime wasn't welcome, especially as it meant I'd missed Mikey's bedtime. Cass being home, lounging on the couch, a cold bottle of beer open and ready for me, though, now that was a welcome treat.

Over the past few weeks of Cassius being here, everything had been perfect. Not that it hadn't always been great when he visited.

This time felt different. No doubt because it was.

This was his home now.

We had a closet half filled with his clothes to prove it. Not only that but a new routine that worked as effortlessly as breathing.

"Tired yet you still have time to read?" He quirked his brow and eyed the paperback in my hand.

After we'd put Mikey to bed, we'd had a couple of beers before I'd dragged myself to bed. He'd since spent some time on the running machine and showered, discovering me under the covers, devouring one of five books I'd put on special order at our small bookstore.

"Call it time to unwind."

"Was today's shift better than yesterday's at least?" He rubbed the towel over his head, gaze still on me as he waited for me to answer.

"Definitely. I got home on time for starters."

He threw the towel into the laundry basket and grinned. "And we appreciate that."

The follow-up wink was one I'd received a million times before, but from the way my heart tumbled, you wouldn't have thought so.

I still wasn't quite sure what to do with that—with the flutters of awareness coming quick and fast since our wedding day.

"I'm sorry."

Sure, he'd shot me a teasing smile, but this couldn't have been what he'd signed up for, right?

The dip of his eyebrows shadowed his eyes. Not enough to hide the concern in them. Cassius sat on the bed facing me, saying, "Sorry about what? Doing your job?"

Tugging the inside of my cheeks between my teeth, I sighed. "Let's just sleep."

"Hell no, not until you let me know what's going

on with this weird self-flagellation shit happening right now."

Cassius was nothing if not dramatic. It was enough to pull forth a smirk, and I rolled my eyes.

"There's no flog in sight."

"Thank fuck for that. No kink shaming, but, dude, my idea of pain is maybe a bite on my nipple every now and then."

Startled, my brain hooked onto that image with worrying ease. "You like your nipples being bitten?"

"I do, especially if my cock's being given some TLC. But not enough to draw blood or anything."

My dick twinged at the thought of nibbling and lathing his nipples. Since his chest was bare and he was clad only in a pair of sleep shorts, the visual was there for the taking.

Fuck, his nipples were a shade darker than his skin. It wouldn't take much attention on them to make them even darker.

"Are you eye-fucking my nipples?"

Snapping my gaze to his, I parted my lips, only to clamp my mouth shut at his shit-eating grin and quirked brow.

"Fuck off," I grumbled, ignoring the heat in my cheeks. If I peered down, I suspected my whole chest would be a ridiculous shade of red.

The asshole lifted his hand to his pec and ran his

fingers over his nipple. Unable to look away, I followed the movement, stomach clenching when his nipple became taut.

Fuck my life.

It was pointless denying I watched his every move, so I did what any self-respecting man would do. I threw a pillow at him, slammed my back onto the mattress, and hid my face behind my book.

If Cass's deep laughter and the bounce on the mattress were anything to go by, he found my fascination hilarious. Which I supposed was better than calling me a perv and telling me to keep my eyes to myself.

"Aw, come on, husbutt. You're allowed to look at my pretty nipples."

I ignored him, despite looking ridiculous with an open paperback literally on my face.

A wobble of the mattress was the only warning I got that he was on the move, but it was too late to defend myself.

He landed on me in a sprawled mass of limbs and loud laughter.

"*Oomph.* Fuck, get your giant ass off me."

Light filled my vision, then his grinning face when my book fell off.

"I have a perfect ass. There's nothing giant about it."

"*Perfect*?" I sassed, adding a scoff for good measure. "Who told you those lies?" I held back my grin, struggling to focus on his expression since he was legit spread out on top of me, face barely hovering more than a couple of inches above mine.

The daggers he shot at me were easy to see, though.

"Lies, you fucker. Take that back."

He shifted on me, and fuck if his groin didn't rub against mine. With two pairs of shorts and a single sheet between us, there was no protection from the semi I sported.

"Dyl?" His tone sounded strangled, and he froze on top of me.

The air thickened, charged. The space around us faded out so all I saw was the man above me. All I felt were his strong, muscled limbs and his rock-hard dick temptingly pressed against mine.

I held my breath, hoping the action would calm my racing pulse.

"Are you hard?" His voice dropped low, the depth awakening my nerve endings with its gruffness.

Because of course Cass would just come out with it like that.

"No?"

The pitch of my voice earned me a smirk.

"I'm not hard." The defense was weak. The words ridiculously hollow.

"*Half*-hard is a technicality." Eyes sparkling with mischief, Cass was having far too much fun with this.

The fuckface.

Two could play at that game.

I squared my jaw and shifted my hips. The movement dragged my dick over his. While it had been years since I'd seen and felt his dick, I remembered just how big he was when erect. And holy fuck, he was rock solid.

With no idea if my plan backfired or not since I barely held back my groan, I took pleasure in the widening of his eyes and the hitch in his breath.

Before I could form a syllable to call him out, his mouth was on mine, capturing my breath and stealing my oxygen.

My brain short-circuited, struggling to compute.

Cass made it impossible to think, to consider anything beyond his warm mouth, his exploring tongue, or how much I liked the feel of the scruff of his jaw against mine.

A spark of heat bubbled in my stomach, quickly flickering fully to life and sending a wildfire of need burning through me.

With my one hand on his cheek, I used the other to claw at his back, holding Cass close.

Eight years was the last time chemistry had flamed so bright. Eight years since feeling so comfortable, so right, despite the alarm bells trying to break through the need fogging my mind.

The alarm shattered around us in the form of a cry, the two of us pulling apart. Wide-eyed and panting, I stared up at Cass, at his wide, confused eyes.

Another shriek.

Mikey. Fuck. Mikey was crying.

"I've got him."

Cass stood before I could speak. Something he was surprisingly good at—getting in there first.

"You're wiped. Get some sleep. We have to be in the city by nine."

A bucketful of cold water if ever I heard it.

"Yeah, okay," I managed between choppy breaths. How the hell was Cass so unaffected?

The man simply shot me a smirk, the same kind I'd received a million times, before he left the room.

There was no sign of, well, anything untoward. Any hint that what had just happened had rattled him in the slightest.

I was losing my goddamn mind.

I turned off my bedside light, leaving Cass's on.

Another time, when my brain wasn't mush and I wasn't so dog-tired, perhaps I'd analyze once again how it was that my bed had become ours.

The best friend in me who expected nothing less from Cass told me to get over myself and simply accept it. Which, technically, I had, right?

I sighed as I closed my eyes, settling my thoughts and relaxing as my pulse finally calmed.

Tomorrow everything would be back to normal.

We'd not mention this again and focus on our meeting with Cass's lawyer.

There were documents we needed to sign for the adoption application, and he'd also heard from my parents' lawyer.

I refused to worry, confident Granger would do everything in his power to get this settled. Cass being the driving force behind that completely.

Another deep sigh and Cass's off-key singing as he hushed Mikey reached me. Warmth wrapped around me, and I soaked it in—Cass's soft voice, the taste of him still on my lips, and the occasional gentle sigh I could just make out from Mikey.

It wasn't possible for life to get better than this.

CHAPTER 15
CASSIUS

THE MEETING WITH GRANGER TOOK JUST FIFTEEN minutes.

We literally had to sign some initial paperwork, and we received news from Dylan's parents' lawyer, which was almost laughable.

Laughable in as much as it was clear their lawyer knew he wouldn't be winning any court time but was willing to open up negotiations with a face-to-face meeting.

Needless to say, Granger had already formed a polite version of a "not in this lifetime" response and just needed Dylan to sign off on it.

It meant we had plenty of time for our flight out to Chicago to take in the League Championship Final. Pearce, my asshole friend who'd abandoned the Eagles to go play for the Jetts, had scored us tickets.

Sure, I'd griped when he'd called me a couple of nights ago, giving him shit about his team playing in the finals, but I was happy as hell for him.

Not that I'd be wearing a Jetts jersey any time soon. But between his team and the Mountain Lions, I'd be reluctantly rooting for his team's win.

As soon as we entered our hotel suite, I stretched out on the bed. It didn't matter how much legroom business seats claimed to offer, it still felt like my knees had been under my chin.

"I'm just going to call Mama T to check on Mikey," Dylan said as he sat on the mattress beside me, leaning against the headboard.

"Sounds good. Tell everyone I love them."

A delicate smile curved his lips, awakening the flutter of wings that seemed to be present every time we were together. And even when we were apart and I thought about Dylan. The same sensations had been my constant since our wedding day. I swore I was losing my goddamn mind.

"I think I'll grab a quick shower. It's a short flight, but I still stink of airplane farts." The words spilled out of me, earning me a chuckle and cutting through the lust fogging my mind and controlling the flurry of awareness.

"You do that. I'll grab one after."

Even as I bobbed my head, my gaze drifted to his mouth. The last time we'd been in bed together, I'd practically jumped him.

Or hell, maybe he'd jumped me.

Either way, it had ratcheted me up in a way I hadn't experienced in so long.

When Mikey's cries had smacked us with a reality check last night, I'd hightailed it out of there with a hard dick and feeling even more confused.

A good night's sleep snuggled up to Dylan hadn't done a thing to mute my spiraling thoughts.

But now, unable to pull my focus from his lips, I couldn't help but wonder if it would be a bad thing to explore this chemistry between us. There was no denying that's what it was. Because that kiss on our wedding day and his dick rubbing against mine last night had been hot enough to create sparks.

"Hey, Mama T."

I jerked at his words, not realizing he'd made the move to call my mom. How long had I been staring at him? If the pink in his cheeks and the wariness in his gaze as he stared at me despite the conversation he was having were anything to go by, an uncomfortably long time.

That was my cue to leave.

And ideally get rid of this tent in my pants with a cold shower.

Grabbing our toiletry bag, because yes, we shared, I headed into the bathroom, turning on the shower as soon as I entered.

As I set about soaping up, I tried to focus on the water sluicing over my body. Calming, non-sexy thoughts refused to come. Maybe I really did need to turn the temperature to cold.

I looked down at my bobbing cock. Likely a mistake since all that did was make me harder. Hornier.

Sinking into Dylan…

Fuck, not a memory I should have been delving into when all I could think about lately was doing so again and again.

He'd been my first and my last.

I gripped my cock, unable to keep myself in check.

What would he think if he knew he was the only man I'd been buried balls deep into?

Would he get off on that? Like the idea so much he'd be willing to open for me?

My hand picked up speed, working my cock, allowing a dip of my fingers to grope my balls on the third stroke.

Would he bend for me this time? Though top would be fucking hot. To kiss and suck his tongue into my mouth. But to be able to have an uninhibited view as I dicked him good and hard…

"Fuck." The word tore out of me with a shaky gasp. My knees trembled, weak as heat licked at my skin and bubbled in my gut.

I rubbed the underside of my cock, just beneath my helmet. A shudder rippled through me at the sensation.

Dylan's mouth on me, licking that exact spot before taking me deep.

"Oh fuck." My hold tightened, accelerated. Water bounced off my fast-working hand.

I needed… something. More friction. More lube than the shower gel that had almost washed away.

More—

My head jerked as a sound broke through my pounding pulse.

Dylan.

Standing there.

Gaze glued to me. Pink-cheeked and wide-eyed.

A flash of heat, a sharp tingle in my spine, and I parted my lips.

His tongue dipped out, just the peak, a sliver as he swiped it over his bottom lip, and I was gone. Lost in his lighter shade of brown eyes.

My orgasm barreled through me. I should have looked away, but he pinned me down, all heat and interest and scorching desire. I couldn't stop this from happening.

The first rope of cum spilled out of me. I didn't look to check. Didn't stop working my hand.

Our gazes remained locked, and fuck knew how I kept my eyes open from the pleasure tearing through me.

Another spurt and I groaned.

I lost his eyes and grieved for them for a split second until I saw where his gaze landed.

Another tempting peek of his tongue as he roamed my body, settling resolutely on my cock.

And fuck, another spurt and I was sure my legs were going to give way.

A ripple of goose bumps danced over my skin as my whole body shuddered. Heavy breaths mingled with the sound of spraying water.

And still, Dylan stood there. Soundless. His chest moving rapidly.

Taking him in fully, I soaked up the expanse of skin on display. He wore his cock-hugging boxers. But there was no tenting in sight.

Fuck no. Even better was his rigid cock head poking out, a good inch visible and refusing to be contained.

Want roared to life, so raw, so immediate that I

moved before I could process my intent. Left the shower before I could second guess myself.

"Cass?" The breathy question from Dylan did nothing but ramp up my desire.

Hooking my fingers into his boxers, I paused, not breaking eye contact. "Let me."

Unsure if that had been an order or a question, I all but vibrated as I waited for something, anything from Dylan, letting me know I could have this.

"You want…?" The slide of his Adam's apple was punctuated by a loud click.

"My mouth on you… yeah."

"Fuck."

His groan, combined with a quick nod, was all I needed.

I dropped to the floor, tugging down his boxers in the process.

It had been eight long years since I'd been near his cock, and I hadn't been this close.

My memory didn't do him justice.

I took my fill, keeping my hands to myself, considering all the things I wanted to do to his weeping length.

At Dylan's breathy "Cass," I snapped my attention up, capturing his wild-eyed gaze. His previously heaving chest had nothing on the fast gushes of air punching out of him now.

He didn't need to say anything else. I read the need in his half-lidded stare. Understood without words how fucking hot for this moment he was.

And then I was on him.

With our gazes locked, and I was sure with yearning dancing in mine, I leaned in and tasted him. As Dylan gasped at the contact, I groaned. The combined sounds were desperate and filled with need.

Taste exploded on my tongue, and I traced his slit, dipped in, and captured the gathered beads.

This time he moaned, loud and fervent, a plea if ever I heard one. With that one sound, urgency swept through me. I wanted this, needed this moment with Dylan more than I needed any-fucking-thing in the world.

Surrendering, I closed my eyes and sucked and lapped, exploring every perfect inch of his length.

Every tremble beneath my fingertips was a reward. Every needy gasp of my name a step closer to my undoing.

When he palmed my cheek, my eyelids snapped open.

With parted lips, Dylan looked wanton. Fucking beautiful.

Lost in his gaze, adrift under his scrutiny, I

sucked harder, bobbed my head up and down, refusing to break this connection.

"Fuck, Cass." Raw emotion captured his plea.

My fingers twitched on his ass cheek, and I dragged him closer, holding my breath and not releasing until his words became nonsense and his hold on me shifted to my hair, where he gripped.

I pulled off with a gasp and watery eyes, my heart thundering, my dick throbbing despite my release a few short minutes ago.

"You're so fucking hot."

A smirk tilted my lips when he spoke, and when he wiped a couple of stray tears from my cheeks, he bit his bottom lip.

"So fucking beautiful."

At his praise, I returned my mouth to his cock, my hand still holding him firmly. Feeling heady and light, feeling so damn right about everything unraveling, I focused on his scent, his taste. Committed both to memory. Hoped this was just the start.

I tightened my grip on his ass, a physical anchor in the maelstrom of need storming through me and threatening to carry me away.

Yielding to my hunger was easy. Consuming him my fucking mission.

His soft pants turned into loud groans, my name the hottest sound spilling from his lips.

My world narrowed around him, to his taste, his eager grunts.

When his voice pitched and strained, turned ragged, and a reverent "Cass" passed his parted lips, both our restraints snapped.

I drank him in and accepted every last drop of cum. With a swallow, he gasped, his body trembling under my touch. A second later, he slumped against me, vulnerable, sated.

His glazed eyes connected with mine, igniting a new ache in me. The small, almost shy tilt of his lips had me guiding him down to the soft mat on the tiled floor.

My "Are you o—" was cut off when he bridged the gap between us, his lips connecting with mine. With his taste still in my mouth, I slid my tongue against his. Dylan's breath hitched, and my cock throbbed. He liked how he tasted on my tongue. *Fuck yeah.*

Relief, heady and perfect, barreled into me when he gripped my cock. I ached, fucking yearned for him.

For his mouth. For his hand. For his ass. Anything and everything he would give me.

With a firm touch, he stroked me, fast and hard. His kisses didn't stop, his attention never wavering despite my brain imploding.

I wanted to see, wanted to watch how I fucked his hand. But his kisses… warm, soft, perfect, I couldn't stop. Didn't want to.

He pulled away the tiniest of distances. "Come for me."

I shuddered at the longing in his voice, thrilled at the growled demand.

"Next time you can fuck me bare and so fucking hard, I'll—"

He didn't get time to finish. There was no chance when his dirty words shot me over the edge until I was free-falling.

We watched my release streaming over his hand. Each pulse, each shudder as he milked me sent my pulse into overdrive.

How the fuck would I survive this?

"Oh fucking… fuck… Dyl…." I petered out, then claimed his mouth in a bruising kiss, even as I gave a final shudder in his hand.

He met me stroke for stroke, his lips moving against mine like we'd been born to do this.

Fuck… maybe we had.

We eased the kiss, an unspoken agreement, knowing we both needed to come up for air. Parting, we both released trembling breaths, our foreheads pressed against each other's.

I could never regret this. Not ever.

But unlike last time, I didn't think I could ignore it either. Not again.

"Will you shower with me?"

Tentatively spoken, his words washed over me with the warmth of an embrace.

He wasn't running either. That had to mean something, right?

"Yeah." I stood, not releasing my hold on him. "Not sure my knees could take much more."

Dylan's lips twitched, the action pulling my gaze. Red and swollen, his lips looked thoroughly fucked. Jesus, and that was just from my mouth on his. What would they look like after he sucked me off? I was desperate to find out.

My dick gave a valiant twitch, but not a chance it would stand to attention after coming so hard. Twice.

"I would say something about your age, but since we're the same age…," he sassed, and I grinned, what little uncertainty trying to gather in my gut fizzling away.

We stepped into the large shower and turned the water back on. Honestly, I'd been impressed I'd switched it off. Autopilot was a hell of a thing.

"You need help washing down?" I quirked my brow and kept my tone light.

Dylan studied me, and I fought hard to remain relaxed under his scrutiny.

"I'll never say no to a back rub."

And fuck it, I kissed him again. A slow, tender brush of lips, a gentle swipe of tongues, and I smiled against his mouth. Dylan eased away with a satisfied grin.

"You like the idea of rubbing my back, huh?"

Amused, I snorted and shook my head. "Turn your fine ass around."

He did so, but not until he instigated another brief kiss. By the time his back was to me, my heart was in my throat and my hands were filled with shower gel.

This was really happening.

I massaged his pale, warm skin, digging my thumbs into his muscles as I went. Throaty groans escaped him as I continued to work my fingers over him.

"Not sure I can ever handle hearing your groans again without thinking about sex." I punctuated my words with a nip to his shoulder and lathed the sting with gentle kisses.

"So we're going to talk about this?" he asked, peering over his shoulder to look at me.

"I'd prefer to bury my fingers in your ass and sink into you, but since my dick's not going to get up for a while, maybe we should."

A muffled snort left him, and he turned around.

That Dylan snaked an arm around me, his hand settling on my back, I interpreted as a win.

"That's mighty generous of you."

I bobbed my head, taking the moment to explore his body. When I reached his cock, desire unfurled in my gut. He was rock-hard.

"Jesus. Apparently not generous enough if you're hard enough to hammer nails."

Should I do something about that? Make an offer?

In the time it took for me to worry my lip and wonder if it was bad that I wasn't already jacking him off, Dylan's free arm curled around me. He pulled me close, blocking my view.

He peered up at me, amusement easy for me to read in his features.

"This isn't tit for tat. We don't have to keep score."

I parted my lips to ask whether he remembered who he was talking to, but Dylan pushing me against the wall had me slamming my mouth shut and tore a grunt out of me.

"And yes, I know I'm talking to an athlete who literally scores for a living, and I know that shit counts for you," he challenged, humor coloring his words, "but that's not us."

While that took the teasing out of my sails, I latched on to his words, asking, "So there's an us?"

"Says the man to his husband." Dylan quirked his brow high. And fine, he got me there, and I sure as shit realized how ridiculous I sounded. But wading through the unknown didn't come with an instruction manual.

Not that I would have likely read that shit anyway.

"Fine, but you know what I mean."

Twitching his lips, I suspected at my pouting, Dylan smacked my ass. I jumped at the contact and shot him the stink eye.

"Let's get dry and we'll talk." He switched off the water and left the shower.

Unable to move, I fixed my gaze on his glutes, mesmerized by just how perfect they were.

When he grabbed a towel and turned, hard cock jutting out, I all but swallowed my tongue. Was it only a matter of fifteen minutes or so ago that I managed to wrap my lips around him?

The tingles in my balls let me know we would be absolutely up for doing that again. An achy jaw or not.

"You look like you want to eat me up." The heat in his eyes belied the teasing in his tone.

"I'm thinking about it."

Warm, soft skin wrapped around hard steel

pushing deeply into my throat…. A shudder rippled through me at the memory.

"I—" He cleared his croaky throat.

I liked that a hell of a lot. How affected he was.

"Here." A shaky breath escaped Dylan as he threw me a towel. "I think we need beer."

With a chuckle, I dried off and considered walking into our room naked. Getting a rise out of Dylan was always fun. Now, getting a rise in the most literal sense took my joy to a whole new level.

But he was right. We needed to talk.

After I pulled on a pair of shorts, sans boxers, I accepted the cold beer from Dylan. Sitting on the couch in the living room of our suite, he looked surprisingly relaxed considering I could still see the hard outline of his dick trapped behind a pair of shorts.

"So…." Yeah, that was all I had.

Dylan's huff of laughter cut through some of the awkwardness making this moment weird.

Sex we could apparently do. Be best friends, parent together even, but talk real shit like this… Jesus, this was so out of both of our comfort zones.

"You know we overshare all the time, right?"

Truth. "So why is this so weird?"

He took a pull of his beer, maintaining eye contact. When he finished, he shrugged, his discomfort mirroring my own. "We usually just know what the other person is thinking or feeling, so we don't need to really talk things out like this."

"That. That right there. You're absolutely right."

I reached out and we clinked bottles, both of us snickering but not clearing the awkwardness completely.

We'd shared so much with each other over the years. From that time we'd blurted out our sexualities, to the time Dylan had watched someone OD on a callout and proceeded to get so drunk, worrying me so much, that I'd jumped on a flight the same day to go and see him.

Then was the time he'd done the same for me when I'd freaked out about anal sex.

Which I suppose brought us full circle.

"So, we what?" I eyed Dylan carefully, trying to get a read on his expression. "Say what we think the other person is thinking or feeling or something?"

Dylan's brows shot high. "I think that's the worst idea in the history of ever." His laughter was loud and abrupt, and I loved the sound of it. I let it wash over me and absorbed as much of it as I could.

"You have the best fucking laugh."

His laughter petered out, his eyes springing wide as pink flushed his cheeks.

"Yeah?" A vulnerability I rarely heard dipped his tone low. "You've never said that before."

"Because I'm a fucking idiot."

"Well…." He cleared his throat, a cocky grin forming. "That's something we both already knew."

"Fuck off."

Still looking at me with heat in his cheeks, he gnawed on his bottom lip. Jesus, it had been years since I'd seen him do that. Dylan always seemed so in control and certain about everything.

I saw the moment it happened. The instant he'd made some sort of decision. With a determined expression, he all but squared his shoulders.

At any other time, I may have ribbed him for it—him doing his resolute cop thing. But I was ensnared, caught completely in the unspoken conviction staring back at me.

My breathing shallowed as I waited him out. Thank Christ I didn't have to wait long. I wasn't sure my lungs could handle it.

"I don't regret what we did."

Air whooshed out of my lungs, relief in the ragged sound.

"I…." He trailed off, his cheeks blazing. "Fuck, I… I suppose I'm saying, I have no idea what this means for us, but I'm okay with it."

"You're 'okay' with it?" I wasn't sure whether to laugh, mock, or be butt hurt.

From the narrowing of his eyes, Dylan apparently wasn't so sure which way I was going either.

"You know what I mean."

"I do?" I challenged. Sure, I'd agreed we usually knew what each other was thinking or really meant or whatever, but the fuck was I meant to do with his "I'm okay with it"?

"Are you being deliberately obtuse?"

"Well, I can't do the splits, but I can manage a high kick."

The groan and roll of his eyes were well deserved. It wasn't my best comeback, but my emotions were out of control. Considering the two mind-blowing orgasms, I was surprised I'd managed anything punny at all.

Our communication skills needed some work. But I totally had this.

"I've come a lot over the years."

Dylan's brow furrowed. "Uhm… okay?"

"And only one other time have I come as hard as I just did in the bathroom."

He seemed a little shell-shocked by that admission.

"It's not like I've been a monk over the years. I've had plenty."

"Jesus." Dylan rubbed a hand over his face. "Is there a point to this, or are you just saying that I'm one notch in so many you can't even give me a number?"

"What? No?" Shit. I was worse than Dylan at this. I shook my head. "That's not what I mean at all." A stir of unease muddled my gut at his words. Honestly, I didn't think I could give him a number. Well, maybe if I really thought about it.

Except one. One number I could definitely give him.

"You're the only man I've had sex with." The admission shot out of me so much louder than I intended that his head jerked back a little.

When his face shuttered, uncertainty crawled across my skin. That wasn't the reaction I was going for.

"Uhm... that's not true." Disbelief and I was pretty fucking certain disappointment colored his words.

"Yes, it is." The hell was he arguing with me about this for?

His jaw ticked. "I know you've hooked up with lots of guys."

Understanding immediately, I released an exasperated sigh. "We are so shit at talking stuff out. I just don't get it." I shook my head, more than aware he was staring at me with wide-eyed confusion.

He didn't correct me, though. No doubt because it was obvious I was right.

"I mean sex. Full-on penetration. Not hand jobs or bjs. You're the only guy I've had… you know, inter-course with," I said, thoroughly proud of myself for being crystal fucking clear. "And you know I wouldn't be able to let anyone but you near my ass."

"I would?" The question released on a shaky exhale, whisper soft and still confused. "I don't know that." With his words, his expression morphed, no longer shut off.

Softness filled his gaze. And Jesus H. Christ, it was like he was looking at me for the first time.

Awareness swept through me, leaving me feeling open and vulnerable under his intense scrutiny.

"You mean, all this time, you haven't been with another man?"

"No." My throat was dry, but it seemed wrong to take a large gulp of beer.

"I'm sorry."

"What? Why?"

Genuine sadness poured off him, confusing the hell out of me.

"Why wouldn't you be all, I don't know, caveman or happy that I haven't dicked anyone but you?"

Shock widened his eyes, and in the next breath, a loud laugh burst out of him. "Fuck." He laughed harder, louder. The sound wrapped around me, and my lips twitched.

Well, at least his sadness had been wiped away. That was something.

When he sobered, he slowly shook his head. "I suppose I'm sorry because I thought after what we… you know… I just thought you were okay." A one-shoulder shrug followed. "I know you're still not completely comfortable, but I'd hoped you no longer held back."

Embarrassment licked across my skin. Sure, this was Dylan, and he knew pretty much everything, but still… "I tried twice after you." I huffed out a humor-less breath. "It didn't work out."

Both were memories I'd tried to turn to dust.

"You didn't say anything."

"Not my finest hours." A self-deprecating smile curved my lips. "Not something I really wanted to hash out."

After a moment, he bobbed his head. Well, he definitely didn't look pissed off anymore. Maybe a little sympathetic. Perhaps concerned.

"So yeah… this conversation has gone way off track."

The room seemed extra quiet as Dylan stared at

me. It was oh so tempting to fill in the silence. The truths beginning to fill the space between us started to feel deafening, a little overwhelming in what they could mean for us.

When he pursed his lips, I inhaled slowly, counting as I held, waiting for him to speak.

"Did you know I only top?"

I froze, my breath caught in my lungs, my brain struggling to catch up. It was as if his words were suspended in the air, in this new space between us filled with tension and chemistry I struggled to navigate. And what a labyrinth it was.

Emotion and need and new information. And my dick… fuck, my dick that should still be flaccid after being so well taken care of throbbed when Dylan's words hit their mark.

He only tops?

Fuck, did that mean…? With my mouth turning drier than a parched landscape, I swallowed hard, the sound scratchy and loud in the otherwise silent room.

"So when we…?" Fuck, I couldn't finish the sentence. And wasn't that a hell of a thing since I rarely kept shit to myself.

"When we fucked…." Dylan's intense gaze contradicted his teasing tone.

"Jesus." I palmed my cock, right there in front of

him. How could I not, as with one more word or heated look, I was sure I'd be jizzing in my pants.

Based on Dylan's quirked brow as his gaze traveled to my hand gripping my dick, he didn't seem to mind one bit. Between the heat pulsing between us and the building charge I swore held enough current it would be able to power the whole building, it was time I stopped being a fucking pussy.

"So, have we officially consummated our marriage yet, or do we need to replicate that night for us to finally do this for real?"

His chest heaved, eyes flared, and he'd never looked sexier than he did in that moment.

Possibility was a heady concept. And that was what this was, right? What I was suggesting?

"You saying you want a real marriage?"

The acceleration of my heart was loud. Fast enough to have my breathing pick up speed. Before I could answer, he tilted his head, gaze fixing to mine, and I knew, just fucking knew, he was going to fucking own me.

"It already feels like what we have is real."

His whispered words latched on to any last remaining doubts, obliterating them at contact.

"It is real," I croaked, not even questioning what was happening anymore.

A subtle shift transformed his expression. A

warm, genuine smile crept across his face, and my breath hitched as I took him in. Handsome didn't even begin to describe the man before me.

Dylan was all rugged gorgeousness, a fucking masterpiece of masculinity and charisma. And I knew he didn't see himself that way. It made him more beautiful. His unawareness, the light pink that would often touch his cheeks, just like now, when he realized he held me captive.

Because that was exactly what I was. Ensnared by him. By the light scruff on his jawline, by his light brown eyes that he thought were dull and boring, but I found mesmerizing. Every single thing about this man had me spellbound.

As his eyes twinkled while he sat with the slightest of smirks on his kiss-swollen lips, letting me drink him in, my heart legit skipped a beat.

This was it. The beginning of everything I never knew I wanted and didn't even consider I could ever have.

That I loved the man before me was a no-brainer. Could I fall *in* love with him?

Holy fuck. I was certain I was already halfway there.

"Okay, then."

His words pulled me up short. With my head foggy, I struggled to know what he was referring to.

Was he answering a question? Caught up in eye-fucking Dylan and having an epiphany or something, I stared at him, hoping he'd clarify without me admitting I was clueless.

A twitch of his lips and he rolled his eyes, but he didn't leave me hanging. "Let's do this."

Exhilaration coursed through me, like a victorious battle cry pulsing behind my rib cage. A satisfied, over-fucking-joyed smile broke out on my face, and screw it all to hell, I launched at him, tugging Dylan into my arms and holding on for dear life.

CHAPTER 16

DYLAN

FORGET WALKING ON AIR, I PRACTICALLY LEVITATED AS I made my way back to my seat, happiness keeping me buoyed.

It didn't even matter that our heated kiss was interrupted by a knock on the door revealing Eddie and Lottie—Pearce's husband and their daughter. Sure, I'd needed to throw some clothes on, and my cock had cried out for attention from Cass, but joy was a hell of a thing.

Through an early dinner and even through the stream of conversation dominated by Lottie, who was basketball obsessed and a preteen going on sports agent, and Cassius talking B-ball, my smile barely strayed. It kinda helped that Cass and I only released hands when we needed two hands on our burgers.

I was just a few feet away from my seat, and my gaze narrowed. A woman was in my spot, all but shoving her cleavage under Cass's chin. Admittedly she was covered up in a jersey and her hands were to herself, but still, I didn't like it one bit.

I rolled my eyes at myself as I moved closer. Men and women regularly threw themselves at Cass. They had for years. It was not a new development.

And while I didn't necessarily like it over the years—I could be a selfish prick and wanted time with Cass by myself—now jealousy raised its ugly head.

"Thought I'd lost you." Cass grinned up at me as he took Eddie's and Lottie's drinks from the holder and passed it over.

"No chance of that." I stared pointedly at the woman in my seat. Her eyes widened when she peered up and back, her brows shooting high.

"Dylan, right?" The woman stood with a friendly smile.

"That's me." Some of the green worked its way out of my system. That she knew who I was meant she hadn't been hitting on Cass, right?

"I'm Taylor, Garret Baker's wife."

Okay, so definitely not hitting on Cassius. Relief barreled through me, and as I flicked my gaze at Cass and took in his arched brows and the amusement he wasn't trying too hard to conceal, it was a comfort that he read me just as easily as he always did.

"Good to meet you. Baker's having a great game."

Her smile stretched wide. "Thanks. I've got everything crossed they keep it up." She glanced back at Cassius. "I best get going. Great seeing you again, Cass. And congratulations on hooking yourself to Dylan." While I wasn't sure what expression she was pulling, from Cass's chuckle, I had my ideas.

"Thanks, Taylor." He accepted her friendly hug. "I think I got lucky snagging myself Dylan too."

Heat touched my cheeks even as I rolled my eyes, pretending I thought he was ridiculous rather than soaking up his words.

Taylor left with a small wave, leaving me peering down at Cassius. Once more, his one eyebrow arched high.

"Shut up," I grumbled with zero heat. The asshole had read my initial reaction easier than he read the basketball rulebook.

At his chuckle, I sat with a smirk. I swore it was a permanent fixture, and it seemed even Eddie had noticed. From some of the amused looks he had shot us over dinner, he'd been as bemused as he was entertained by our behavior.

Love drunk was a thing, right?

Because every time Cass held my hand or swept his gaze over me, my heart seemed to swell.

"This is yours." I passed him his drink, our fingers grazing and lingering as he took it off me. Heat licked at my spine as well as rushed to my cheeks.

At the holler of Cass's name, I cleared my throat and forced my simmering desire to the back burner. Cass waved at the couple of fans who'd called out to him, which had been happening since the moment we stepped foot in the arena.

Thankfully, the seats were packed with more than a few celebrity faces and a whole lot more athletes. Plus, with the game halfway through and Pearce's team playing hard, it meant most fans were more focused on the fast-paced play rather than stopping Cass for a selfie.

"A seven-point lead," Cass said, leaning forward to look at Eddie.

"Eighteen points, nine rebounds." Eddie grinned widely, his arm around Lottie as he relayed his husband's gameplay.

"A hell of a first half," I added. Sure, I wasn't a pro like Cass or a former pro like Eddie, but I knew basketball as well as I knew the law. It was hard not to when I'd lived and breathed it all through school, courtesy of Cass's obsession.

"He's been the best player on the court this first half." Conviction rang through Lottie's words, and there was no arguing with her. Especially as she was likely right. "The Mountain Lions look nervous."

Cass chuckled and reached out to fist-bump Lottie.

"They only shot one of fifteen from the three-point range." Eddie's composure was gone. Nothing but glee when he talked about the game.

I could relate. Every time Cass played and he kicked ass, pride was always my companion. Hell, even when his team lost, it was still there. How could it not be when he played his hardest and lived his dream every single day?

Just then the players rejoined the court. We all stood, just like virtually everyone else, and cheered for our team. Pearce passed us, turning to Eddie and Lottie, pressing his fingers to his lips, and sending them a kiss.

I cast a look at Eddie, his face wide open with his feelings for his husband. Hell, love practically poured off the man.

I wondered if that was how I looked when staring at Cass. If that was what others saw.

Love had always been the glue that held us together. That and respect.

Love started to feel a whole lot deeper. Thicker,

warmer, a sturdy rope of rightness that strengthened with each passing day.

We sat down and I leaned into Cass, my hand instinctively finding his. Angling to look at me, he smiled, his gaze roaming my face.

"You okay?" he whispered, his lips practically touching my ear so I could hear him over the volume.

"Yeah. Are you?" I flicked my eyes to his and tilted my head. While his team never got close to the playoffs this year, I had no doubt there was an edge of disappointment or envy that came with that.

"I'm here with you. Had an extra six weeks at home by your side." He dotted a kiss to my neck. The touch sent a delicious shiver down my spine.

Cass pulled away, his heated gaze returning to mine. And I kissed him, just a barely there brush of his lips. I couldn't not. And from the smirk Cass shot my way, he was more than okay with my PDA.

The news of our marriage was already out in the world. This right here… holy fuck, I was totally claiming the asshole. And yeah, his smirk was filled with smug satisfaction. The man totally knew it.

"Fuck off," I mumbled, hoping no cameras were trained on us and could read my lips.

The buzzer sounding tugged our attention to the

court. And not a moment too soon. The last thing I wanted to do was dry hump him or something.

The third quarter kicked off with a three-pointer from the Jetts in the first seconds of play. They were on fire. Already in the lead, they came out wanting the win.

And that was just the beginning as they dominated the court.

Pearce was everywhere. His whole team seemed to have double of their players as they intercepted so many passes, it was a struggle keeping up.

By the final quarter, we were barely in our seats. There seemed little need when we were celebrating so many points.

Not that the Mountain Lions weren't battling. They were.

But there was no close call, just preemptive cheers as the clock entered the final ten seconds. And then we cheered for the Jetts when the buzzer sounded, and chaos ensued.

The roar threatened to blow the stadium roof off. The celebratory hollers were contagious as even Cass and I shouted alongside the packed crowd.

Eddie and Lottie headed to the court to congratulate Pearce while Cass and I stood, grinning down at them.

"I want you to have this moment." I wrapped my arm around Cassius's waist and peered up at him.

He'd made it to the finals twice before but never took a win.

"It would be something." He glanced down at me, but there was no envy in sight, just joy for his friend.

"Is winning the playoffs still your big dream?"

Still looking at me, he was quiet a beat, his gaze searching. "One of them."

"One?" Color me surprised. "I thought this was *the* big dream." It was all he spoke about growing up, including when he played at college. Even over the past few years, he didn't shy away about his biggest dream being to finally win the playoffs. "When did that change?"

He cupped my cheek, and his thumb rubbed lightly over my bottom lip. My pulse skyrocketed, headfirst into the unknown as his gaze intensified.

I needed air in my lungs, but for the life of me, I couldn't remember how to breathe. Not when every cell in my body was focused on Cassius and the way he looked at me. The way he leaned close.

"The moment I realized I could have something I hadn't even dared dream of or even imagine."

I dragged in a jagged breath, wondering when I'd

turned into this guy. The one who practically swooned at hearing pretty words.

And fuck… I thought they were about to get prettier. I had no issues in helping him say them.

"And what's that?" The breathy question escaped me, but I had no time to be embarrassed. Not a chance when Cassius looked at me like I was his whole world.

"You and Mikey. Loving you both is all I'm ever going to need. You're my dream."

Holy shit. Did he just lay that on me here and now when I couldn't jump his bones and ask him to fuck me and prove it?

A shuddery breath escaped my lungs. "Tell me that I complete you and I'll—"

Cass hissed the word "Asshole" even as he grabbed me up close, buried his face in my neck, and dug his fingers into my sides.

My laughter was loud, this whole thing crazy inappropriate. But what else was a man to do when his husband whispered words that made logic and reason threaten to dive out of the window without a parachute in sight?

He nipped at my neck, and I swallowed my groan.

"You're an asshole."

As he eased away, I kept my hand on his waist

and squeezed. "When our dreams align so damn perfectly, how the hell am I meant to react when I'm sure there's at least five cameras on us at the moment?"

I wasn't even exaggerating.

Cassius wasn't the first player to have a husband in the League, but he was legit the fourth. Or was that third since Gale Sutton had married his teammate Jayden when they'd still been active players? Either way, our relationship came with attention, all of which we'd managed to stay far away from. Until now.

"Fair." He cleared his throat and glanced around. When his focus returned to me, he straightened and held my hand so we could walk out of the row of seats. "Don't think I've not got a whole heap of shit to say to you, though, when we get back to the hotel."

I cast him a "what, me? What did I do?" look.

"Dreams align," he whispered as his thumb stroked over my skin. "And don't get me started on you quoting rom-coms at me."

Amused, I shook my head. "That you know that's from a rom-com doesn't really give you much credibility here."

In response, he simply stared at me.

I paused just before we left our row of seats.

Dipping my voice low and stepping into his space, I said, "And if you believe for one second that you'll be able to think of anything but having your dick in my ass when we get back, you're underestimating me."

With that, I turned and stepped into the aisle, heading to the court, where I knew Cass wanted to go. I didn't miss the hitch of his breath or his grumbled "Jesus H. Christ" as he followed my lead.

DESPITE OUR TEASING AND THE COMBUSTIBLE TENSION between us, we survived celebratory drinks with Eddie, Pearce, and the majority of the Jetts. This was after Pearce's parents collected Lottie to take care of her.

"Tonight was fun." The words were whispered against Cass's back as my hands roamed his chest.

He groaned, just as the door of our suite unlocked.

"And I need you naked in bed, hand off your cock, while I go and prep." Just the thought of him needy and desperate while he waited sent a thrum of anticipation dancing along my skin. "Can you do that?" I asked, not letting him go as we entered the room.

He spun in my arms, and as soon as we were clear of the door, he pushed it shut. Dark, smoldering eyes burned with an intensity that had me catching my breath. Fuck, he was so damn gorgeous and looked sexy as hell as he stared at me with uninhibited lust.

The flush of desire tinted his cheeks, and his parted lips released ragged breaths.

"Not sure I can wait that long."

I smiled at the gravel in his voice, my nuts drawing up at how desperate he was. "You'd prefer my mouth rather than my ass?" Down for either, I left the decision to him, waiting for him to make up his mind as I trailed my fingers over his chest.

When he darted his gaze to my lips, a groan spilled from him. "You have a really pretty mouth."

I snorted. "Pretty, huh? Now I know your dick's addling your brain." I skimmed my fingertips over his rock-hard cock that strained against his pants.

He grunted at the contact. "It will be pretty as fuck with my dick in it."

Well, there was that, and zero argument from me.

Stepping even closer, he clamped his hands on to my ass and squeezed. The movement tugged against him, our groins rubbing. This time both of us moaned.

"So bed and mouths…?"

Indecision warred on his face, so I made it easy on him, knowing he was desperate but how much he craved the connection of taking my ass. I felt it too. This bone-deep need to have him sinking inside me, fucking me hard like no one but him ever had or would.

The whirlwind of our marriage had changed everything. The last twenty-four hours especially had thrown all our emotions, our plans, pretty much everything in the air.

His words from the game filtered into my mind. *"Loving you both is all I'm ever going to need."*

Those words unraveled me while tethering us together in a way I'd never thought possible.

I knew what we needed, the both of us. Something we should have done on our wedding night. Something I wished we'd been ready for then. But we were here now, and it was never too late to start.

Scooting up to reach Cassius's lips, I pressed my mouth firmly to his but didn't let it go deeper. "Give me ten minutes." I spoke against his mouth and dotted another kiss to it before easing away and grabbing a second toiletry bag I'd stowed away.

"Make it seven and I'll wake you up with head in the morning."

I laughed loudly and glanced at Cassius as I

backed into the bathroom. With a teasing smirk and half-lidded eyes, the man was all sin and smiles.

"Done," I said, my chest constricting when I took my fill of him before I stepped out of sight and got to prepping.

After being as thorough as I could in the seven-minute challenge, I found Cass spread out on the mattress, lube on the bedside table, and his cock weeping.

My dick jerked, liking the visual a whole lot.

"You're magnificent."

His eyebrow quirked at that, his lips twitching, but sensibly he didn't call me out or let loose whatever ridiculous thing was on his mind.

I threw the towel on the other side of the mattress and crawled my way from the bottom of the bed until I straddled him. I settled on his lap with a sigh while a shuddery breath left Cassius.

Rolling my hips so our cocks brushed, I watched him carefully.

There was little doubt that desperation clung to him, but the edge of nerves was visible in the slight tightening of his eyes.

This issue he had, he owned. Joked about it with his friends, even though they didn't know the reason behind his concerns. They just thought he had a slight phobia. But with us, there was no need to hide or pretend.

I wanted him to share his thoughts and fears. Which, considering we'd been so bad at expressing what we wanted and how we felt earlier, seemed almost laughable.

But this was different.

Maybe because I'd been there to witness the whole thing all those years ago.

Before I could ask if he was okay, Cassius ran his trembling hands over my thighs. The journey continued until he cupped my bare ass cheeks and squeezed, kneading my glutes with dexterous fingers.

A shuddery groan passed my lips. Touching like this got my engine going big-time. Every caress, every tender stroke, I loved.

"I want to try something." His nervous eyes snapped to mine, and a dry swallow followed. With his dick standing proud, I wasn't too concerned he couldn't handle whatever he had planned. Horniness was a heck of a motivator.

"You can try anything with me."

He nodded, his focus moving to my groin, then my face.

"You need me to help you?"

Tugging his bottom lip into his mouth, he gnawed the side. Another swallow and he bobbed his head.

When he moved one hand, fingers finding the crack of my ass, my breath hitched.

Fuck. That's what he wanted.

Shooting him a soft smile, I angled my arm around my back, my palm pressing to the back of his hand. Since I was already lubed, I was good to go.

Guiding his hand, I tilted forward so I leaned more fully over him. Our gazes caught. Wide-eyed, he breathed heavily. By the time our fingers reached my entrance, his pupils were blown.

I wrapped my fingers around his, leaving our pointer fingers out. Another half an inch and I swirled our fingers around my opening, spreading the lube.

His breath hitched, and I paused, not pulling my gaze from his.

I leaned down and kissed him, a gentle sweep of our lips. "Okay?" I asked as I pulled away, only stopping when I could see his expression clearly.

"Yeah. Keep going."

Jesus, this man, his trust, it was everything.

Another swirl of our fingers and we breached my hole.

I clamped my teeth on my bottom lip and relaxed at the invasion. Our fingers slid in easily without much resistance, having already prepared myself with three fingers in the bathroom.

Surprise sent a fresh pulse of lust into my veins when Cassius took over, guiding our fingers in and out.

"Fuck," I gasped with a ragged moan.

"Good?"

I nodded and dropped my head a little before jolting when he pushed in as far as our fingers would go and picked up speed.

"Holy fuck." My hips moved and jerked, riding our fingers, eager for more. "So fucking full, but I want your cock."

His "Fuck yeah" was captured by my mouth when he tilted up and slammed his mouth to mine. The kiss was deep, dirty, full of tongue and desperation. And so much want and need, I wanted to crawl inside him and never leave.

"Sit on me," he said with a gasp as he broke the kiss.

I nodded as we removed our fingers and reached out for the bottle of lube. Spreading some over his rigid cock, I jacked him off, enjoying his moans and the wildness in his eyes. His hands were on my hips, urging me up.

As I lifted, I held his dick with one hand and settled over him. When he nudged against my opening, I clamped onto my bottom lip. When I bore down and he breached me, my lips parted, and a guttural groan tore out of me.

"Fuck, that's it, baby."

And then I eased down, taking him in, luxuriating in the stretch and burn.

By the time I was fully seated, Cassius trembled beneath me, his grip so tight on my hips, I'd be admiring the bruises for days.

"Move and fuck me," I ordered, even as I started to do the exact thing to him.

He met me stroke for stroke, his grip never wavering as I rode him hard, begging for him to be so deep that I'd feel him forever. Those words spilled out of me, all my desires, the need to make him mine.

"Fuck, Dyl. Give me your mouth."

As I leaned down, he met me halfway, angling up from the bed. Our mouths met—a clash of teeth, a tangle of tongues. And we didn't stop. Continued moving. Kept up the pace until I was on my back, my ankles on Cass's shoulders as he slammed into me with hard, delicious thrusts.

"So. Fucking. Good. Perfect." Each piston of his hips jolted out his desperate words.

All I could do was nod as he pummeled into me while my hand flew over my cock.

Cass canted his hips and lifted mine, diving back

in. The shift had me seeing stars. The head of his cock swept against my prostate again and again until, with parted lips, I gasped, groaned, and shouted my release.

A guttural "Fuck" fell from Cassius as he stilled before he jerked and pulsed. I shuddered at the sensation, at the knowledge of his cum being deep inside me. It was hot as hell, easing the possessive craving to make him mine.

I stroked his forearm planted next to me and followed up with a kiss on his warm skin. The action had his gaze connecting with mine.

A new warmth seemed to settle there.

The desperate heat was gone, dissipating with our release. This was something different. More tender. More honest.

And then he smiled. The raw openness filling his features tugged at the tether between us. Strengthened it further.

Still inside me, Cass carefully maneuvered so his lips touched mine. A soft caress of swollen lips, a gentle dip and stroke of tongues, and we lazily kissed.

Wrapping my arms around him, I held him close and welcomed his weight as our kiss remained tender. This was the first we'd shared like this, slow, with no urgency. Each caress was like a promise of affection, and I savored each delicate touch, committing this moment to memory.

Time seemed to stand still as our lips brushed with the softness of butterfly wings. Each trace of his lips told me more than a thousand clumsy words ever could.

We were in this together, and I didn't want that to ever change.

CHAPTER 17

CASSIUS

LIFE HAD CONTINUED SINCE GETTING BACK FROM Chicago. With our schedules and routines remaining the same, nothing had changed since our time away. When Dylan worked, I cared for Mikey, and when he was home, we did the day-to-day chores while spending quality time together.

With one pretty incredible exception.

My mouth was on his—heck, on any part of his body—whenever I got the chance. Not only did it make life sweeter, but I was happier than I ever had been.

Heading into the backyard where Dylan pushed Mikey on the swing set we'd installed last year, despite him being too small to play with it last summer, I paused on the back deck.

A grin stretched on Mikey's face as he leaned

back, staring up at the sky, swinging back and forth without a care in the world. Thankfully, it was a swing with a strap of sorts, so there'd be no falling. One arm fracture earlier on in the year had been enough to age both Dylan and me, and I hadn't even been living here and parenting.

I had no idea how Dylan had done it. And pretty much by himself.

Of course, he had Mom and Pop, but day in, day out, he'd been here, the sole carer for Mikey.

Not for the first time today, the thought made my heart hurt.

When Dylan called my name, I shoved my melancholy and guilt as far away as I possibly could.

What was the point in rehashing the time I'd missed or how many days exactly I'd held back the truth from Dylan and Mikey?

"Hey, I'm going to head to the store and pick up some onions and tomatoes for the salsa."

"Not without laying one on me first, you're not."

At his teasing tone, I grinned, my heart tumbling with affection for the man who continued to show me every day how incredible he was. More specifically how incredibly right for each other we were.

And as I stepped into his space and leaned down to press my mouth to his, seeking more than just a whisper of a kiss, I embraced him, just as I'd made an unconscious decision at some point over the past couple of weeks to no longer question what was happening.

Acceptance was my mindset of choice, and it was a hell of a thing.

I sighed into his touch and melted into his kiss. At Mikey's giggling and calling our names, we pulled away with smirks and heated cheeks. Getting lost in Dylan was easier than sinking a layup on an open court.

When we turned to Mikey, he indicated he'd had enough by lifting his arms and saying, "Out. No more."

I undid the strap and pulled him out, taking the opportunity to hold him close and press kisses all over his face. Contagious, glorious giggles escaped, a sound that was in my top five favorite sounds ever.

"I'm heading to the store. What are you going to do with Dada?" I asked, smiling internally at the name Mikey settled on calling Dylan. Try as he might to get our boy to call his dad "Daddy," Mikey refused, the name never sticking.

"Me come."

"To the store?"

"Yes."

"The store's not all that exciting, Mikey," I challenged, somehow holding back my smile. Our kid was no fool. He also played me better than a seasoned point guard orchestrating the perfect play. That I was in the habit of picking him up a treat of some sort whenever we went to the store together I suspected had a lot to do with his request.

I was also a sucker and struggled to say no.

"What do you think, Dyl?"

If I was expecting a rescue from him, I should have known better. His far-too-innocent smile wasn't fooling me. Hell, did he whisper that a trip to the store on a Friday evening sounded like fun into his son's ear?

"Just think of the extra shower time I can have if I have the whole house to myself." The teasing tone in his voice did nothing to distract me from the heat in his eyes.

Fuck yeah.

He'd just come off his four-day roster yesterday and had been exhausted at the end of every shift. On top of that, Mikey was just getting over a rotten summer cold, meaning he'd been miserable. That meant we'd all been miserable.

So tonight, I hoped Dylan wouldn't be asleep by eight thirty and Mikey got a full night's rest. Fucking my husband into the mattress would be the perfect way to spend the evening too.

Not that our mutual hand jobs two nights ago

weren't spectacular—I'd blown my load with a smile on my face and captured Dylan's groans with scorching-hot kisses. But since sex was on the cards, it was difficult to think of anything but the sensation, the absolute bliss of being buried inside him.

I cleared my throat, pulling my heated gaze away from Dylan, and willed my cock to behave.

"Looks like you're coming with me to the store, kiddo."

"Yay." He wriggled in my arms to get down. As soon as his feet hit the grass, he bolted to the house. Probably to get my keys. The kid did like to organize shit. When Dylan had commented on it and compared him to me, I'd swallowed down the bittersweet feeling of him liking to organize parties for his dolls and teddies.

"Take as long as you want." Dylan bounced his eyebrows up and down.

I shook my head, then claimed another kiss, gripping his butt and squeezing before I pulled away and smacked his ass for good measure. He grunted as I dipped my voice low. "Such a fucking tease."

"And you love it."

"Yeah, I do."

A crackle of awareness zipped between us, the words caught up in the small space.

Shit, should that have been "you"?

"Weady!" an eager Mikey hollered from the patio, keys raised in one hand, one of the canvas bags we used for shopping in the other.

I chuckled as I took in his triumphant expression. Mikey really was an extraordinary kid.

"And that's my cue." I pressed a chaste kiss to Dylan's mouth, allowing a brief glance to read his expression. His smile was soft, and while the heat was no longer evident, affection seemed to be lit from within.

All that emotion was currently directed at me.

"I'm going to own you tonight, Mr. Britton."

Startled, his brows shot high. Not giving him time to respond, I threw him a smug smirk and got out of there before he could call me out that not once had we discussed either of us changing our names or taking on each other's.

But fuck if I didn't love the idea of him taking mine. Dylan and Mikey.

It didn't take long to get to the store, Mikey chatting the whole way about the drawings he'd done earlier while relentlessly talking about the pet dog on a show he loved and what we should call our pet dog.

I snorted at the name choice as I released him from his car seat. "You think we should call a dog SuperKitty?"

With a grin, he nodded. "Yeah, and we gets mask."

"Uh-huh." Setting him down, I reached for his hand before locking my SUV and heading into the smaller of the two stores in town. There tended to be fewer people here, and usually locals, so there was less chance of folks asking for autographs or a selfie.

While it could be invasive, I'd always just grinned and bore it, recognizing it was a part of the job. If it wasn't for fans, I wouldn't have this job or be living my dream of playing B-ball.

But having Mikey, though, stepping up and being his dad, I finally understood why Pearce and Eddie got frustrated by people approaching them when they were with Lottie.

People approaching me when I was with Mikey, honestly, it pissed me the hell off. Not that I ever caused a scene, though there were a couple of times I calmly told them I was with my son, so it wasn't the time.

The lack of boundaries made my blood boil.

We entered the store, and I held a little tighter to Mikey's hand. He was a good kid, but that didn't mean he couldn't be a slippery creature and make a run for it, thinking it was hilarious for me to chase him.

"How about you keep working on names that

aren't going to give this imaginary dog of yours an identity crisis?"

I smiled at an older woman in the shop and continued on our way toward the fresh produce.

"What's ibempipy cwisis?"

I chuckled. "*Iden*tity crisis... well, it's when the dog might start thinking it's a cat and get confused."

Mikey stopping in his tracks pulled me up short. I peered down, our gazes connecting.

"You okay?"

"We needs a kitty so no ibempipy cwisis. Doggy *and* kitty."

I bit back my laughter just imagining how that request would go down with Dylan. "Perhaps that's something we need to talk to your dad about. We might need to wait till you're a little older too." I absolutely threw Dylan a boon, slipping the age proviso in.

"I's *free* now."

We stopped before the tomatoes, and I released Mikey's hand to grab a plastic bag. "I know you are, kiddo. I was thinking maybe eight or nine."

"But kitty and doggy *now*."

Shit. With his bottom lip sticking out, Mikey looked the picture of defiance.

"How about you help me count out five tomatoes?"

His expression didn't change. Correction: a more stubborn set of his jaw made it crystal clear what he thought about counting tomatoes.

"I can't do this alone, Mikey. Tomatoes and onions, then how about a little treat?"

Since bribery was always a winner, when he shouted, "No," so loud it echoed around the small store, I blanched in surprise.

"Hey, now." I scooted to his level. "You don't want to help me?"

"No."

Well, at least he didn't scream the word this time.

"No worries. Two minutes and we can be out of here." Plastic bag in hand, I angled to gather the tomatoes, not paying too much attention to which ones I grabbed. The threat of Mikey entering DEFCON Toddler Mode had me swiping up five before snagging another bag to throw some onions in.

The kid's tantrums were thankfully few and far between. But hell, when the kid had a meltdown, it was like he was possessed by a gremlin or something.

"Done." And not a moment too soon. The kid was eerily quiet, meaning he was building up to a—

My heart punched a deep, loud thud just as my stomach bottomed out.

Where the fuck is Mikey?

"Mikey," I called, my feet taking me to the end of the small aisle, all while I couldn't hear anything beyond my deafening pulse. "Mikey," I hollered, my heart constricting as I turned back before doing a 360.

Fuck, fuck, fuck.

Sweat broke out on the back of my neck as I called again, this time catching the eyes of a middle-aged woman.

"Hey, have you seen a kid? My son. He's three. I turned around and he was gone." My pitch was high and frantic as I looked at this woman before continuing to stare around me in wide-eyed panic.

"No, I'm sorry. Mikey, did you say?"

I bobbed my head, the blood rushing in my ears close to deafening.

The fuck should I do? Should I start walking around the store?

But what if he came back and I wasn't here?

"Fuck." I clutched my chest, pretty damn sure I was close to having a heart attack.

"Hey, I'm sure he's fine and just got distracted. Why don't you stay here, and I'll go and get the manager. If I see him, I'll bring him right back, okay?"

"Yeah, okay. Sure." Breathing raggedly, I nodded.

"Actually, why don't you stand at the other end? That way you can see the main entrance."

Fuck. I just reacted, sprinting down to the other end of the short aisle. What if he'd wandered off? What if someone had taken him?

Oh my god.

A fresh tsunami of panic swept over me, and if I wasn't careful, it was going to drag me under.

A young guy in his twenties walked by; his eyes widened when he saw me. Whether that was because he recognized me or was freaking out about the expression on my face, I didn't know.

"Have you seen a kid? He's three. My son." Desperation clung to every word.

"No, man, sorry. I've just come in, and I didn't see any kids by themselves."

I nodded before I froze, digesting his words. "So you saw a kid with someone else? He's about this tall." I indicated to just above my knees, knowing he was taller than most three-year-old kids. "His skin tone's about two shades lighter than mine. A mess of wild black hair."

The guy had paused as he'd listened to me, his brow furrowing. Finally, he shook his head. "No, I don't think so. There was a girl, I think, with her mom. White skinned."

A stuttered breath pushed out of my lungs. "Okay. Thanks."

"Mikey," I called again, just as a woman wearing pressed slacks and a blouse appeared. A label on her chest indicated her as the manager. *Thank Christ*.

"Hey, your child is missing?"

"Yeah. Maybe three or four minutes now." Shit, was it longer than that?

"Okay, let's not panic." She pulled out a two-way and spoke into the device. "Melvin, do you copy?"

"Melvin, copy."

"We've got a missing child. Stage-one checks, please. Over."

"Stage-one checks, copy. Over."

"Okay, this is what's going to happen."

I bobbed my head and tugged my cell out. Jesus, what would I tell Dylan?

"Melvin is sending one of the team to the parking lot as we speak. He's also locking the main entrance and will be sending someone to look at the cameras."

"Thank you." I swallowed hard, aware that there were more than a few people standing and watching. Good, maybe they could start looking to see where Mikey was. "And the police?"

She nodded, aiming for a reassuring smile I was sure, but all I felt was blind panic and sick. "We have a procedure to follow, but 999 times out of a thousand, the child's just wandered off, probably got stuck into some candy. Maybe found a nice spot to hide in and nap."

But there was that one in a thousand.

She looked at her phone. "It's been officially five minutes based on your timeline, which means we call the police."

"Fuck. Okay, let me call my husband."

"That's fine, but I need the details of your son first. Name?"

"Mikey Turner. He's three. Brown skin…" I continued reeling off the details, aware that each second that passed, there was still no sign of Mikey.

"Okay. I'll make this call. Why don't you start searching? The team will already be doing so, and I imagine—" She glanced around her and returned to me with a soft smile. "Yes, before you know it, every single person in the store is going to be looking for him. We'll find him in no time at all."

She was right. At some point during the conversation, the few people who'd been in the store started walking around, baskets and a couple of shopping carts abandoned, calling Mikey's name.

Thank fuck for small towns.

Emotion clogged in my throat, fear and gratitude colliding as I started back down the aisle, heading toward the fresh produce. With a trembling hand, I hit Dylan's number and held my phone to my ear.

Just as he answered, "Hey, all okay?" a hollered "He's here. I've got him" reached me.

"Fu-ck." The word tumbled free, broken and dripping with emotion.

"What's wrong? Cass? Cassius?"

But I was moving in the direction of the voice, the buzzing in my ears not stopping until my gaze landed on Mikey.

"Jesus. He's here. It's okay," I gasped into the phone.

"What the fuck is happening?"

"I'm sorry. It was Mikey," I said with a trembling voice, dropping to my knees and tugging Mikey into my arms. "I couldn't find him, but he's safe. I just freaked out."

Mikey wriggled in my arms, but tough shit. I needed him close. Needed to soak him up to know he was okay.

A loud sigh traveled down the line. "Okay." Another breath. "Do you need me?"

"No." I stood with Mikey in my arms, my focus landing on Kelsey. "I promise we're fine. We'll be back soon."

"Okay. Just call if you need me."

We ended the call and fuck it. I stepped forward

and hugged a startled Kelsey tightly. "Thank you so much." I ignored the sliver of guilt that I'd never ended up calling her. Saying that, she hadn't reached out to me either.

After a moment of stiffness, she patted my back, then pulled away, a soft smile directed my way. "You can thank Millie."

My gaze dropped to her daughter, who stood wide-eyed peering up at me.

"You are amazing, Millie. Thank you."

"S'kay." She shuffled her feet, her focus drifting to Mikey, who'd stopped wriggling and was looking at me.

I caught his gaze. "Where'd you go?" I shook my head at him, relief tangling with frustration. But with relief riding high, the last thing I wanted to do was be upset with the kid.

He shrugged, and out popped his bottom lip.

"I was so worried. You know you can't wander off like that. I always need to be able to see you. Know where you are."

His bottom lip trembled. "So-wey," he mumbled with a sniff.

"Jesus, kid." I hugged him close again and pressed a kiss to the top of his head. "Just never again, okay?"

Accepting the hug, he bobbed his head.

Refocusing on Kelsey, I smiled. "Where'd you find him?"

"Hiding under the produce stand."

I shook my head, bewildered, and turned to look at the store manager, who stopped by my side.

After a quick discussion and my eternal gratitude with how quickly the store had reacted, she left us alone, the store reopened, and the folks milling around offered me pats on the arm.

"I best be going." Kelsey took a few steps away, holding her daughter's hand.

"Perhaps we can take the kids for a treat and a play in the park one day next week." Ignoring the wince that I was going against Dylan's wishes, I smiled, letting her know my invite was genuine.

Dylan would have to understand. How could he not?

He was worried about Kelsey's husband more than anything. He'd made it clear that Kelsey was a nice woman, and her kid was great.

"Uhm… I'm not sure—"

"Please, Mommy."

Looking at her daughter, Kelsey seemed to be debating something with herself. A tentative curve lifted her lips, and she nodded before glancing at me. "Sure," she answered. "Millie would love that."

"Excellent. How about Monday, say 9:00 a.m. at

the Covered Bridge playground?" Dylan would be back on shift then, and I had no other plans.

"Yeah, that'll work." A more certain smile formed. "I really need to go. I'm relieved Mikey's okay."

"Me too." While my heart still beat fast, the panic had dulled. "Thanks again."

Refusing to let Mikey down, I grabbed the bags I'd packed up and made my way to pay. Before I put my SUV into Drive, I shot Dylan a text, letting him know I was on the way home.

The siren call of a beer was loud. Maybe even something stronger with how close I'd come to a heart attack.

CHAPTER 18
DYLAN

Uneasy and glancing at the time again, I strummed my fingers on my desk.

"You're driving me insane."

I snapped my attention to Suzie, who sent a pointed look to my hand.

"Sorry."

Rolling her eyes, Suzie stood and headed to the coffee machine. "You could have said no to him."

Immediately, I shook my head. "How the hell could I have said no?"

"Because Mikey's your kid."

"*Our* kid," I reminded her.

"So it's really working out, then?"

For the first time all morning, my shoulders lost some of their tension when I thought about Cassius and just how amazing life was with him.

"And from your goofy expression, I'm going to go with yes."

Not bothering to hold back my grin, I stood and grabbed my empty coffee cup from my desk. "It's fucking awesome." I did a quick double check of our surroundings to make sure nobody had sneaked into our back office. Still alone, I leaned against the coffee station. "He's so incredible with Mikey."

"But he always has been, right?"

"Yeah." He seriously had. "But it's more than that. He's stepped up with parenting and is so amazing at it. He was born to be a dad."

Just thinking about that heart-stopping moment when he'd called last week about Mikey made my pulse kick up, but Cass, even with his fear, had reassured me and had kept me from racing to the store despite knowing Mikey was safe.

And that was the thing—I'd always trusted Cassius implicitly. Trusted him with every part of myself, and that included being a dad to Mikey.

"And you're giving this marriage a real go?" Suzie side-eyed me. "Like, this is more than just a friends-with-benes arrangement and more than because of your asshole parents?"

"Yeah." An almost giddy chuckle escaped me. The past few weeks had been amazing. Our routine had already been awesome and had been working so well. But now, since the playoffs, life was the sweetest it had ever been.

Every time I thought about the man, let alone got my hands or mouth on him, my whole chest filled with so much sunshine and joy, I wouldn't be surprised if I'd burst one day.

"Everything is perfect and so goddamn easy."

"Easy... hmmm."

"What?" I asked as she stepped out of the way and I focused on making my own coffee. "What does *hmm* mean?"

"Easy doesn't exactly sound sexy or great for a marriage foundation." While there was no bite in her tone, the pointed look she shot my way let me know she was concerned.

She didn't need to be. Not about this. Me and Cass.

"Easy as in...." I struggled to find the words to explain myself. "I don't know. Effortless. Right. Because it is, so fucking right. We just fit."

I ignored her quirked brow and the twitch of her lips. Yes, I was gushing, but so what? Feeling this way, my heart full to overflowing, shouldn't have to be contained.

Plus, he was my soul mate, which was something I wouldn't ever be sharing with anyone. But all the times we'd smiled and teased each other about that term, now… I felt it deeper. Had never been more certain about anything before.

"And it wasn't *easy* easy. Admitting what was going on. Hell, realizing what was going on between us took a shitload of work." *And courage.* It had been terrifying, in fact, admitting I wanted more. Even more so, taking it.

The gurgle of the machine finished.

"I'm happy for you. I seriously am. He's got some time left before the season starts, right?"

My heart pinched at the thought.

Missing Cassius for the past ten years had been the norm. With our new relationship, I suspected it would make it feel ten times worse. But we'd handle it.

"Preseason training starts in a couple of months. We're still considering buying a new place a little out of town to help with his commute."

Bobbing her head since she already knew this, Suzie blew on her coffee as she returned to her desk. "Makes sense."

It did, but there were very few places available between us and the city. Land was a possibility. We could build a house.

"And what if he gets traded?"

My stomach flipped even at the thought. While the Eagles hadn't had the best season, they'd not been bad. And Cass had been on form. Plus, he'd reassured me he had a "no trade" clause in the contract he signed last year.

"He's safe with his contract. Signed for five years."

It had been a relief to discover that, too, especially as I was aware a League team could only have two maximum contracts on their roster. Ollie was the other player to score one. Though his was coming to an end at the end of the next season.

"That's good."

It was.

The phone rang, and I picked it up on the second ring. "Zumbrota Police Department, Sergeant Turner speaking."

"Hey, Sarge, it's Mary over at Chill Haven."

"Hey, Mary, all okay?" I placed my coffee down and picked up my keys. That the manager of the small ice cream shop called was odd. That her voice was tight raised my hackles, and I indicated for Suzie to get ready to move.

Alert in an instant, she jumped up and started for the exit.

"I think you need to get down here, Sarge." A crackle and a muffled "I swear if I have to…" followed, but I couldn't make out the rest as the phone seemed to be pulled farther away from her mouth.

"Mary? You there?"

Janice on the front desk nodded at me on the way out, but by the time I reached the cruiser, the call had cut off.

"What's going on?" Suzie asked, pulling out and switching on the sirens.

"Not sure yet, but nothing good from the sounds of it." My focus took in the streets and the sidewalks as we traveled the 82 and passed East Twelfth Street. The store was on East Eighth Street.

Nothing out of the ordinary caught my eye, mainly locals' cars on the road, a couple of trucks passing through. When we pulled onto Eighth Street, my stomach bottomed out.

"The fuck!"

"Shit. Sarge, maybe you need to let me take this."

That was not happening.

My jaw cracked as a pulse of anger slammed into me when I spotted the small group outside the store, but it was the man and woman front and center who had me seeing red. My gaze jumped to Cassius as I stepped out of the cruiser. A quick check over him and Mikey, who was in his arms, and I was able to draw in a breath.

But fuck if fire wasn't going to explode from my

exhale when I saw Cass's tense jaw, livid expression, and the daggers he shot at my parents.

I ate up the pavement in a few fast strides, coming in from the side. The small gathering of locals that I spotted bobbed their heads at me and stepped clearly out of my way. A couple of people from the group of eight surrounding my parents peered over and fidgeted.

A glance at Cassius and we made eye contact. His shoulders indicated a deep breath, but his expression remained fierce and all levels of pissed off. I reached him side-on, Suzie moving from my six, keeping an eye on the now-muttering mob.

"You good?" I shifted into his space, my voice low.

"Just peachy."

His smart-ass response helped to silence some of my concern.

"Mikey?"

At the sound of my voice, Mikey pulled his head off Cass's chest and looked at me.

Rage, with an intensity that whitened my vision, barreled into me when I took him in.

Puffy red eyes and a trembling lip, Mikey looked terrified.

A hand landed on my arm, and I flinched before realizing it was Cassius's.

"He's okay. I've got him. He's upset but will be okay." He pressed a kiss to Mikey's head, and our boy snuggled back to Cass's broad chest, facing me this time, his sad eyes hurting my heart. "Nothing that cuddles won't fix tonight, and maybe an ice cream."

When Mikey didn't immediately grin at the magic promise of ice cream, I knew something fucking bad had happened here.

I spun on my heel, staring hard at the pinched-lipped faces of my parents.

It had been years since I'd seen them, and I got a sliver of satisfaction knowing time had not been kind to them. But that's what misery and spite looked like: deep wrinkles to encase vindictive words and hollow eyes that were windows to empty hearts.

"What did you do?" I grated.

Dad glanced away, gaze on the sidewalk like the coward he always was. Mom, arms folded, shook her head at me, disgust in her features that simply made me wonder how my sister and I had escaped intact.

"We have rights, as that boy's grandparents, to see him. The state of Minnesota says so." With her head held high, she looked around at the group, receiving nods. The reactions buoyed her, and she stood even taller. "It's criminal, what you're doing.

Allowing this poor child to be living in a house of sin. We're here t—"

"You're here causing a scene and being a nuisance." Suzie's voice was hard. She squared her shoulders and took a step so she remained before me —an impenetrable wall between me and my parents. Though I expected she was saving me from myself and doing something that could cost me my badge. "I need to ask, ma'am, did you touch that child or attempt to take the child?"

"What? No, I was just trying to pick him up so I c—"

"I'll ask again, ma'am, did you at any time attempt to touch or take the child away from his father?"

"That man's not his father. That man—"

"That man is his legal guardian," Suzie interrupted. "Any attempt to take a child without permission could result in kidnapping charges. Were you aware of that, ma'am?"

I was eager to slap the cuffs on her right now. It was only Cassius's warm palm on my back that stopped me diving into the fray.

"It's not kidnapping if I'm saving a child from—"

"Ma'am." Suzie's hand went to her cuffs, and her voice turned to steel. "I need you to step back right now." She took a long, slow look at the crew of who I expected were people my parents attended church with. "The rest of you, I suggest you go get into your cars and get out of our town—"

"Look here, you can't order us to leave town. This is a free country," a balding man with a saggy gut warbled.

"That may be so." Suzie glanced to the small group of locals, her gaze settling on Kelsey, who stood by the ice cream store's front with her daughter in her arms. "Mrs. Dellinger, you mind stepping over here so I can just clarify something?"

I winced inside when Kelsey blanched, but she moved forward regardless.

"Yes, Officer?"

"Were you in the vicinity when Mr. Britton was approached by Mr. and Mrs. Turner here, and the group they're with?"

Kelsey nodded and offered a shaky "Yes, ma'am. I was."

"And did you witness Mrs. Turner or any of the individuals in her party touch Mikey Turner?"

For the first time, I felt sick that Mikey and I shared the last name of the people before me.

"I didn't see her touch him. She reached for him and tried to, but Cassius managed to pick him up first."

Not ideal, as if she'd laid one finger on Mikey, I'd

have no issue with charging her. But I was hella relieved she hadn't touched my boy.

"Thanks, Mrs. Dellinger." Kelsey nodded and stepped away, making eye contact with me. I sent her a small smile, grateful she was here.

"Uhm, actually," Kelsey said, her eyes widening as though surprising herself, "I don't know if it's important or not, but I did hear Mrs. Turner tell Mikey she was taking him away." With a shuddery breath, she stepped farther away, and fuck how my stomach twisted in gratitude.

She absolutely did not deserve the likes of Nolan. I swore then and there, if she wanted to get out, I'd help her any way I could.

"That's super helpful, thank you, Mrs. Dellinger." Suzie glanced at me before refocusing on the group. I followed her gaze, noticing at least five were looking increasingly uncomfortable, shuffling from foot to foot. And a couple shot nervous glances at my mom.

That's right, assholes. Mess with my boys and you're going to get your asses handed to you.

"Sergeant, I believe the maximum penalty for attempted kidnapping is seven years."

Suzie was on the money. Like me, she'd also know those charges wouldn't stick, but fuck if how my mom's head snapping in my direction, her lips parting as the color drained from her face, didn't make me want to try my hand.

As quickly as she paled, her face turned fire-engine red.

"I think we should leave."

I startled at hearing my dad's voice.

"What? No, they can't—"

"Rita, it's time." He reached out and took hold of Mom's arm.

"But, no, they can't—"

"The restraining order will be filed by this afternoon," I said, my voice deathly calm. That I now had enough evidence with this vitriolic whatever it was meant at least something positive resulted from Mikey's upset.

And fuck it, because I absolutely wanted to spit in my mom's eye, I angled to look at Cassius, taking in his handsome features and the fierceness in his gaze.

I didn't have to say a thing as he leaned down and pressed his lips to mine, sweeping over them for a couple of beats before we pulled away.

It was tempting to flip my parents off, but since I still wore my badge, I figured I needed to at least attempt to remain professional. But damn, it was hard.

Turning to me, Suzie offered me a nod before her gaze raked over Mikey and Cass. "I'm going to grab some names so I can file a report. Why don't you take fifteen and go get Mikey an ice cream?"

Thankful, I bobbed my head before ushering Cassius and Mikey off the sidewalk, receiving a few pats on my arm along the way and a "We wouldn't have let anything happen to your lovely son or that handsome husband of yours" from Mrs. Jacobs.

Her words pulled a chuckle out of me, right along with a fresh wave of gratitude.

What an unbelievable shit show.

And as Mikey finally licked at his dripping ice cream and I shared a whispered conversation with Cass, my words from a few weeks back came to mind.

Yeah, maybe living in my small hometown wasn't so bad after all.

CHAPTER 19
CASSIUS

IT HAD BEEN A DAY.

While Mikey had thankfully been mollified by ice cream, it would take more to stop my scowl from slipping into place. And likely something even more excessive to ease the fury that filled Dylan's gaze when I caught him staring into nothing.

While the air had cooled—the norm for late summer in Zumbrota—I sat on the back porch, wearing an Eagles hoodie and sipping beer. Dylan had been starting a second bedtime story when I'd kissed Mikey goodnight.

I understood his reluctance to leave our boy.

Fresh fury sliced at my gut.

Dylan's parents would be served tomorrow with restraining orders. I didn't even want to see their reaction. As far as I was concerned, if I never had to see them again it would still be too soon.

Poor Mikey had been petrified as the crowd had all but swarmed us just as our group—me, Mikey, Kelsey, and Millie—had been about to step into the ice cream store after the kids had enjoyed a long, giggle-filled play.

And when Rita had made a grab for Mikey, spewing her hatred, only my boy's wide-eyed panic had stopped me from losing my shit.

The opening of the patio door drew my attention to Dylan. Silhouetted by the backlight of the kitchen, he looked pale, almost ethereal. Combined with the lost expression on his face, I reached out for him, urging him over.

In a few steps, he took hold of my hand and settled at my side, scooting down a little to fit more comfortably under my arm. And fit he did. Perfectly so.

How had I managed all these years without Dylan being mine? The flicker of a smile tried to form as he released a heavy exhale, just as I called bullshit on my thoughts.

"You're smiling. How come?"

Dylan wasn't even looking at me, reaffirming just how well he knew me.

"All these years we weren't together as a couple,

do you think we both kind of knew this was how we'd end up?"

Dylan shifted against me, no doubt surprised by the direction of my thoughts. Understandable since despite sort of knowing everything, we didn't go over and over what we were to each other. Beyond married.

Describing us as a "couple" was likely the first time either of us referred to each other that way.

Honestly, I didn't know how we worked so well and seemed to know without words what the other was feeling.

"Maybe," he answered after a beat. "You never seemed interested in looking for a serious relationship." Peering up at me, he shot me a lopsided smile.

"Back at'cha."

Dylan snorted.

"You're the only person I trust with everything." Heat crept up my neck, but I didn't pull away from the eye contact, even though I sounded like a big baby.

"If you say 'including your heart,' I might come in my pants."

An abrupt laugh shot out of me. "You're such a fucker." I continued chuckling, Dylan joining in. My laughter petered out, but amusement remained bubbling in my chest as I asked, "And if I did say 'including my heart' and meant it, what then?"

But fuck yes, I really did.

With his chuckle dwindling, Dylan angled back. Shadows cast on his face, two streaks of light spilling from the door, one highlighting his parted lips, the other his chiseled cheekbone.

"I'd ask if we could change my and Mikey's last name to Britton."

Air froze in my lungs. And even though my lips parted, I couldn't speak. Couldn't form the words needed, not when happiness swelled in my heart, filling me to the brim while clogging my throat with emotion.

He waited patiently as joy, so fucking pure and magical, zipped around my system and finally had my hands working. Snatching hold of him, I hauled Dylan close, maneuvered him so he sat on my lap, where I hugged him tightly.

"Fuck yes," I whispered against his skin, following up with two tender kisses on his neck. "I want that so much. Fuck."

With trembling hands, I clutched his face, stroking his soft bristles as I stared up at him.

Sweet emotion peered back at me. As his ragged breath whooshed out of him, I tugged his mouth to mine, capturing his lips and kissing him.

I poured everything into our kiss. My joy. My certainty.

He matched every stroke, every tender caress until we pulled apart, panting.

"And if I tell you I'm falling in love with you… what then?"

My breath hitched as I absorbed Dylan's softly spoken words.

How did I get so lucky? How was this my life?

Not breaking eye contact, I slowly shook my head, saying, "I'd ask you to show me every day for the rest of our lives."

The mush was strong, but with Dylan's deep swallow and wobbly smile, I'd stand in front of a packed-out stadium and shout my feelings for the man with a sonnet if he looked at me this way.

"Yeah?" His gaze searched mine, and I nodded, my grip tightening on his waist.

"Always."

The lightest of chuckles spilled out of him, more of a huff of disbelief, possibly amazement. And I got it. Related 100 percent.

The shit show of the day faded into the background as Dylan pressed his mouth to mine and pulled away, saying, "Let's take this to our room and I can start showing you."

Fuck yes.

My mouth on his and buried balls deep, wringing every ounce of pleasure from Dylan, was how I wanted to spend every night we had together.

PANIC STARTLED ME AWAKE. GASPING, I CLUTCHED AT my chest and sat up, taking ragged, deep breaths.

Goose bumps prickled my skin, the sweat covering my body cooling.

The fuck was that about?

Another shaky breath, followed by another, but my panic failed to subside.

Glancing to my side, I was tempted to wake Dylan. My neediness nor the weird feeling in my chest wasn't a good enough reason to disturb him.

We'd made love twice. Once with our mouths, and the second when I'd slowly driven into him, capturing each whimper until we'd finally detonated. Showering had been an effort, and I'd never been more grateful for anything than remembering to cover the bed with a towel rather than having to strip the sheets.

Both exhausted, it hadn't taken us long to drift into sleep, but Dylan had another twelve-hour shift ahead of him. Not only was that enough for him to be dealing with, but the added shit of his parents didn't make life easier.

Handling my racing heart by myself was something I could manage.

After I checked in with Mikey.

Naked, I slipped out of bed, grabbing my sleep shorts and hoodie on my way out. Once out of earshot, I dressed and headed to Mikey's room, practically tiptoeing up the staircase, making sure I missed the creaky step.

Sleeping peacefully, Mikey's one arm rested above his head, his other by his waist. The pounding of my heart settled as I watched his quiet, even breaths.

Fear unlike anything I'd ever known seemed to be my constant since finally stepping up to be Mikey's dad. Would there ever be a day I wouldn't worry? Wouldn't be terrified he'd be hurt, or lost, or taken?

My pulse picked up speed with heavy thumps that threatened to have my knees buckling.

Mikey and Dylan were everything to me. My world.

If I didn't have them, I might as well disappear.

The thought renewed my trembling breaths. I needed to get out of here before I woke Mikey or Dylan. Christ knew how loud my breathing was through the monitor.

Backing away, I left Mikey's room with a last look and a tightness gripping my heart.

Fuck.

I all but stumbled my way into the kitchen, heading toward the faucet. After splashing cold water on my face, I filled up a glass and drank greedily.

It would be fine.

It would all work out.

Dylan would forgive me. He'd understand my reasons and his sister's. He'd understand the deception.

Fuck.

I practically fell onto the couch, hanging my head low and cupping my face.

Dylan was going to lose his shit. He'd never forgive me for this. Not ever.

Nausea cramped my stomach. Fear squeezed my chest.

I could lose them both.

The hell was I going to do?

And that these emotions, the reality of the situation I'd gotten myself in, hit now? I didn't have the emotional capacity to be surprised.

Everything had changed.

We were a family.

And yeah, just like Dylan, I was more than

halfway in love with the guy. More than halfway, meaning absolutely, no-bullshit in fucking love with him.

Knowing I was the biggest fool out there, not telling him sooner, didn't make me feel any better or help me navigate what to do. The regrets were numerous, but I could never regret Mikey.

Not ever.

Even if it meant I lost him because Dylan couldn't forgive me.

"Hey."

I jolted at Dylan's sleepy voice.

"What are you doing up?"

From the widening of Dylan's eyes when I faced him, I could only imagine how I appeared. The state I was in.

"Cass, what's wrong?"

Alert in an instant, he joined me on the couch, taking hold of my hands and urging me to face him.

Looking him in the eyes over the past four years had been difficult, but since May, when we got hitched, doing so proved impossible at times. Now was such a moment.

I didn't deserve his concern, and while terror clawed at me, everything was coming to a head. I had to tell him. How could I not and stand to look him in the eyes and tell him I loved him when I kept something so significant from him?

Fuck, I was going to be sick.

Launching up and racing to the bathroom, I heaved until my stomach was empty. On shaky limbs, I stood before the toilet and closed my eyes.

A cold cloth pressed to the back of my neck, and I sighed.

Dylan was so incredible.

"You're worrying me. What can I do?"

Silently, I shook my head, not sure I could speak without the dam breaking.

"Have you felt ill for long?"

The concern in his voice twisted my stomach. I released a shuddery breath, forcing words to form. "No. I'm okay. Better now." I flushed the toilet and eased away.

Dylan stepped back, concern filling his expression when I finally found the courage to look at him.

"You don't look the best, Cass."

A humorless huff escaped me as I picked up my toothbrush to brush my teeth. "I suppose vomit isn't the best look on anyone."

Tight-lipped, his face pinched in worry.

Jesus, I should latch on to that while I could. When I told him the truth, this expression would disappear into something entirely different. And

I'd deserve all the anger and disappointment. Betrayal was sometimes an impossible pill to swallow.

Fuck.

"You're seriously scaring me."

The panic in his eyes, the raw vulnerability in his voice, they were my undoing.

"I'm sorry. I'm so fucking sorry."

"Jesus, Cass, stop." He was in my space, wrapping his arms around me. "Everything is fine." He held me tighter as I hugged him so hard, I didn't know how I'd be able to let go.

But I needed to do this. Finally tell him the truth and accept the consequences, even though my heart would undoubtedly break.

"I need to talk to you," I managed, easing back but not letting go.

"O-kay," he said slowly. He grabbed my hand. "Let's go to our room."

I nodded and mutely followed him.

The space felt so much like ours, even though it hadn't been all that long. Change in such a short amount of time shouldn't have been possible, but here we were, and I'd never felt more at peace, more loved.

This was my home.

Emotion threatened to nudge me into a babbling

mess, but I swallowed it back. Dylan deserved the truth without me being incoherent.

Asses on the mattress, I considered letting go, suspecting Dylan would be eager to release me once I shattered his trust in me. Since I could be a selfish fuck, I held on tighter, memorizing the feel of his skin, how light his hands appeared under the glow of the bedside lamp.

"Cass." His tone was sterner than before, demanding my attention.

Our eyes connected, and I appreciated the patience visible in his.

"What are you sorry for? Yesterday morning?"

I suspected that meant dawn was fast approaching, and Dylan would have to be at work soon. There was nothing like the double whammy of having an inconsiderate asshat for a husband. Obviously, the asshat was me in this scenario.

"No," I croaked. We'd already discussed his parents yesterday and what happened in depth. That was just before we'd called Granger, our lawyer. While I'd felt like shit that Mikey had been exposed to the confrontation, it hadn't been my fault.

"Okay." With unwavering focus, he leaned into me, squeezing my hands. "That's good. So what's going on?" His expression was open, waiting patiently for me to speak.

I wanted to close my eyes and miss his expression. But being a coward was not an option. He deserved more than that.

With clammy hands and my heart racing at the speed of a hummingbird's wings, I fixed my eyes on his, taking in the familiarity of the warm brown a few shades lighter than my own. Maybe he'd find a way to forgive me.

There was only one way to find out.

With a deep inhale and not-so-steady exhale, I battled through the constriction in my throat trying to prevent me from speaking. "When Paula told us all about her infertility, you know how we all rallied, supported her decision."

If Dylan was surprised by my words and Paula being the topic, he didn't show it. Instead, he nodded, saying, "We were devastated for her. She was so eager to be a mom one day."

"She would have been an incredible mom," I murmured, my tone filled with reverence. "When she first approached me about being a donor, I laughed her off."

There was a slight widening of his eyes, but he remained silent.

"You knew Paula better than any other single person." I pulled a tender smile at the memory of her.

"She was the most... tenacious woman I've ever known."

A slight uptick of his lips and Dylan added, "You mean bullheaded."

"That too." My tone turned subdued as I continued, "She also knew exactly what she wanted, but to her credit, it didn't take too much convincing." A bittersweet huff of a half laugh escaped me. "I've not always been known to think things fully through."

Dylan's brow shot high, and his lips pinched. "You could say that. You have moments of being pretty reactive." The pointed look he shot me told me he was absolutely thinking about our shotgun wedding.

Not a chance would I ever want to take that back. I told him as much, adding, "Reactive means also relying on your gut instinct, right?" Since he didn't call me out, I carried on. "And there are two major decisions I've ever made that I said yes to *almost* immediately. And only because I knew in my heart, hell, in every fiber of my being that they were the right call to make. That they'd be life-changing and amazing."

The words continued to race out of me in an impassioned torrent as I willed Dylan to believe me.

"And I can't regret them, not ever. That doesn't mean I was always right or that I always made the right call, especially as it meant I betrayed you, but fuck, Dyl, I love you and Mikey so fucking much that me doing stupid shit and just thinking of the now and not the bigger picture can't be wrong, right? Like, I know it's wrong that I didn't—"

"Cass." Dylan squeezed my hands when he cut off my babbling. "Take a breath for me."

I did, kind of wishing he would have just let me unravel and release everything I'd been holding back. An inhale and a wobbly exhale and I nodded.

"Better. Okay?"

"Yeah."

"So these two major decisions. One of those wasn't joining the League, right?"

With a shake of my head, I tugged my bottom lip into my mouth, taking a moment to center myself.

"One was marrying me?"

"Fuck yes." The words punched out of me. "I think we were always meant to be here, together, as a family, and I don't know how we could have gotten there without getting married. And that hot-as-hell kiss."

His lips twitched. "It was pretty life-changing."

It seriously was.

"And I know when I jumped all over Granger's suggestion that we should get married for Mikey it was fast and done with literally five seconds of thinking time… and I know I didn't in my wildest dreams expect this would be where we ended up—"

"But your dream changed," he cut in, and fuck my heart and how it bounced around in my chest. That night watching basketball, surrounded by a sea of nameless faces, had brought everything into sharp focus. Just how much Dylan meant to me and how much my love for him had changed into something so much more special.

"It did. It has. You and our life together with Mikey are all that matters."

Dylan swallowed hard, his Adam's apple dipping with the loud click of a dry throat. And when his quiet question "And what's the other one?" sliced through the air between us, there was no escaping the truth.

"I'm Mikey's biological father."

CHAPTER 20

DYLAN

HE FINALLY SAID THE WORDS.

They fluttered between us like delicate leaves that could so easily be shredded in a harsh breeze.

But it was the single tear trickling down his cheek that I focused on. It made a slow trek down his skin, leaving a shiny path behind. It paused on his chin, waited a while, before finally dripping onto his sweatshirt.

With my pulse fluttering in my neck like a butterfly caught in a storm, my breathing stuttered as I drew in his words.

He really was Mikey's dad.

If I'd never received Paula's letter, would I have ever suspected or even worked it out for myself?

"Please, say something." Cass's voice trembled, eyes wide and pleading.

"I know," I croaked, thankful I was sitting. As the relief of everything—the letter I received from Paula via her lawyer on Mikey's second birthday, the ability to acknowledge that Mikey was so much like Cassius that it was uncanny, no longer holding this back from Cass, or him from me—combined, my legs might have buckled. "It's okay."

And it was.

It had taken me six months to make peace with Paula's revelations in her own messy handwriting. Until finally it all made sense. Our wedding, our relationship, all so unexpected, but I swore Paula had known.

The Cassius from four years ago hadn't been ready. Nor the one from a year ago. But now he was.

His heart so big, so wide, so open… which truly had never been the problem. Cass was the most loving and affectionate and loyal person I knew.

"You knew?" Cass shook his head as his gaze roamed my face, his eyebrows pulled low in confusion. "I don't understand." His breaths were heavy, his chest rising too fast, but his palms remained solid and still in mine. Kept clinging tightly to me as I did to him.

But I needed to let go. If only to let Paula tell Cassius in her own words.

"Let me get something." I made to stand, but Cass gripped me tighter.

"You're not going to leave?"

How was it possible for my heart to fracture and heal itself while swelling with love in the space of a simple panicked question?

"I'm not going to leave," I promised. Tempted to kiss him, I broke away instead. We needed all this out in the open, fully and without regret.

I felt his eyes on me as I stepped into our small closet, finding the box and the note with a speed that would tell Cass how many times I'd read the letter.

As I approached him, I held the letter out to him. This time a tremble shook the well-read paper.

I chuckled lightly, laughing away my nerves as he took it. "It's from Paula."

Cass's hand froze in the middle of unfolding the thick paper. Fresh tears welled in his eyes, and in a single blink, two tears rolled down his cheeks. "How…? I don't…."

My heart hurt taking in his broken expression. I wanted to go to him, hold him close, and promise him everything would be okay. Did I believe that? God, I wanted to. And peering down at the man who'd always held a piece of my heart, only now to have snatched it out of my chest with all his sweetness and love and sunshine laughs, I refused to even consider an alternative.

We'd gone through so much together for this to disintegrate around us.

"This was with her lawyer, but I didn't know about it. I received it last year on Mikey's second birthday." The second anniversary of my sister's death went unsaid. "She'd want you to read this."

"Now and not—"

The shake of my head cut him off. "Please, just read it."

After wiping his tears away on his hoodie, Cass took a long, shuddery breath and opened the letter.

I watched as he read the words I suspected I could recite without effort:

Dylan,

Do you remember the time we snuck out when I was ten and we didn't stop running or laughing until we reached the river? I think then was the first time I truly realized that's what life should always be like for us. We should always be laughing, running, and holding hands, even though you were a little embarrassed to do so.

It's also the first time that I realized just how special Cassius was, especially to you.

That was the moment I figured out, at just ten years old, under the stars while exhilarated and terrified that Mom and Dad would discover we were missing from our beds, what love should look like.

The way you lit up and your whole body relaxed when Cassius was already waiting for us and gave you an unabashed hug in the way only he knows how to do.

I don't think either of you knew then, and I truly hope you're finally beginning to figure it out, but we'll always be family, and our love, yeah, that can grow and morph and bloom into something truly spectacular if you're open to it.

It was that selfless kind of love that brought us Mikey. I don't need to see him to know that's his name. The way he's wriggling around right now, always on the move, legs and arms pushing against me, I kind of figure he's going to be so much like one of his parents. I'm just not sure when that time will come... for one of his dads to step up and realize that being selfless and being honorable is an amazing gift, but love—real, life-changing love—is transcendent.

But he'll get there. Maybe not yet—well, definitely not right now while I'm eight months pregnant and wondering about what life you've created for Mikey.

I know it's amazing, though. Know you're giving Mikey everything he needs. How could you not when you're just as selfless as the man who I seriously hope is at your side, loving you both in that incredible, shameless way he does. Because I want that for you.

But I need him to come to you. Need for him to know without a shadow of a doubt that you both are his world. His life.

And I'm sorry, Dyl, so fucking sorry that I'm laying this all on you. Sorry that I knew the risks with the pregnancy, with the delivery, and didn't tell anyone, but Mikey's worth it. I know he is.

Every time you tuck him into bed, I know you'll smother him in love. Just like I know you'll help him find a friend who he can sneak out to go fishing with and maybe fall in love with one day.

And I miss you. Miss you all. But I don't want you to be sad, and I don't want you rolling your eyes at me either. I'll always be your little sister, but that means I see so much more than you realize.

And because of that, I need you not to be mad at me or at him.

Keeping this from you is perhaps unfair, and I know it will be just about killing him. But at some point, he'll make it right and let you know. And I need you to forgive him and be a family. Need you to both love that boy of ours together with your whole hearts and until your last breaths.

And now I'm crying again because of these damn hormones.

Dyl, remember I love you, and Mikey is worth the secrets. Just like he's worth it too.

Love you with my whole heart, Dyl, and thank you for being Mikey's dad. Thank you for making him happy every day and showing him the love that you always showed me.

Love you, big brother.
Paula

WHEN CASSIUS REACHED THE END, HIS WET EYES darted to me. He was a mess, and I could totally relate. It had taken me maybe twenty read throughs to do so without body-racking sobs.

That my sister had known there was a high mortality rate during labor had hit me harder than anything, even the news of Cass's involvement. And while she hadn't come out directly and said he was the donor, she'd made it clear as day that he was.

"I can't believe you've known all this time." Emotion wrapped around his words. "How do you not hate me?"

Fuck it all to hell.

Two steps and I was before him, tugging him up off the bed and wrapping him in my arms. "I could never hate you. Ever." I held on tightly, pouring in my heartache and my love and my relief that the subterfuge was over.

I couldn't have gone against my sister's last wishes by confronting him for anything. Plus, I understood where she was coming from. Eventually.

Cassius, like me, had been young when Mikey was born. Heck, we still were. He'd also been in a very different place and stage in his life when he'd agreed to be the donor. Since Mikey's birth, I'd witnessed the changes firsthand. Seen how he reined himself in, observed how he prioritized me and Mikey.

And that all had to be done in his own time, without the pressure of him being aware that I knew the truth.

Clinging to me, Cass buried his face against the crook of my neck. With ragged breaths, he sniffled, hanging on for dear life.

"I hated keeping this from you. Fucking hated it."

I dropped a kiss to his head. "I know." Because of course he had. This was Cassius. He told me pretty much everything on his mind and what was going on in his life. And this was one hell of a secret to keep to himself.

"I don't ever want to hold anything back from you again. Even if we can be shit at talking things out."

He pulled a chuckle out of me, as he was absolutely right. Off-loading what was on our minds and then moving on and not actually discussing things tended to be our go-to. But feelings and shit were hard, dammit.

"We can do that."

Tilting back, he peered down at me, the whites of his eyes a little pink but dry. He searched my gaze, saying, "Mikey is still your son. I'd never—"

"Hey." I stopped him and cupped his cheek. "He is. He's also your son too."

A loud swallow and he nodded. "But I didn't want you to be worried—"

"Baby, stop."

He closed his mouth, softness entering his gaze. A shaky breath later and he nodded.

I tugged him down to the bed to sit. Our knees touched as we held hands. "When you proposed in your roundabout way, that was the moment you were ready to be Mikey's dad. I accepted that then. Even if I hadn't known and he didn't have your genes, you would still be his dad."

Closing his eyes at my words, he leaned forward and pressed his head to my shoulder. "Thank you. I love him so damn much. I want to be the best dad ever."

"You already are," I reassured.

When he angled away, a shy smile curved his lips. "We're pretty fucking incredible at it, huh?"

A huff of laughter escaped me, adoring this man before me, ego and all. "Yeah, I think so."

"And you really meant it yesterday about changing your names?"

I bobbed my head. "Definitely, and not just to be rid of the connection with my parents, but we're together, and us all having the same last name…." My cheeks heated but I pushed on, saying, "I'm yours, and so's Mikey."

Dropping his eyelids, Cassius took a raspy breath before he nodded and stared at me with an intensity that caught my breath. "I'm yours too. I always have been. I might not have understood it or known it, but that doesn't make it any less true."

Not sure how much more my heart could take after all the early-morning declarations, I answered quietly, "I know. I also know I have to be up in ninety minutes."

"Shit, I'm sorry."

"No, now's as good a time as any. At least it's all out there now."

We undressed and got back under the covers, wrapping our arms around each other. With my head on Cass's chest, he stroked my hair. I sighed into his touch, so relieved we'd said our piece.

Eyes closed, I whispered, "Next day off, let's meet with Granger and get your name on the birth certificate and the application for our name changes."

I didn't have time to react beyond inhaling Cass's breath as he shifted and slammed his mouth to mine. We kissed until we were breathless. We swallowed each other's release as the first rays of sunlight breached the small gap in the curtains. And we whispered words of love as the sun rose and my alarm sounded.

My exhaustion would kick my ass, but with the taste of Cassius still on my tongue and my heart full, I would have done it all again without hesitation or regret.

After dropping Mikey off with Mama T and Pop, we'd jumped on the 52, my hand never leaving Cass's thigh. The norm over the past few weeks, but especially since a few mornings ago.

To say both of us were needy fuckers would have been an understatement. But I was here for it. Every wistful glance, every tender touch, and every single hot and sweet moment.

Since finally revealing all that was in our hearts, it was quite possible we were worse than ever with the need to be close. It made my three shifts the longest ever, but hell if I didn't make the most of each minute with Mikey and Cassius the moment I stepped through the front door, usually to the sound of Mikey's happy giggles and Cass preparing family dinner.

We dealt with the crummy traffic on the way to Minneapolis and arrived in the city in time to grab a coffee from Northern Coffeeworks.

I'd made Cass stay in the car while I'd ordered the drinks. Getting bombarded by his fans would have slowed us down.

"You know, Dogwood's much better, right?"

I shot Cass the stink eye over the rim of my coffee cup. "No way. Northern roasts their own beans. Their coffee's the best."

"You know I actually lived here, right?"

A thrilled pulse of joy at the past tense of that word warmed me, but I still challenged him with "And?" as we left the elevator, hand in hand. "I also know you've got shit taste in coffee."

I snickered at his incredulous look. Dogwood actually made amazing coffee, but screwing with Cass was always fun.

"Take that back."

I snorted into my drink, only stopping at the sound of a throat clearing.

Granger stood in the foyer of his office, eyebrows high and amusement in his gaze. "Ah, the newly-weds are here."

With a gentle squeeze of my hand and a kiss to my temple, Cass grinned. "That we are."

PDA had always been our thing. Now we were worse than ever.

"You've really got the old-married-couple vibe locked down." Granger smirked and indicated to follow him into a meeting room.

"It's like we've been married for twenty years," I said, digging my elbow into Cass's side for good measure.

He jerked away from me, only to then snag me by the waist and tug me close.

The asshole was ridiculously strong and wiry for such a big guy. I could totally take him still.

Probably.

Maybe.

With my Taser.

We jostled a little, stopping when Granger once again cleared his throat.

My gaze snapped to him. Humor twisted the lawyer's lips as he stood, arms folded, watching us.

There was no holding back the heat flooding my cheeks. In my defense, Cass and I together often resulted in this testosterone-fueled ridiculousness. This was nothing new but likely a surprise to somebody who didn't know us well.

Affection took many shapes and forms. And yes, we hugged and snuggled and now sucked each other off—obviously not in public—but we also had tickle fights and trapped each other in headlocks. We dared each other and got into mischief more than two grown-ass men probably should. And dads to boot.

It didn't mean we couldn't be sensible, but I enjoyed how we behaved with each other.

Though perhaps in front of the lawyer who was working hard on getting all the paperwork straight for me and Cassius wasn't our smartest move.

Straightening, I cleared my throat. Professional face it was.

"Thanks for meeting with us today." I stepped forward and shook Granger's hand. I ignored Cass's chuckle and low "Kiss ass" and instead offered our lawyer a friendly smile.

"My pleasure. You guys want to take a seat and we can get started?"

"Sure thing."

As I sat, Cass and Granger shook hands and pulled each other into a small hug.

A dull thud at the action startled me. It was deep in my chest, though hard enough to rattle my bones. The hell was that?

"You look good," Granger said, patting Cass's shoulder affectionately as he pulled away.

Another thud and my stomach twisted in distaste.

"Marriage suits you, Cassius."

I sucked in air, a little wide-eyed and mildly freaked out.

Jealousy? Seriously?

That it was the reassuring words of Cass being married that had me breathing again—pretty significant since I hadn't realized I'd been so close to passing out from lack of oxygen—was a terrifying and telling sign.

The hell was I ever jealous of Cassius?

And now, when I had zero need to be since I knew his heart was mine…?

Fuck. If the asshole realized, there'd be no letting go of this. It was bad enough at the basketball game a while back. Now, he'd never let me live it down, taking too much pleasure in seeing the green-eyed monster in me.

I schooled my features, aware that two sets of eyes were on me, and Cass's were filled with amusement and a smug arch of his eyebrow. With a roll of my eyes, I glanced away from him, determined not to give him more teasing ammo.

As Cass sat, I forced myself to look his way, offering a relaxed smile. *Yeah, nothing to see here.*

Studying me intently, this time with a satisfied smirk, Cass reached out and took my hand.

Fuck my best friend and his ability to know me so damn well.

At least he didn't call me out.

Granger got straight into it, explaining the process of adding Cassius to the birth certificate and how that changed the adoption process a little. For the better.

A relieved smile split my lips, and I squeezed Cass's hand.

"I just need you both to sign some paperwork, and directly after this, I want you to head to the clinic for a swab for DNA testing. While I don't technically need it—"

"You don't?" Cass asked.

"Not when you both sign this paperwork for the

fertility clinic so they can release the details of the insemination."

"So why the swab?" I asked.

"For peace of mind. While the fertility clinic has an excellent reputation, having the DNA confirmation from you"—Granger looked at Cass—"and Mikey will provide no room for contest. They'll give you a swab to take home for Mikey too. I suspect you'll be able to mail it in."

That was a relief and sounded straightforward.

"The adoption can take up to six months; however, I don't imagine it taking that long, considering all of the contributing factors. Plus, we really want to get you in court before you, Cassius, are so restricted by your schedule."

Money, I imagined, would help speed things along. While that made me uncomfortable, not a chance I'd challenge it in this instance. Funny how double standards worked at times.

"Let's hope the judge is an Eagles fan," I only half teased.

Granger handed over papers to sign for the adoption, the fertility clinic, the name changes, and the birth certificate. With so much going on, it would be easy to become overwhelmed, but as soon as I'd finished with the pen and Cassius took my hand, ease settled through me.

"As you know, Mr. and Mrs. Turner were served with the restraining order."

Didn't we just. We'd received the news they had been a couple of days back.

Rather than feeling satisfaction, I simply felt relief. I just wanted an end to their hate-filled drama and for this to be the last time we saw or heard from them.

Was I sad?

My sadness had been swept away years ago. And I was glad for it.

The last thing I wanted was for them to take up any space in my life, let alone my head or my heart.

"And what happens next with them?"

"I reached out to their lawyer, letting them know the developments. Obviously they already knew about the restraining order. I spelled out in no uncertain terms that your parents didn't have a leg to stand on. Even the most basic of grandparents' rights of supervised visits would be unlikely considering their actions from a few days ago. Add in the paternity clarification, and if they tried to fight this, they'd be in for a long and expensive time of it. Even then, I am confident no judge would provide them with the outcome they're seeking."

"And have you heard back?" Cassius asked as his thumb worked slow circles on the back of my hand.

"Not yet." Granger aimed his focus on me. "Do you think they'll pursue this?"

"Honestly, it's fifty-fifty. Either the humiliation will make them back away, not being able to handle any more, or it'll have the opposite effect and they'll push in an attempt to save face."

Granger bobbed his head. "As soon as I hear anything, I'll let you know."

"We'd appreciate that. Thank you," I offered.

Fuck, why did I feel tired all of a sudden?

Looking objectively at the case, everything was in our favor, but I just wanted the uncertainty to end.

After that, we wrapped up the meeting, and we left, heading straight to the car.

"You want to hang out in the city for a bit?" Cassius asked as he unlocked his SUV.

A visit to his empty condo sounded tempting, but I just wanted to collect Mikey, hear his carefree laughter, and spend the rest of the day with my boys. I stepped into Cass's space and angled up to make eye contact. "You mind if we just go home once we have Mikey?"

With a caress of my cheek with the pad of his thumb, Cass's curve of his lips was gentle, understanding. "Of course not, baby. Let's go get our boy."

CHAPTER 21

CASSIUS

How did I get so damn lucky? A thought I was well aware of played on repeat recently.

And why was it that Dylan's kisses were so addictive? Seriously, I couldn't get enough of the man.

Fortunately, Mom was so used to me being, well, me, I didn't think much shocked her these days. Even when I snatched a kiss from my husband when he left the room to use the bathroom.

I took a swig of my lemonade, my gaze traveling to Dad on the rug coloring with his grandson, though technically he didn't know that it was more than love that bound them together.

That would change when we told them the truth.

When we realized Dad had baked his kick-ass bread, the scent hitting us as soon as we arrived to collect Mikey, all it took was one brief silent exchange for Dylan and me to settle in to share a meal with them.

Sandwiches, but on killer fresh bread, should have been basic, but damn if it wasn't delicious. Maybe everything tasted sweeter with the loved-up lens I now stared at the world through.

"I'll do that, Mom." I took the plate off her and set about loading the dishwasher.

With a smile, Mom settled down at the kitchen table. "So everything really went okay?" she asked quietly after flicking a quick glance in Mikey's direction. Playing hard with his papa, his attention wasn't on us.

"It did. I just want it to all be over, though."

A flash of protective indignation morphed Mom's features. Still pissed off from when she'd heard about what Dylan's parents had done—and attempted— she struggled to temper her reaction. I suspected it wouldn't take much for her to give in to her desire to jump into her car and throw down with them.

Little got my mom as angry as someone messing with her boys.

"If I see that woman in the street—"

I cut her off before she spiraled into a tirade with a "Mom, it's okay." My own anger morphed whenever I thought about what happened, but I didn't want to cling to such emotions. Not now when everything finally felt right in my heart.

"I know." She shook her head, the smile she shot me a little tight.

Pushing the dishwasher door closed, I turned and leaned back against it. "Dyl and I aren't worried. All we're focusing on is being happy and making a life together."

Mom's gaze softened, emotion welling in her eyes. "I'm so happy you boys figured things out. You're so wonderful together."

Wholeheartedly, I agreed. Not that it wasn't nice to hear that my folks felt the same way.

Had we come out and actually told them that our relationship had evolved and I loved Dylan as so much more than my best friend? That'd be a no. But I didn't need to.

The first time we'd seen my parents when our relationship had developed, they'd known without explanation. We'd just received extra-tight hugs when we'd left that first time, and while Mom had whispered a "I'm so happy for you both," Dylan later told me Pop had told him, "It's about damn time you boys pulled your heads out of your asses."

Apparently, it hadn't just been Paula who'd seen what Dylan and I truly meant to each other.

"Daddy, I's drew this for you."

I startled at the sound of Mikey calling Dylan "Daddy" and smiled, looking at my boy. As soon as I did, my stomach tumbled. Air trapped in my throat as I all but fell to my knees, hand outstretched to take Mikey's coloring.

Struggling to form words, I parted my lips and simply stared at my son.

"I use-ed lellow, like Eagles."

Fuck. With my heart hammering and emotion close to welling over, I took the picture Mikey had drawn and colored with a shaky hand.

"You did this for me?" At my croaked question, Mikey bobbed his head.

"Yeah."

Somehow managing to tear my eyes away from my sunshine boy, I peered at the picture through glassy eyes. An assortment of lines and circles and a mass of yellow and blue were scribbled across the page. Not having a clue what it was, I asked, "Do you want to tell me what you drew?"

Nodding eagerly, he moved forward, backing up so he was pressed against my chest. I knelt back so he sat on my thighs.

This kid…. I pressed a kiss to the top of his head, ignoring the sting of happy tears trying to escape.

"It our famwy. That's Dada, me, and you, Daddy."

Unable to hold back, I wrapped my arms around him and hugged Mikey close, soaking up all the happiness he gifted me every damn day.

He giggled and wriggled, so I set about dropping kisses all over his head and face.

"Hey, why are you having all the fun without me?"

My attention snapped to Dylan, and his smile slipped as his concerned gaze roamed my face.

Sending him a watery smile, I slowly exhaled. "Mikey was just showing me the picture he drew of the three of us."

"Yeah?" he asked, stepping fully into the kitchen and dropping down before me and Mikey. "Can I see?"

Completely in his element having an engaged audience, Mikey showed Dylan his picture. As he explained we were playing B-ball together, he said who was who. When he pointed out me, his daddy, Dylan's breath caught.

For the barest of seconds, fear held me hostage. What if this was too much, a slap of reality in the face of—

"It's the best thing you've ever drawn."

Hearing the emotion in Dylan's voice, I swallowed hard. When he leaned in, kissing Mikey on the forehead and me on the lips, a shaky breath wheezed out of me.

Apparently that was enough showcasing for one day, as Mikey wriggled free and dashed back to the rug. We followed his progress until a soft sniff caught my attention.

Tears spilled down Mom's cheeks, and at her side, Pop looked a little choked.

Standing with Dylan, I held his hand. He nodded when we made eye contact, which was all the go-ahead I needed.

After checking Mikey remained occupied, I sat at the kitchen table, my eyes still damp as I faced Mom. Dylan stood behind me, hand on my shoulder.

"Mom, Pop, there's something I need to tell you."

A squeeze of encouragement from Dylan followed my words.

Mom, having wiped her few remaining tears, stared at me warily. At her side sat Pop, his expression open.

How the hell did I do this? Did I just blurt it out? Start at the very beginning?

I parted my lips, not quite sure what to say or where to start. Unlike me for sure, and from the growing looks of concern on my folks' faces, they agreed. It was rare for me to be stumped.

"Cassius?" Mom encouraged.

Why was this a struggle? They adored Mikey.

I swallowed, knowing my concern rested in their reaction to me and what I'd done. Or rather the secret I'd held.

But if Dylan could forgive me—

"Cassius is Mikey's biological father."

Relief that Dylan had my back was a heady, wonderful thing.

Two pairs of blinking eyes stared my way.

Dad caught up first with a tilt of his head, saying, "Paula came to you, asked you to be Mikey's dad."

While it wasn't a question, I needed to clarify. "Well, at the time I was just the donor, but now, yeah, I'm Mikey's dad." The difference was important. If Paula had survived, I would have stayed in my lane, somehow, someway. But she hadn't.

Pop glanced over his shoulder, peering at his grandson. A twinge of guilt awoke in my gut. As if knowing my emotions were once again going crazy —the norm lately, it seemed—Dylan squeezed my shoulder and pressed a kiss to my head.

The support he gave was everything.

Pop focused on me again. "I always thought there was something, a resemblance, but I thought I was just being an old fool."

When tears sprang in his eyes, I blinked back my own quickly. "Oh, Pop, I'm sorry."

"I just thought it was because I've always thought of Mikey as ours, as our grandson."

"That's because he always has been. Blood or not," Dylan said softly.

Aware Mom had yet to say anything, I shot her a wary glance, not sure what to expect. The tension around her eyes and the hard set of her jaw had not been it, though.

She was pissed, like super, steam-coming-out-of-her-ears pissed.

Shit.

I needed protection. A barricade.

"Mikey," I called, not at all too proud to let my son block me from Mom's wrath. "Can you come over here a second? Nana wants a big cuddle before we head home."

Something close to a squeak left Dylan as I shot Mom a but-look-at-how-amazing-your-grandkid-is smile.

Dutifully, Mikey trotted over, holding on to a crayon and a piece of paper. Straight into his nana's arms he went, where he scrambled onto her lap.

"Loves you, Nana." He launched at her, wrapping his arms around her neck and squeezing.

If I hadn't already set up a trust fund in his name, I would have opened one immediately. It was like we'd rehearsed just how to win his nana over while stopping his dad from getting his ass whooped.

Of course Mom hugged him back, but not before flipping me off.

Laughter burst out of me. Mom, in all my years, had never flipped me off, though I sure had deserved her middle finger directed my way more times than I could count.

"I love you, baby boy."

My laughter died away at the sincerity in her tone, and when she closed her eyes and breathed him in, my heart swirled with fresh emotion.

"You're so lucky having two daddies who love you so much," Mom said to Mikey as she pulled away and looked him in the eye. "But shall I tell you a secret?"

From the twitch of Pop's lips, I could only imagine the expression on Mikey's face at the offer of a secret. If it was anything like his large, exaggerated head bobbing, he looked ridiculously cute.

"You know you have a dada and a daddy?"

Mikey nodded again, this time peering over his shoulder and looking us over with wide-eyed curiosity.

When he returned his attention to Mom, she said, "Well, did you know you have the exact same nose as your dada and the same smile as your daddy?"

Mikey lifted his hands and placed them on his face, and fuck if my heart didn't melt.

"But your eyes, they're just like your mommy's."

Dylan's grip on my shoulder tightened. I reached up and held his hand.

"Dada tolded me that."

Mom smiled. "He did?"

Mikey bobbed his head.

"But did your dada tell you about these freckles on your nose?"

Mikey shot an incredulous look at Dylan so fast and with such betrayal that it jolted a snort out of me.

"He didn't, huh?" Mom continued, her lips settling into a soft smile. "Well, those freckles are special."

"They is?"

"They sure are. If you look at Papa, he has the same ones on his nose."

Jesus H. Christ. This was one way of Mom getting me back. There was nothing like kicking my ass by making me feel so damn much, all I wanted to do was cry.

Touching Pop's face, Mikey studied his papa carefully. "I sees them."

"You do, huh? And do you know what those freckles mean?"

Mikey shook his head. "No, Nana."

Since Mom wore her heart on her sleeve, how she melted at Mikey's words told me just how much she adored him.

"They're because your papa has such a love for chocolate chip cookies and is so messy that all those crumbs got left behind. I suspect it means you're a chocolate chip cookie monster. Am I right?" Tickling his belly until Mikey was breathless, Mom finished by planting a raspberry on his tummy.

"Papa, can you get that *giant* cookie from the pantry for Mikey? I think it'll be the perfect treat for supper, just before bedtime." Her gaze settled on me, a satisfied smirk on her face.

I huffed out a laugh. "Well played, Mom. Well played."

If Mikey on a sugar high at bedtime was her form of punishment, I'd take it on the chin, and since Dylan chuckled, I figured he could cope with the penance too.

CHAPTER 22
DYLAN

Time sped by too quickly. In just under two months, the luxury of having Cassius at home would be over. Already I dreaded it, but we'd make it work, just like every other League player with a family did.

But that was a concern for future me.

What I should have been doing was making every moment count. In theory, I *was* doing that.

Almost every minute not at work, I was with Mikey and Cass.

With the exception of tonight when I was having a couple of beers with Suzie.

Our four-day roster had finished at six thirty. We'd thrown on some civvies before going to The Backward Bridge, usually the quieter of the two bars in our town.

"You still thinking about moving out of town?"

Suzie picked at the bowl of curly fries, just the crispy ones left over as we'd all but inhaled our meal.

"Yeah, but not yet. We're going to see how this season plays out first. No point in upping sticks if it works out just fine. If it's not, we'll look into it."

Living in town was convenient, but I could adjust if need be.

"And what about you?"

Suzie's brow dipped. "What about me, what?"

I rolled my eyes. She'd been unusually quiet about her love life. It wasn't like Zumbrota was a hive of activity for single residents, but throw in gays and lesbians and all the letters in between, and the likelihood of meeting anyone local became pretty slim.

"Didn't you head into the city last week? You've been really tight-lipped about that."

"That's because it was boring as shit, so I cut the night early."

Frowning, I raked my gaze over her. "You sure there's nothing wrong?"

When she smiled, it seemed genuine. She added, "Nothing at all. Just tired."

I raised my bottle to that. We'd had two quiet days followed by a callout last night, with Briggs and Mason needing support. And today after I'd spotted

Kelsey at the pharmacy wearing a dark pair of shades, I'd spent the rest of the afternoon pissed off.

It had been a few weeks since she'd stepped in at the ice cream store, and I still hadn't done a thing to help her.

And I'd tried.

Today, though, Suzie had given it a go, suggesting she have a quiet word to see if it made a difference.

It didn't.

But there was only so much we could do without harassing the poor woman. Then was the fact that it would be easy to make life even worse for her. That's the last thing Kelsey needed.

The message alert on my phone went off. Immediately, I smiled, seeing Sexy Husbutt.

I'd attempted to change the name Cassius had set one time. When he'd complained and whined so damn hard, then had sucked my brains out through my cock, I gave in willingly and returned it.

> Sexy Husbutt: I am a fucking genius. Mikey ate all his spinach. I'll await my reward when you get home. 😊🥒💦

I snorted, fingers flying across the screen.

> Me: Looks like your eggplant has exploded prematurely. You should see someone about that. And spinach, really? How? What did you promise him?

"There's only one person who can get you to smile like that."

I side-eyed Suzie, not even trying to control my grin.

"Jesus, will this honeymoon phase ever stop?"

As three dots appeared, I shot out, "I hope fucking not."

Suzie snorted. "Cheers to that." She clinked my bottle.

> Sexy Husbutt: 👍 No promises. Just a bit of healthy competition.

> Sexy Husbutt: Premature 🥒 sounds like a you problem, especially after yesterday's ☝️ 🫗 🫗

Heat flamed my cheeks, and I quickly closed my phone. The last thing I needed was a reminder of how hard I'd come down Cass's throat last night while he'd had two fingers up my ass, teasing my prostate.

"Geez, do I want to know what that exchange was about?"

"No, you do not," I said quickly, taking another pull of my beer to get myself under control. With my half-hard dick trying to take notice, I swallowed my beer and thought about how I'd had to hunt through the garbage bin outside Powell's Butchers yesterday, looking for a stolen wallet.

A surefire way to calm my excited dick down.

"You guys are sickeningly sweet, but I'm happy for you."

"I'm happy for me too." I bounced my eyebrows at her, earning me a chuckle.

"I suppose you want to head on home to that man of yours."

Well, I did, but... "I'm good here for a while."

Shooting the shit with Suzie seemed like a luxury these days, and that was all down to me and my eagerness to be at home. I had no desire to change that, but it didn't mean I wasn't aware that Suzie, who I counted as a good friend, and I hadn't spent much time off the clock together.

"Honestly, it's all good. I'm beat. Crawling into bed and not waking up until ten sounds like heaven."

Didn't it just.

That wouldn't be happening for me, but waking up wrapped around Cassius and with Mikey jumping on the bed was pretty damn perfect.

"Right. I'm off." Suzie placed her empty bottle on the bar and tucked some cash under it.

"Hold on, I'll walk you out." We lived in opposite directions, but still.

She waved me off. "Finish your beer."

This was my second light beer, and I was only halfway through.

Before I could argue, she gave me an up-nod and headed out.

Alone, I tugged out my phone, grinning when I saw a new message.

> Sexy Husbutt: Hope you're having fun. You want me to send you a 🍆 pic to reassure you that premature 💦 is never a problem? 😄

Holding back my chuckle, I put my phone away and pulled out some bills. The beer didn't have anywhere near the pull of Cassius.

I said goodbye to Jeremy, the bar manager, and made my way out, calling out to a few of the patrons as I went. The crowd tonight was a friendly bunch. And barring one young couple, they were locals. It was only Thursday, so nowhere near the busyness of a weekend.

That should mean a quiet night for the department at least.

The cooling night air greeted me when I stepped out onto the street.

It wasn't that late, but the streets were empty. The norm for our small town, especially with the bar off the main drag.

I headed in the direction of my parked car. When I turned the corner, surprise slammed into me just as quickly as concern.

"Kelsey?"

I picked up my pace, taking a surreptitious look around the area. With no cars currently on the side street and no one milling around, I returned my gaze to her.

One wide, frightened eye peered back at me, her whole body trembling as she stood by my car, Millie on her hip, a bulging backpack at her feet.

"What's happened?" I asked as soon as I was before her. But I needn't have. A fresh cut on her lip would have told me enough, but it was her swollen right eye, so banged up it was closed, that had me gritting my teeth.

Staying silent, she continued to shake. And the look on her face I knew well, had seen so often over the years. She barely held it together.

Without words, I picked up the heavy bag and unlocked my car doors. I opened the back one, carefully took a sleeping Millie from her arms, and silently guided Kelsey inside.

She did so almost robotically, a noticeable wince and a painful gasp as she angled and finally sat.

Once she was safely inside, I closed the door quietly. A few careful steps later, I tugged open the driver's side back door and settled a sleeping Millie in Mikey's car seat, strapping her in.

Grateful she slept soundly, I could only hope Millie hadn't witnessed what had gone down tonight.

With both of them stowed away, I took a deep breath. Questions burned on my tongue, my brain firing through the best way to support Kelsey. Ultimately whatever happened would be her decision, but fuck if I didn't want to give her options.

Taking a calming breath, I fired off a quick text to Cass, letting him know I'd be home in a few minutes and that Kelsey and Millie were in the car with me. Reading what I'd left unsaid would unfortunately be too easy.

> Sexy Husbutt: Okay ❤

His message came through before I climbed inside my car.

"Are you okay to come back to my place? Mikey's

asleep. Cassius is awake and expecting all three of us." I kept my words soft.

"Yeah. Okay."

Without another word, I started the engine and drove home. In no time at all, I pulled onto the drive, cutting the engine just as Cass appeared in the open doorway at the front of the house. Even from here I could see the concern etched on his features.

"Are you okay if I pick up Millie?" I made eye contact with Kelsey through the rearview mirror, receiving a nod in response.

Once out of the car, I indicated for Cass to come over. He did so immediately. "Can you collect the backpack from the front seat? Kelsey might need help getting out of the car."

I suspected she needed an X-ray, too, but at the moment it was about getting her safe.

"Of course." Cassius pressed his mouth briefly to mine. I let the touch center me before I eased a still-sleeping Millie out of the car seat, then waited until Cass, bag in hand, carefully supported Kelsey out of the car and toward our home.

Each step looked painful, and as Kelsey stepped under the porch lights, fresh anger burned in my gut. Seeing the damage, too, Cass shot his tight gaze to mine, his lips set in a harsh line.

Once in the hallway with the front door locked, I

quietly said Kelsey's name. When she made eye contact with me through her one open eye, I held back my wince, saying, "I'm going to put Millie in my bedroom. It's just through the hallway there, okay?"

Another nod from her and I set about tucking Millie into our bed, an errant thought about being thankful we had clean sheets on it rolling through me.

Jesus, this was a shit show, but I was so relieved Kelsey had gotten out and come to me.

I just hoped she had the courage and conviction to allow us to help her and get her out for good.

With Millie settled, I found Cassius and Kelsey in the kitchen, the first aid kit open and him handing her some Tylenol and a glass of water.

When I entered, I smiled softly at Kelsey and made my way over. The last thing I wanted to do was push her, but we needed to do this right.

"I want to allow you to rest and to settle, but there's some things we need to figure out first, okay?" I watched her expression carefully, taking in the swelling, the cuts, and the bruises. When my gaze met hers, her sadness beat at me, but what else I saw there sparked hope in my chest.

Defiance. Anger.

Just what she'd need to get through this.

"Kelsey, what do you want to happen here?"

She shifted on the kitchen chair as she set down the glass, wincing at the movement. Without breaking eye contact, she whispered with quiet, unwavering strength, "I want to leave. I want Millie and I to be safe. I want him arrested and a restraining order made against him. I never want to see Nolan again and would be happy if he rotted in jail."

I shouldn't smile. Shouldn't find such joy in her words. But fuck if I could keep my grin at bay. "I'm so fucking proud of you, Kelsey."

A shuddery breath escaped her, and she blinked, releasing a single tear.

"Will you let me help you?"

At Cassius's "Us," I looked at him, seeing the fierce determination in his expression.

"Us," I clarified. "Will you let us help you?"

"Please."

I nodded, wishing I could hug her, but I was too damn frightened to touch her, not sure where exactly she was hurt.

Over the next two hours, I took photographs of her face, her bruised ribs, and the giant bruise on her thigh. And while she was desperate for a shower, I talked her out of it until after we formalized her statement, explaining that we needed to make sure all boxes were checked so that charges brought against him would stick.

In that time, I'd called the chief, letting him know what was going down and what the plan was. He agreed, sending Briggs over since he was on duty so he could take an official statement from Kelsey.

First thing in the morning, not only would we be helping Kelsey with a restraining order—though Cass had already woken his lawyer up to have him looking at speeding that process up—but Nolan would be arrested.

Since there were multiple callouts over the years to Kelsey's address, it helped to strengthen her case. That she'd never previously pressed charges was neither here nor there. Nor was it uncommon for DV cases.

Once her statement was taken, Kelsey showered while Briggs had left, taking her clothes for evidence. It was now time to get her to the hospital, but we wouldn't be going to our small local hospital.

"I think we should all go." With his arms folded, Cassius wore a deadly serious expression.

"You seriously want to wake up Mikey now, at 10:00 p.m.?" It felt later than that.

"I can call Mom and Pop. They can come here and take care of him." Something flickered in his eyes before he shook his head. "No, not that. What if

Nolan comes here looking for them?" The pointed look he shot me told me loud and clear, he knew he'd gotten me.

Because, yeah, what if that happened and I wasn't here? Just the thought of Cass or Mikey being anywhere near Nolan terrified me.

The guy was a piece of shit. Once he realized Kelsey and Millie weren't home after the bar kicked him out, he'd be pissed. Fuck knew what he'd do.

I had little doubt he'd look for her and suspect I had some sort of involvement.

Cass was right and he knew it.

Fuck. It also meant we had to head to the city sooner rather than later in case Nolan left early.

Swallowing back my fear, I bobbed my head. "Okay. Text your mom, though, so she doesn't worry if she comes over in the morning or something and we're not here. I'll pack Mikey's bag, and you grab things for us."

Relieved eyes stared back at me. "Thank you."

I hugged him, appreciating how incredible he was.

"I feel pretty useless, but I don't want to be away from you."

"You're not fucking useless. You've spoken to Granger." That he was paying for the support Kelsey would need went without saying. "You're also offering up your condo to Kelsey and Millie. That's not nothing."

"But it's just me throwing money at—"

"No. It's *you* being kind and generous and caring so much, you'll use whatever is in your arsenal to help those around you. That, baby, is not nothing."

His gaze softened at my words, and while I wanted to lean into him and love on him, we had more pressing matters.

CHAPTER 23
CASSIUS

I stayed at my condo to look after a sleeping Millie and Mikey, which was better than dragging Millie to the hospital while Kelsey was treated and scanned.

Fortunately, by the time the kids woke at seven, Kelsey had been tucked in bed next to her daughter, and Mikey had woken with a wide grin in the middle of me and Dylan.

I'd since urged Kelsey and Dylan to try to get more sleep while I entertained the three- and four-year-old with coloring, multiple TV shows, and I'd encouraged them to make a fort out of the sofa cushions and the blanket throws.

I smiled at their giggles. They were watching something on the iPad in their fort and were surrounded by teddies we'd made sure to stuff in one of Mikey's bags. Quiet chatter and high-pitched squeals after the night we'd all had were the most soothing of sounds.

"Please tell me the coffee's fresh."

I grinned at my bleary-eyed husband. Even disheveled and bone-tired, he looked delectable.

"It's a fresh pot, and we even have creamer."

My fridge had been bare. Fortunately, I had several cafés and restaurants on speed dial, so I had ordered us all breakfast. I'd also ordered groceries, which had been delivered about thirty minutes ago, so my pantry and refrigerator looked much healthier.

"I love you."

Not sure if Dylan was talking to his coffee or me, I leaned into him when he stopped at my side where I'd been standing, watching the kids.

"You are talking to me, right?"

After taking a sip, Dylan snorted out a light chuckle. "Yes?"

"Asshole," I mumbled, moving to stand before him so I could kiss him good morning properly. When Mikey woke and I'd gotten out of bed with him, Dylan's kiss had been by rote. Come to think of it, I was sure only one eye had opened. He'd been super quick to offer me a grateful hum when I told him to sleep.

Not two seconds later, his breathing had changed, and he'd been out for the count.

After capturing a kiss from him, I sighed, content at the contact. He peered up at me, his gaze soft.

"Thanks for looking after the kids."

"No need to ever thank me for being Mikey's dad."

A slow shake of his head and he trailed his fingers over my jaw. "You know you're perfect, right?"

I quirked my lips, a shit-eating grin settling quickly. "I've been told a time or two, but feel free to tell me that as often as you want."

Chuckling, he dotted a brief kiss on my lips before all but inhaling the rest of his coffee.

"Are you still tired?" I asked.

"Yeah, but I'll be okay. I also called the station."

I sat beside him on the kitchen stool, waiting for him to give me more. While there was lots of work-related stuff he never shared with me, he knew I was in this.

"The chief charged Nolan this morning. He was still drunk. The house was trashed, and he took a swipe at Jack."

"Shit, really?" My eyebrows shot high. "Dumb fuck move."

"Definitely. What's even better is Jack saw it coming and let it happen."

Shock slammed into me. "So that means what?"

"On top of the DV charge, he's also being charged with assaulting a police officer. That and criminal damage since at some point during the night, he must have driven his car and ended up crashing into the bus stop over on Tenth Street."

What a dick for brains.

"And that's good, right?" I pressed.

"With his priors, it's likely he'll be doing time."

My shoulders sagged, knowing that the little girl giggling with our boy would remain safe, as would her mom.

"I've spoken to Bernard in security," I said, referring to the building's main security guy. "He knows they're going to be staying here for as long as they need. I've also told him Nolan's name. He won't be allowed access."

Hopefully the latter wouldn't be an issue if Nolan didn't make bail.

"I want to help her and Millie set up a home. Wherever she wants. Help her find her feet. I just want to know she's okay." How could I not?

Kelsey had saved me twice. She was an incredible woman and mom. That I was in the privileged position to make a real difference in her life was a no-brainer. I'd help Kelsey however I could.

Reaching out, Dylan held my hand. "You're

amazing. Thank you. And thank you for yesterday… today… for offering up your home."

Immediately, I shook my head, frowning. "This is not my home. You know that. That's wherever you and Mikey are."

"I'm sure there are songs about that," my asshole husband teased.

"Most likely," I shot back. "There're plenty about soul mates and falling in love with your best friend too."

The smile he sent me shot directly to my chest. I clung to the feeling, memorized this moment along with the hundreds of others we'd already shared. Each one reminded me how incredible he was. How much I loved him.

And with Mikey's innocent giggles drifting through the condo, I brought Dylan's hand to my lips and pressed a kiss to his warm skin. An unspoken vow to keep loving them both, for now and for always.

EPILOGUE
DYLAN

EIGHTEEN YEARS LATER

THIS WAS SO MUCH WORSE THAN THE HUNDREDS OF games I'd watched Cassius play over the years. And from the way he gripped my hand and the hoarseness of his voice from shouting, I figured it was a nightmare for him too.

Watching my son's team be on the brink of a spectacular win was too much for my heart to handle.

With a minute on the clock, it could so easily go the other way. Five points was nothing with those sixty seconds still on the board.

"Fuck, I don't think I can watch." I winced as the Coyotes intercepted the pass from Ethan and groaned when the Coyotes scored.

"Come on, Britton." Cass clapped, encouraging our son.

He'd played incredibly all his way through college. This summer he was even going to Montview Academy. Then just one more year, where he'd promised to finish his degree—like his dad finally did fourteen years ago—and then he was holding on for the draft.

"He's got this." I pushed confidence in my voice. But that didn't stop me from asking, "Right?"

If Mikey's team, Barth's Renegades, lost, our boy would rally, as he always did. But that wouldn't stop him from being devastated.

"They can do this," Cass confirmed, nothing but conviction in his tone.

Thirty seconds on the clock and I wished I'd brought a hip flask.

Twenty seconds and Jackson, the Renegades' forward, scored, and I shouted my happiness along with half the stadium in this final game.

Cameras flashed, and the volume was close to bringing the roof down.

"Come on, come on," I chanted, willing Mikey to intercept.

I gasped. He did. "Come on, Britton," I yelled, my voice scratchy.

The whole stadium jumped to their feet.

Five seconds.

"Fuck, fuck, fuck."

That Cassius wasn't chuckling and laughing at how I was losing my shit told me he was right there with me.

When he launched the ball, I watched Mikey's face rather than the hoop.

One beat passed, then two...

He grinned, shouted in glee, his head immediately turning, gaze finding mine, his dad's, and the buzzer sounded.

Smiling so wide, I pumped my fist in the air, hoping Mikey felt just how happy we were for him. That and so fucking proud.

A second later, he was in the middle of his teammates, and I was wrapped up in Cass's arms.

"Holy shit, they did it." I smacked a loud kiss on my husband's lips, pulling away, grinning manically.

Cass, eyes wet with pride, nodded, then shook his head, nodded again, clearly not knowing how to react to the team's win.

"Let's go down."

Taking hold of his hand, I hauled him down with me, passing through the crowd. Thankfully, it was fairly easy. I was pretty sure most people in the stadium knew who Cassius was at least. If not because of his own impressive career, then because he was one of the dads of the Renegades' star players.

On the court, I sidestepped the cameras, hoping they wouldn't collar Cass for an interview.

Since he'd retired from the League thirteen years ago, he'd been balancing his time between working on investment profiles—and making a ridiculously tidy profit—and doing charity work.

It was the latter that we worked on together, finally bringing to life a passion project to support LGBTQ+ youth kicked out of their homes, I'd dreamed up when I'd been seventeen and left home. It was then I'd promised myself that one day, I'd help kids who weren't as lucky as I was. Those who didn't have the Brittons as the best surrogate family ever.

Mikey spotted us first and was before us in the next breath, wrapping his sweaty giant arms around me and his dad.

"I'm so proud of you." I pressed a kiss to his cheek, having to go on my damn tiptoes to do so.

Cassius followed suit, without straining his neck, though. "Proud of you, son. You feeling good?"

"Amazing." Mikey pulled back, all bright-eyed and filled with so much unfiltered happiness, emotion caught in my throat.

Paula would have been just as proud. Hell, my

sister would have been decked out in the Renegades' colors and cheering the loudest.

"We're still good to go to the family party at Coach Maple's house?"

"Of course," Cass answered.

Tiller, Mikey's college team coach, was kick-ass at his job. He'd also arranged for a barbecue at his house for the team and their families. That was with the expectation that the players would last maybe an hour before they went and celebrated without their parents cramping their style.

That was more than okay with us.

Before I could ask where his girlfriend was, Millie appeared, smiling widely and throwing herself into Mikey's arms. As they kissed, I looked away, searching for Kelsey and Tim, her husband. I knew they were coming, but we must have sat on opposite sides of the arena.

Since we had plans to catch up for drinks tomorrow—something we didn't have much chance to do since she'd settled in Michigan not long after her divorce—I wasn't concerned about searching for them in this massive crowd.

When Millie and Mikey finally came up for air, Millie hugged Cassius and then me.

"You doing okay? How's your voice holding up?"

Millie laughed. "I don't think I'll have a voice

tomorrow. I was screaming so loudly. Mikey was amazing." Happiness shined brightly in her eyes.

"He did. Your folks still around?"

She shook her head. "No, they've already gone to the hotel."

Mikey called her over, and she smiled as she headed to him.

"They all look so young." I shook my head, watching Mikey with his friends and his girlfriend. With the world right there at their feet, they had so much living to do. So many exciting days ahead of them.

Likely some heartbreak and tough times too.

But we'd be there whenever our son needed us.

"They are." Cass looped his arm around me, and I melted into his touch.

"Do you ever wonder what would have happened if we'd both liked green gummy bears?" I asked, feeling nostalgic.

The sound of his hearty laugh pulled my attention. Face alight with humor, he always looked extra handsome when he was like this. "Gummy bears? God, it's been a long time since I've even thought about gummy bears, let alone had one."

"You mean you've forgotten how you wooed me with red gummy bears?"

"Wooed? Is that what I did when we were what, five?"

I quirked my brow in challenge, a smirk directed his way.

"I would have still shared them with you. Hell, maybe I would have given you all my favorite green ones."

"Hmmm." I hip-checked him. "I would have let you eat all my red ones, too, if those had been the only ones you liked."

To be where we were now, to have lived this incredible life together, what wouldn't I have done to make him mine?

Cass's grip on my waist tightened as he leaned in close and breathed me in, right at the juncture of my neck and shoulder that he loved. "I think we need to go to the store after the barbecue and buy a giant bag of gummy bears."

With his warm breath skating across my skin, a delicious shiver danced down my spine.

"You do, huh? Any particular reason?"

"Let's see how many we can eat off each other before one of us is begging to come."

I barely held back my groan. "Asshole." I nudged him. This man of mine was incorrigible, in the most delicious of ways. Seeing Mikey heading back toward us, I whispered out the corner of my mouth,

"You are so on, and you are so going to blow before me."

As he shifted his body with a grunt, angling a little toward me to hide his groin, I grinned. Yeah, getting each other hard at the most inappropriate times was something that would never get old.

Another eighteen years and I suspected nothing would change. Those dreams we had, that we talked about all those years ago, at a game not so dissimilar to this, every day I pinched myself, grateful we were living them.

As Cassius pressed a kiss to my head as I spoke to our son, I knew he did the exact same thing.

***

Writing the Zone Defense series has been such incredible fun—so much so, check out the bonus scene (link in RoMMance with Becca & Louisa Facebook group or for newsletter subscribers: https://BookHip.com/PGTZZJG) set at Montview Academy.

As soon as I created Cass's character in No Wrong Moves, I knew he needed his own HEA with his BFF. If you've entered this series a little late, be sure to check out book one, No Take Backs. There's also spin-off series, Fast Break, where you'll find Tiller's story, Mikey's college coach. The college series starts with Rules, Schmules!

ABOUT THE AUTHOR

I live and breathe all things book related. Usually with at least three books being read and two WiPs being written at the same time, life is merrily hectic. I tend to do nothing by halves, so I happily seek the craziness and busyness life offers.

Living on my small property in Queensland with my human family as well as my animal family of cows, sheep, chooks, and dogs, I really do appreciate the beauty of the world around me and am a believer that love truly is love.

To check for updates head to my website:
HTTPS://BECCASEYMOUR.COM
HTTPS://LANDING.MAILERLITE.COM/WEBFORMS/
LANDING/R9F0I4
Plus, join my Facebook group, which I share with the awesome Louisa Masters here:
HTTPS://WWW.FACEBOOK.COM/GROUPS/
ROMMANCEWITHBECCALOUISA/

facebook.com / beccaseymourauthor

x.com / beccaseymour_

instagram.com / authorbeccaseymour

bookbub.com / authors / becca-seymour

tiktok.com / @beccaseymourwrites

Milton Keynes UK
Ingram Content Group UK Ltd.
UKHW011040201123
432908UK00005BA/609